Please Leave in Book

CA
CH Apr 14
HE
KI
LH Sept 2017
LU Sept 2018
M/C Oct 2019
PA
PE
RI
SB
SO
TA
TE
TI
TO
WA
WI

SUSPECT

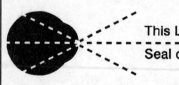

This Large Print Book carries the
Seal of Approval of N.A.V.H.

SUSPECT

ROBERT CRAIS

WHEELER PUBLISHING

A part of Gale, Cengage Learning

Detroit • New York • San Francisco • New Haven, Conn • Waterville, Maine • London

GALE
CENGAGE Learning

Copyright © 2013 by Robert Crais.
Wheeler Publishing, a part of Gale, Cengage Learning.

Wheeler Publishing Large Print Hardcover.
The text of this Large Print edition is unabridged.
Other aspects of the book may vary from the original edition.
Set in 16 pt. Plantin.

**LIBRARY OF CONGRESS CIP DATA ON FILE.
CATALOGUING IN PUBLICATION DATA FOR THIS BOOK
IS AVAILABLE FROM THE LIBRARY OF CONGRESS**

ISBN-13: 978-1-4104-5513-0 (hardcover)
ISBN-10: 1-4104-5513-0 (hardcover)

Published in 2013 by arrangement with G. P. Putnam's Sons, a member of Penguin Group (USA) Inc.

Printed in the United States of America
1 2 3 4 5 6 7 17 16 15 14 13

for Gregg Hurwitz
friend, dog man, writer.
and his beautiful pack,
Delinah, Rosie, Natalie,
and Simba.

■ ■ ■ ■

Prologue:
The Green Ball

■ ■ ■ ■

Maggie stared at Pete with rapt, undivided focus. His dark face was smiling, his hand was hidden inside the heavy green bulk of his USMC flak jacket, and he cooed to her in the high-pitched, squeaky voice she loved.

"That's a good girl, Maggie. You're the best girl ever. You know that, baby girl Marine?"

Maggie was an eighty-five-pound black-and-tan German shepherd dog. She was three years old, and her full name was Military Working Dog (MWD) Maggie T415, the T415 being tattooed on the inside of her left ear. Corporal Pete Gibbs was her handler. He had been hers and she had been his since they met at Camp Pendleton one and a half years ago. They were now halfway through their second deployment as a patrol and explosives-detection team in the Islamic Republic of Afghanistan.

Pete cooed, "We good to go, baby girl?

You gonna find the bad thing for daddy? You ready to work?"

Maggie's tail thumped the dirt hard. This was a game they played often, so Maggie knew what was coming, and lived for the joy of this moment.

Al-Jabar Province, 0840 hours, the Republic of Afghanistan. It was 109 degrees, and would reach 120.

The desert sun beat hard on Maggie's thick fur as a dozen Marines unassed three Humvees and formed up in a loose column twenty meters behind her. Maggie knew the other Marines, but they meant little to her. Pete was relaxed around them, so Maggie tolerated them, but only when Pete was near. They were familiar, but not pack. Pete was pack. Pete was hers. Maggie and Pete ate together, slept together, and played together 24/7. She loved, adored, protected, defended, and felt lost without him. When the other Marines came too close, Maggie warned them with a low growl. She had been bred to guard and protect what was hers, and Pete was hers. They were pack.

Now, this moment, Maggie was totally focused on Pete. Nothing else mattered or existed. There was only Pete, and Maggie's joyful expectation of the game they were about to play, when a voice called out behind her.

"Yo, Pete. We're good, bro. Roll out."

Pete glanced at the other humans, then smiled wider at Maggie.

"Wanna see it, girl? Wanna see what I got?"

Pete took a fluorescent green ball from beneath his flak jacket.

Maggie's eyes locked on the ball, and she stood like a shot, up on all fours, whining for Pete to throw it. Maggie lived to chase the green ball. It was their favorite toy and her favorite game. Pete would throw it hard and far, and Maggie would power after it, chasing it down with a feeling of purpose and bliss; catch it, clamp it tight in her jaws, and proudly bring it back, where Pete was always waiting to shower her with love and approval. Chasing the green ball was her absolute favorite game, but now Pete showed her the ball only as a promise of the bliss to come. Maggie knew the routine, and was cool with it. If she found the smells Pete had taught her to find, she would be re-warded with the ball. That was their game. She must find the right smells.

Pete tucked the ball back under his flak, and his voice changed from squeaky to firm. He was alpha, and now he spoke in his alpha voice.

"Show me what you got, Maggie Marine.

11

Find the bad things. Seek, seek, seek."

Seek seek seek.

Maggie was trained as a patrol dog and an explosives-detection dog, making her a dual-purpose dog. She would attack on command, chase and apprehend fleeing persons, and was stellar at crowd control, but her primary job was sniffing out caches of ammunition, artillery ordnance, and roadside bombs. Improvised Explosive Devices. IEDs. The Afghan insurgents' weapon of choice.

Maggie did not know what an IED was, but this was not necessary. She had been taught to recognize the eleven most popular explosive components insurgents used in their bombs, including ammonium nitrate, detonator cord, potassium chlorate, nitrocellulose, C-4, and RDX. She did not know these things could kill her, but this did not matter, either. She sought them for Pete because pleasing Pete meant everything. If Pete was happy, Maggie was happy. They were a pack of two, and Pete was her alpha. He would throw the green ball.

At Pete's command, Maggie trotted to the end of her leash, which was tethered to a metal D-ring on Pete's harness. She knew exactly what Pete expected because Pete had trained her, and they had performed this same mission hundreds of times. Their job was to walk along the road twenty meters ahead of the Marines to find the IEDs. They went first, and their lives and the lives of the Marines behind depended on Maggie's nose.

Maggie swung her head from side to side, checking the high scents first, then dipped her head to taste the smells close to the ground. The humans behind her might be able to identify five or six distinct smells if they concentrated, but Maggie's long shepherd's nose gave her an olfactory picture of the world no human could comprehend: She smelled the dust beneath her feet and the goats that had been herded along the road a few hours earlier and the two young male goatherds who led them. Maggie smelled the infection that one of the goats carried, and knew that two of the female goats were in heat. She smelled Pete's fresh new sweat and the older sweat dried into his gear, his breath, the perfumed letter he kept in his trousers, and the green ball hidden beneath his flak. She smelled the CLP he used to clean his rifle, and the residual gunpowder that clung to his weapon like a fine dust of death. She smelled the small grove of palms not far from the road, and the trace scents of the wild dogs that had slept beneath the palms during the night and defecated and urinated before moving on. Maggie hated the wild dogs. She spent a moment testing the air to see if they were still in the area, decided they were gone, then ignored their scent and concentrated on searching for the scents Pete wanted her to find.

Smells filled her nose as fully as light filled her eyes, all blurred together like the hundreds of colors a person sees without seeing on library bookshelves. But as a person could focus on each individual book to see its colors, Maggie ignored the smells in which she had no interest, and concentrated on finding the smells that would bring the green ball.

Their mission that day was to clear a five-mile dirt road leading to a small village where insurgents were believed to cache arms. The squad of Marines would secure the village, protect Maggie and Pete while they searched, and recover any weapons or explosives that were found.

The miles crept past slowly, and they drew closer to the village without Maggie finding the smells she sought. The heat grew brutal, Maggie's fur became hot to the touch, and she let her tongue hang. She immediately felt a gentle tug on her leash, and Pete approached.

"You hot, baby? Here you go —"

Maggie sat, and thirstily drank from the plastic bottle Pete offered. The Marines stopped in place when she stopped, and one called out.

"She okay?"

"The water's good for now. We reach the vil, I want to get her out of the sun for a while."

"Roger that. Another mile and a half."

"We're good."

A mile later they moved past another palm grove and glimpsed the tops of three stone buildings peeking over the tops of the palms. The same Marine voice called out again.

"Heads up. Vil ahead. We take fire, it'll come from there."

They were rounding the last curve in the road toward the village when Maggie heard the tinkle of bells and bleating. She stopped, pricked her ears, and Pete stopped beside her. The Marines stopped in place, still well behind.

"What is it?"

"She hears something."

"She got an IED?"

"No, she's listening. She hears something."

Maggie tested the air with a series of short, fast sniffs, and caught their scent as the first goat appeared through the shimmering heat. Two teenage boys walked near the front and to the right of a small flock, with a taller, older male walking on the left. The taller male raised a hand in greeting.

The Marine behind Maggie shouted a word, and the three oncoming men stopped. The goats continued on, then realized the men had stopped, and milled in a lazy group. They were forty yards away. In the rising, windless air, it took a few seconds for their smells to cover the distance.

Maggie didn't like strangers, and watched them suspiciously. She sampled the air again — sniff sniff sniff — and huffed the air through her mouth.

The taller male raised his hand again, and the molecules that carried their smells finally reached Maggie's nose. She noted their different and complex body odors, the coriander, pomegranate, and onion on their breath, and the first faint taste of a smell Pete taught her to find.

Maggie whined and leaned into the leash. She glanced at Pete, then stared at the men, and Pete knew she was onto something.

"Gunny, we got something."

"Something in the road?"

"Negative. She's staring at these guys."

"Maybe she wants the goats."

"The men. She doesn't give a shit about the goats."

"They carrying?"

"We're too far away. She smells something, but the scent cone is too big. These guys might have residue in their clothes, they might be packing guns, I dunno."

"I don't like it we're standing here with the buildings right there. If someone lights us up, it's going to come from the vil."

"Let'm come to us. You guys stay put, and we'll give'm a good sniff."

"Roger that. We got you covered."

The Marines spread to the sides of the road as Pete waved the goatherds forward.

Maggie swung her head from side to side, hunting for the strongest scent, and felt alive with anticipation. The scent grew stronger as the men approached, and she knew Pete would be pleased. He would be happy with her for finding the scent, and reward her with the green ball. Pete happy, Maggie happy, pack happy.

Maggie whined anxiously as the men drew closer and the scent cone narrowed. The older boy wore a loose white shirt and the younger a faded blue T-shirt, and both wore baggy white pants and sandals. The taller man was bearded, and wore a dark loose shirt with baggy long sleeves and faded pants. The sleeves hung in folds, and draped when he raised his arms. His body reeked of days-old sour sweat, but the target scent was strong now. It came from the taller man, and Maggie's certainty flowed up the leash into Pete, who knew what Maggie knew as if they were one creature, not man and dog, but something better. Pack.

Pete shouldered his rifle, and barked at the man to stop.

The man stopped, smiling, and raised his hands as the goats now herded around the boys.

The man spoke to the boys, who stopped, and Maggie smelled their fear, too.

Pete said, "Stay, girl. Stay."

Pete stepped out ahead of her to approach the tall man. Maggie hated when Pete moved away from her. He was alpha, so she obeyed, but she heard his heart beat faster and smelled the sweat pouring from his skin, and knew Pete was afraid. His anxiety coursed through the leash, and poured into Maggie, so she became anxious, too.

Maggie broke position to catch up with him, and shouldered into his leg.

"No, Maggie. Stay."

She stopped at his command, but gave a

low growl. Her job was to protect and defend him. They were pack, and he was alpha. Every DNA strand of her German shepherd breeding screamed for her to put herself between Pete and the men, and warn them off or attack them, but pleasing Pete was also in her DNA. Alpha happy, pack happy.

Maggie broke position again, and once more put herself between Pete and the strangers, and now the smell was so strong Maggie did as Pete had taught her. She sat.

Pete kneed her aside, and raised his rifle as he shouted a warning to the other Marines.

"He's loaded!"

The tall man detonated with a concussion that slammed Maggie backward so hard she was thrown upside down. She lost consciousness briefly, then woke on her side, disoriented and confused as dust and debris fell on her fur. She heard nothing but a high-pitched whine, and her nose burned with the acid stink of an unnatural fire. Her vision was blurred, but slowly cleared as she struggled to rise. The Marines behind her were shouting, but their words had no meaning. Her left front leg collapsed with her weight. She shouldered into the dirt, but immediately stood again, propping

19

herself on three wobbly legs that stung as if being bitten by ants.

The bearded man was a pile of smoking cloth and torn flesh. Goats were down and screaming. The smaller boy was sitting in the dust, crying, and the older boy stumbled in a lazy circle with splashes of red on his shirt and face.

Pete lay crumpled on his side, groaning. They were still joined by the leash, and his pain and fear flowed into her.

He was pack.

He was everything.

Maggie limped to him, and frantically licked his face. She tasted the blood running from his nose and ears and neck, and flushed with the need to soothe and heal him.

Pete rolled over and blinked at her.

"You hurt, baby girl?"

A burst of earth kicked up from the road near Pete's head, and a loud crack snapped through the air.

The Marine voices behind her shouted louder.

"Sniper! Sniper in the vil!"

"Pete's down!"

"We're taking fire —"

The crazy loud chatter of a dozen automatic weapons made Maggie cringe, but she licked Pete's face even harder. She wanted him to get up. She wanted him to be happy.

A heavy crack of thunder so close it shook the ground exploded behind her, and more dirt and hot shards blew through her fur. She cringed again, and wanted to run, but went on with the licking.

Heal him.

Soothe him.

Take care of Pete.

"Mortar!"

"We're gettin' mortared!"

Another puff of dirt kicked up from the road beside them, and Pete slowly un- clipped Maggie's lead from his harness.

"Go, Maggie. They're shootin' at us. Go."

His alpha voice was weak, and the weak- ness scared her. Alpha was strong. Alpha was pack. Pack was everything.

More thunder shook the earth, then more, and suddenly something awful punched her hip and spun her into the air. Maggie screamed as she landed, and snapped and snarled at the pain.

"Sniper shot the dog!"

"Take that fucker out, goddamnit!"

"Ruiz, Johnson, with me!"

Maggie paid no attention as the Marines ran toward the buildings. She snapped at the terrible pain in her hip, then dragged

21

herself back to her pack.

Pete tried to push her away, but his push was weak.

"Go, baby. I can't get up. Get away —"

Pete reached under his flak and took out the green ball.

"Get it, baby girl. Go —"

Pete tried to throw the green ball, but it only rolled a few feet. Pete vomited blood, and shuddered, and everything about him changed in those seconds. His scent, his taste. She heard his heart grow still and the blood slow in his veins. She sensed his spirit leave his body, and felt a mournful loss unlike anything she had ever known.

"PETE! Pete, we're coming, man!"

"Air support comin' in. Hang on!"

Maggie licked him, trying to make Pete laugh. He always laughed when she licked his face.

Another high-pitched snap ripped past her, and another geyser of dust spouted into the air. Then something heavy slammed into Pete's flak so hard Maggie felt punched in the chest, and smelled the bullet's acrid smoke and hot metal. She snapped at the hole in Pete's flak.

"They're shooting at the dog!"

More mortar rounds whumped just off the road, again raining dirt and hot steel.

Maggie snarled and barked, and dragged herself on top of her alpha. Pete was alpha. Pete was pack. Her job was to protect her pack.

She snapped at the raining debris, and barked at the metal birds now circling the distant buildings like terrible wasps. There were more explosions, then a sudden silence filled the desert, and the clatter of running Marines approached.

"Pete!"

"We're comin', man —"

Maggie bared her fangs and growled.

Protect the pack. Protect her alpha.

The fur on her back stood in rage, and her ears cocked forward to scoop in their sounds. Her fangs were fearsome and gleaming as bulky green shapes towered around her.

Protect him, protect the pack, protect her Pete.

"Jesus, Maggie, it's us! Maggie!"

"Is he dead?"

"He's fucked up, man —"

"She's fucked up, too —"

Maggie snapped and ripped at them, and the shapes jumped back.

"She's crazy —"

"Don't hurt her. Shit, she's bleeding —"

Protect the pack. Protect and defend.

23

Maggie snapped and slashed. She growled and barked, and hopped in circles to face them.

"Doc! Doc, Jesus, Pete's down —"

"Black Hawk's inbound!"

"His dog won't let us —"

"Use your rifle! Don't hurt her! Push her off —"

"She's shot, dude!"

Something reached toward her, and Maggie bit hard. She locked onto it with jaws that brought over seven hundred pounds per square inch of bite pressure to bear. She held tight, growling, but then another long thing reached forward, and another.

Maggie released her grip, lunged at the nearest men, caught meat and tore, then took her place over Pete again.

"She thinks we're gonna hurt him —"

"Push her off! C'mon —"

"Don't hurt her, goddamnit!"

They pushed her again, and someone threw a jacket over her head. She tried to twist away, but now they bore her down with their weight.

Protect Pete. Pete was pack. Her life was the pack.

"Dude, she's hurt. Be careful —"

"I got her —"

"Fuckin' scum shot her —"

24

Maggie twisted and lurched. She was furious with rage and fear, and tried to bite through the jacket, but felt herself lifted. She felt no pain, and did not know she was bleeding. She only knew she needed to be with Pete. She had to protect him. She was lost without him. Her job was to protect him.

"Put her on the Black Hawk."

"I got her —"

"Put her on there with Pete."

"What's with the dog?"

"This is her handler. You gotta get her to the hospital —"

"He's dead —"

"She was trying to protect him —"

"Stop talkin' and fly, motherfucker. You get her to a doctor. This dog's a Marine."

Maggie felt a deep vibration through her body as the thick exhaust of the aviation fuel seeped through the jacket that covered her head. She was scared, but Pete's smell was close. She knew he was only a few feet away, but she also knew he was far away, and growing farther.

She tried to crawl closer to him, but her legs didn't work, and men held her down, and after a while her fierce growls turned to whines.

Pete was hers.

They were pack.

They were a pack of two, but now Pete was gone, and Maggie had no one.

■ ■ ■ ■

PART I

■ ■ ■ ■

■ ■ ■ ■

SCOTT AND STEPHANIE

■ ■ ■ ■

1.

0247 Hours
Downtown Los Angeles

They were on that particular street at that specific T-intersection at that crazy hour because Scott James was hungry. Stephanie shut off their patrol car to please him. They could have been anywhere else, but he led her there, that night, to that silent intersection. It was so quiet that night, they spoke of it.

Unnaturally quiet.

They stopped three blocks from the Harbor Freeway between rows of crappy four-story buildings everyone said would be torn down to build a new stadium if the Dodgers left Chavez Ravine. The buildings and streets in that part of town were deserted. No homeless people. No traffic. No reason for anyone to be there that night, even an LAPD radio car.

31

Stephanie frowned.

"You sure you know where you're going?"

"I know where I'm going. Just hang on."

Scott was trying to find an all-night noodle house a Rampart Robbery detective had raved about, one of those pop-up places that takes over an empty storefront for a couple of months, hypes itself on Twitter, then disappears; a place the robbery dick claimed had the most amazing ramen in Los Angeles, Latin-Japanese fusion, flavors you couldn't get anywhere else, cilantro-tripe, abalone-chili, a jalapeño-duck to die for.

Scott was trying to figure out how he had screwed up the directions when he suddenly heard it.

"Listen."

"What?"

"Shh, listen. Turn off the engine."

"You have no idea where this place is, do you?"

"You have to hear this. Listen."

Uniformed LAPD officer Stephanie Anders, a P-III with eleven years on the job, shifted into Park, turned off their Adam car, and stared at him. She had a fine, tanned face with lines at the corners of her eyes, and short, sandy hair.

Scott James, a thirty-two-year-old P-II with seven years on the job, grinned as he touched his ear, telling her to listen. Stephanie seemed lost for a moment, then blossomed with a wide smile.

"It's quiet."

"Crazy, huh? No radio calls. No chatter. I can't even hear the freeway."

It was a beautiful spring night: temp in the mid-sixties, clear; the kind of windows-down, short-sleeve weather Scott enjoyed. Their call log that night showed less than a third their usual number of calls, which made for an easy shift, but left Scott bored. Hence, their search for the unfindable noodle house, which Scott had begun to believe might not exist.

Stephanie reached to start the car, but Scott stopped her.

"Let's sit for a minute. How many times you hear silence like this?"

"Never. This is so cool, it's creeping me out."

"Don't worry. I'll protect you."

Stephanie laughed, and Scott loved how the streetlights gleamed in her eyes. He wanted to touch her hand, but didn't. They had been partners for ten months, but now Scott was leaving, and there were things he wanted to say.

"You've been a good partner."

"Are you going to get all gooey on me?"

"Yeah. Kinda."

"Okay, well, I'm going to miss you."

"I'm going to miss you more."

Their little joke. Everything a competition, even to who would miss the other the most. Again he wanted to touch her hand, but then she reached out and took his hand in hers, and gave him a squeeze.

"No, you're not. You're going to kick ass, take names, and have a blast. It's what you want, man, and I couldn't be happier. You're a stud."

Scott laughed. He had played football for two years at the University of Redlands before blowing his knee, and joined LAPD a couple of years later. He took night classes for the next four years to finish his degree. Scott James had goals. He was young, determined, and competitive, and wanted to run with the big dogs. He had been accepted into LAPD's Metro Division, the elite uniformed division that backed up area-based officers throughout the city. Metro was a highly trained reserve force that rolled out on crime suppression details, barricade situations, and high-conflict security operations. They were the best, and also a necessary assignment for officers who hoped to join LAPD's most elite uniformed assignment — SWAT. The best of the best.

Scott's transfer to Metro would come at the end of the week.

Stephanie was still holding his hand, and Scott was wondering what she meant by it, when an enormous Bentley sedan appeared at the end of the street, as out of place in this neighborhood as a flying carpet, windows up, smoked glass, not a speck of dust on its gleaming skin.

Stephanie said, "Check out the Batmobile."

The Bentley oozed past their nose, barely making twenty miles per hour. Its glass was so dark the driver was invisible.

"Want to light him up?"

"For what, being rich? He's probably lost like us."

"We can't be lost. We're the police."

"Maybe he's looking for the same stupid ramen place."

"You win. Let's forget the ramen and grab some eggs."

Stephanie reached to start their car as the slow-motion Bentley approached the next T-intersection thirty yards past them. At the moment it reached the intersecting street, a deep, throaty growl shattered the perfect silence, and a black Kenworth truck exploded from the cross street. It T-boned the Bentley so hard the six-thousand-pound sedan rolled completely over and came to rest right side up on the opposite side of the street. The Kenworth skidded sideways and stopped, blocking the street.

Stephanie said, "Holy crap!"

Scott slapped on their flashers, and pushed out of their car. The flashers painted the street and surrounding buildings with blue kaleidoscope pulses.

Stephanie keyed her shoulder mike as she got out, searching for a street sign.

"Where are we? What street is this?"

Scott spotted the sign.

"Harmony, three blocks south of the Harbor."

"Two-Adam-twenty-four, we have an injury accident at Harmony, three blocks south of the Harbor Freeway and four north of Wilshire. Request paramedics and fire. Officers assisting."

Scott was three paces ahead, and closer to the Bentley.

"I got the Batmobile. You get the truck."

Stephanie broke into a trot, and the two veered apart. No one and nothing else moved on the street except steam hissing from beneath the Bentley's hood.

They were halfway to the accident when bright yellow bursts flashed within the truck and a hammering chatter echoed between

36

the buildings.

Scott thought something was exploding within the truck's cab, then bullets ripped into their patrol car and the Bentley with the thunder of steel rain. Scott instinctively jumped sideways as Stephanie went down. She screamed once, and wrapped her arms across her chest.

"I'm shot. Oh, crap —"

Scott dropped to the ground and covered his head. Bullets sparked off the concrete around him, and gouged ruts in the street.

Move. Do something.

Scott rolled sideways, drew his pistol, and fired at the flashes as fast as he could. He pushed to his feet, and zigzagged toward his partner as an old, dark gray Gran Torino screamed down the street. It screeched to a stop beside the Bentley, but Scott barely saw it. He fired blindly at the truck as he ran, and zigged hard toward his partner.

Stephanie was clutching herself as if doing stomach crunches. Scott grabbed her arm. He realized the men in the truck had stopped firing, and thought they might make it even as Stephanie screamed.

Two men wearing black masks and bulky jackets boiled out of the sedan with pistols and lit up the Bentley, shattering the glass and punching holes in its body. The driver stayed at the wheel. As they fired, two more masked men climbed from the truck with AK-47 rifles.

Scott dragged Stephanie toward their black-and-white, slipped in her blood, then started backwards again.

The first man out of the truck was tall and thin, and immediately opened fire into the Bentley's windshield. The second man was thick, with a large gut that bulged over his belt. He swung his rifle toward Scott, and the AK-47 bloomed with yellow flowers.

Something punched Scott hard in the thigh, and he lost his grip on Stephanie and his pistol. He sat down hard, and saw blood welling from his leg. Scott picked up his pistol, fired two more shots, and his pistol locked open. Empty. He pushed to his knees, and took Stephanie's arm again.

"I'm dying."

Scott said, "No, you're not. I swear to God you're not."

A second bullet slammed into the top of his shoulder, knocking him down. Scott lost Stephanie and his pistol again, and his left arm went numb.

The big man must have thought Scott was done. He turned to his friends, and when he turned, Scott crabbed toward their patrol car, dragging his useless leg and pushing with his good. The car was their only cover. If he made it to the car, he could use it as a weapon or a shield to reach Stephanie.

Scott keyed his shoulder mike as he scuttled backwards, and whispered as loudly as he dared.

"Officer down! Shots fired, shots fired! Two-Adam-twenty-four, we're dying out here!"

The men from the gray sedan threw open the Bentley's doors and fired inside. Scott glimpsed passengers, but saw only shadows. Then the firing stopped, and Stephanie called out behind him. Her voice bubbled with blood, and cut him like knives.

"Don't leave me! Scotty, don't leave!"

Scott pushed harder, desperate to reach the car. Shotgun in the car. Keys in the ignition.

"DON'T LEAVE ME!"

"I'm not, baby. I'm *not.*"

"COME BACK!"

Scott was five yards from their patrol car when the big man heard Stephanie. He turned, saw Scott, then lifted his rifle and fired.

Scott James felt the third impact as the bullet punched through his vest on the lower right side of his chest. The pain was intense, and quickly grew worse as his abdominal cavity filled with pooling blood.

Scott slowed to a stop. He tried to crawl farther, but his strength was gone. He leaned back on an elbow, and waited for the big man to shoot him again, but the big man turned toward the Bentley.

Sirens were coming.

Black figures were inside the Bentley, but Scott couldn't see what they were doing. The driver of the gray sedan twisted to see the shooters, and pulled up his mask as he turned. Scott saw a flash of white on the man's cheek, and then the men in and around the Bentley ran into the Torino.

The big man was the last. He hesitated by the sedan's open door, once more looked at Scott, and raised his rifle.

Scott screamed.

"NO!"

Scott tried to jump out of the way as the sirens faded into a soothing voice.

"Wake up, Scott."

"NO!"

"Three, two, one —"

Nine months and sixteen days after he was shot that night, nine months and sixteen days after he saw his partner murdered, Scott James screamed when he woke.

2.

Scott threw himself out of the line of fire so violently when he woke, he was always surprised he had not jumped off his shrink's couch. He knew from experience he only made a small lurch. He woke from the enhanced regression the same way each time, jumping from the dream state of his memory as the big man raised the AK-47. Scott took careful, deep breaths, and tried to slow his thundering heart.

Goodman's voice came from across the dim room. Charles Goodman, M.D. Psychiatrist. Goodman did contract work with the Los Angeles Police Department, but was not an LAPD employee.

"Deep breaths, Scott. You feel okay?"

"I'm okay."

His heart pounded, his hands trembled, and cold sweat covered his chest, but as with the violent lunge that Goodman saw as only a tiny lurch, Scott was good at downplaying his feelings.

Goodman was an overweight man in his forties with a pointy beard, a ponytail, sandals, and toenail fungus. His small office was on the second floor of a two-story stucco building in Studio City next to the L.A. River channel. Scott's first shrink had a much nicer office in Chinatown at the LAPD's Behavioral Science Services, but Scott didn't like her. She reminded him of Stephanie.

"Would you like some water?"

"No. No, I'm fine."

Scott swung his feet off the couch, and grimaced at the tightness in his shoulder and side. He grew stiff when he sat for too long, so standing and moving helped ease the pain. He also needed a few seconds to adjust when he left the hypnotic state, like stepping from a sun-bright street into a dark bar. This was his fifth enhanced regression into the events of that night, but something about this regression left him confused and uncertain. Then he remembered, and looked at his shrink.

"Sideburns."

Goodman opened a notebook, ready to write. Goodman constantly wrote.

"Sideburns?"

"The man driving the getaway car. He had

white sideburns. These bushy white side-burns."

Goodman made a quick note in his book, then riffled back through the pages.

"You haven't described sideburns before?"

Scott strained to remember. Had he? Had he recalled the sideburns, but simply not mentioned them? He questioned himself, but already knew the answer.

"I didn't remember them before. Not until now. I remember them now."

Goodman scribbled furiously, but all the fast writing made Scott feel more doubtful.

"You think I really saw them, or am I imagining this?"

Goodman held up a hand to finish his note before speaking.

"Let's not go there yet. I want you to tell me what you remember. Don't second-guess yourself. Just tell me what you recall."

The memory of what he saw was clear.

"When I heard the sirens, he turned toward the shooters. He pulled up his mask when he turned."

"He was wearing the same mask?"

Scott had always described the five shoot-ers in exactly the same way.

"Yeah, the black knit ski mask. He pulled it up partway, and I saw the sideburns. They were long, here below the lobe. Might have been gray, like silver?"

Scott touched the side of his face by his ear, trying to see the image even more clearly — a faraway face in bad light, but there was the flash of white.

"Describe what you saw."

"I only saw part of his jaw. He had these white sideburns."

"Skin tone?"

"I don't know. White, maybe, or Latin or a light-skinned black guy."

"Don't guess. Only describe what you clearly remember."

"I can't say."

"Can you see his ear?"

"I saw part of his ear, but it was so far away."

"Hair?"

"Only the sideburns. He only raised the mask partway, but it was enough to see the sideburns. Jesus, I remember them so clearly now. Am I making this up?"

Scott had read extensively about manufactured memories, and memories recovered while under hypnosis. Such memories were viewed with suspicion, and were never used by L.A. County prosecutors. They were too easily attacked, and created reasonable doubt.

Goodman closed his notebook on the pen.

44

"Making this up as in imagining you saw something you didn't?"

"Yeah."

"You tell me. Why would you?"

Scott hated when Goodman went all psychiatrist on him, asking Scott to supply his own answers, but Scott had been seeing the man for seven months, so he grudgingly accepted the drill.

Scott had awakened two days after the shooting with a vivid memory of the events that night. During three weeks of intensive questioning by the Homicide Special detectives in charge of the investigation, Scott described the five shooters as best he could, but was unable to provide any more identifying detail than if the men had been featureless silhouettes. All five had been masked, gloved, and clothed from head to foot. None limped or had missing limbs. Scott had heard no voices, and could not provide eye, hair, or skin color, or such identifying information as visible tattoos, jewelry, scars, or affectations. No fingerprints or usable DNA had been found on the cartridge casings, in the Kenworth, or in the Ford Gran Torino found abandoned only eight blocks away. Despite the case being handled by an elite team of detectives from the LAPD's Homicide Special detail,

45

no suspects had been identified, all leads were exhausted, and the investigation had ground to an inevitable, glacial halt.

Nine months and sixteen days after Scott James was shot, the five men who shot him and murdered Stephanie Anders remained free.

They were still out there.

The five men who murdered Stephanie.

The killers.

Scott glanced at Goodman, and felt himself flush.

"Because I want to help. Because I want to feel like I'm doing something to catch these bastards, so I'm making up bullshit descriptions."

Because I'm alive and Stephanie's dead.

Scott was relieved when Goodman wrote none of this down. Instead, Goodman smiled.

"I find this encouraging."

"That I'm manufacturing memories?"

"There's no reason to believe you've manufactured anything. You've described the large elements of that night consistently since the beginning, from your conversation with Stephanie, to the makes and models of the vehicles, to where the shooters were standing when they fired their weapons. Everything you described that *could* be

46

confirmed *has* been confirmed, but so much was happening so quickly that night, and under such incredible stress, it's the tiny things we tend to lose."

Goodman always got into it when he described memory. Memory was his thing. He leaned forward, and pinched his thumb and forefinger together to show Scott what he meant by "tiny."

"Don't forget, you remembered the cartridge casings in our first regression. You didn't remember hearing the Kenworth's engine before you saw the truck until our fourth regression."

Our regressions. As if Goodman had been there with him, getting shot to pieces while Stephanie died. Regardless, Scott had to admit Goodman had a point. It wasn't until Scott's first regression that he recalled the spent casings twinkling like a brass rainbow as they arced from the big man's rifle, and he hadn't recalled hearing the Kenworth rev its engine until the fourth regression.

Goodman leaned so far forward, Scott thought he might fall from his chair. He was totally into it now.

"When the little details begin coming back — the tiny memories forgotten in the stress of the moment — the research suggests you may begin remembering more and more, as each new memory leads to another, the way water trickles through a crack in a dam, faster and faster until the dam breaks, and the water floods through."

Scott frowned.

"Meaning, my brain is falling apart?"

Goodman returned Scott's frown with a smile, and opened his notebook again.

"Meaning, you should feel encouraged. You wanted to examine what happened that night. This is what we're doing."

Scott did not respond. He used to believe he wanted to explore that night, but more and more he wanted to forget, though forgetting seemed beyond him. He relived it, reviewed it, and obsessed about it constantly, hating that night but unable to leave it.

Scott glanced at the time, saw they only had ten minutes remaining, and stood.

"Let's bag it for today, okay? I want to think about this."

Goodman made no move to close his notebook. He cleared his throat, instead, which was his way of changing the subject.

"We still have a few minutes. I want to check in with you about a few things."

Check in. Shrink jargon for asking more questions about things Scott didn't want to talk about.

"Sure. About what?"

"Whether the regressions are helping."

"I remembered the sideburns. You just told me they're helping."

"Not in what you remember, but in helping you cope. Are you having fewer nightmares?"

Nightmares had shattered his sleep four or five times a week since his fourth day in the hospital. Most were like short clips cut from a longer film of that night's events — the big man shooting at him, the big man raising his rifle, Scott slipping in Stephanie's blood, and the impact of bullets punching into his body. But more and more were paranoid nightmares where the masked men were hunting him. They jumped from his closet or hid under his bed or appeared in the back seat of his car. His most recent nightmare had been last night.

Scott said, "A lot less. I haven't had a nightmare in two or three weeks."

Goodman made a note in his book.

"You attribute this to the regressions?"

"What else?"

Goodman made a satisfied nod, along with another note.

"How's your social life?"

"Social life is fine if you mean grabbing a beer with the guys. I'm not seeing anyone."

"Are you looking?"

"Is mindless small talk a requirement for mental health?"

"No. Not at all."

"I just want someone I can relate to, you know? Someone who understands what it's like to be me."

Goodman made an encouraging smile.

"In the fullness of time, you'll meet someone. Few things are more healing than falling in love."

Few things would be more healing than forgetting, or catching the bastards who did this, but neither seemed to be in the cards.

Scott glanced at the clock, and was irritated to see they still had six minutes.

"Can we bag it for today? I'm tapped out, and I have to get to work."

"One more thing. Let's touch base about the new job."

Scott glanced at the time again, and his impatience increased.

"What about it?"

"Have you gotten your dog? Last session, you said the dogs were on their way."

"Got here last week. The chief trainer checks them out before he accepts them. He finished yesterday, and says we're good to go. I get my dog this afternoon."

"And then you're back on the street."

50

Scott knew where this was going and didn't like it. They had been through this before.

"After we're certified, yeah. That's where K-9 officers do their job."

"Face-to-face with the bad guys."

"That's kinda the point."

"You almost died. Are you concerned this might happen again?"

Scott hesitated, but knew better than to pretend he had no fear. Scott had not wanted to be in a patrol car again, or sit behind a desk, but when he learned two slots were opening in the Metro K-9 Unit, he had lobbied hard for the job. He had completed the K-9 dog handler training course nine days ago.

"I think about it, sure, but all officers think about it. This is one of the reasons I want to stay on the job."

"Not all officers are shot three times and lose their partner on the same night."

Scott didn't respond. Since the day he woke in the hospital, Scott had thought about leaving the job a thousand times. Most of his officer friends told him he was crazy not to take the medical, and the LAPD Personnel Division told him, because of the extent of his injuries, he would never be cleared to return, yet Scott pushed to stay on the job. Pushed his physical therapy. Pushed his commanding officers. Pushed his Metro boss hard to let him work with a dog. Scott would lie awake in the middle of the night, making up reasons for all the pushing: Maybe he didn't know what else to do, maybe he had nothing else in his life, maybe he was trying to convince himself he was still the same man he was before the shooting. Meaningless words to fill the empty darkness, like the lies and half-truths he told to Goodman and everyone else, because saying unreal things was easier than saying real things. His unspoken, dead-of-night truth was that he felt as if he had died on the street beside Stephanie, and was now only a ghost pretending to be a man. Even his choice of being a K-9 officer was a pretense — that he could be a cop without a partner.

Scott realized the silence was dragging on, and found Goodman waiting.

Scott said, "If I walk away, the assholes who killed Stephanie win."

"Why are you still seeing me?"

"To make peace with being alive."

"I believe that's true. But not the whole truth."

"Then you tell me."

Goodman glanced at the time again, and

finally closed the notebook.

"Looks like we're a few minutes over. This was a good session, Scott. Same time next week?"

Scott stood, hiding the stitch in his side that came with the sudden movement.

"Same time next week."

Scott was opening the door when Goodman spoke again.

"I'm glad the regressions are helping. I hope you remember enough to find peace and closure."

Scott hesitated, then walked out and down to the parking lot before he spoke again.

"I hope I remember enough to forget."

Stephanie came to him every night, and it was his memories of her that tortured him — Stephanie slipping from his bloody grip, Stephanie begging him not to leave.

Don't leave me!

Scotty, don't leave!

Come back!

In his nightmares, it was her eyes and her pleading voice that filled him with anguish.

Stephanie Anders died believing he had abandoned her, and nothing he did now or in the future could change her final thoughts. She had died believing he had left her to save himself.

I'm here, Steph.

I didn't leave you.
I was trying to save you.

Scott told her these things every night when she came to him, but Stephanie was dead and could not hear. He knew he would never be able to convince her, but he told her anyway, each time she came to him, trying to convince himself.

3.

The narrow parking lot behind Goodman's building was furious with summer heat, and the air was sandpaper dry. Scott's car was so hot, he used his handkerchief to open the door.

Scott bought the blue 1981 Trans Am two months before the shooting. The right rear fender had a nasty dent from the taillight to the door, the blue paint was pocked with corrosion, the radio didn't work, and the odometer showed 126,000 miles. Scott had bought it for twelve hundred dollars as a weekend project, thinking he would rebuild the old car in his spare time, but after the shooting he lost interest. Nine months later, the car remained untouched.

When the air blew cold, Scott made his way to the Ventura Freeway and headed for Glendale.

The K-9 Platoon was headquartered with the Metro Division at the Central Station downtown, but used several sites around the city for training its dogs. The primary training site was in Glendale, which was a spacious facility where Scott and the other two new handlers had been trained as K-9 officers during an eight-week handler school run by the Unit's veteran chief trainer. The student handlers trained with retired patrol dogs who no longer worked in the field due to health or injury issues. They were easy to work with and knew what was expected of them. In many ways, these dogs served as teachers for their baby handlers, but when the school cycle was completed, the training dogs would return to wherever they lived, and the new handlers would be partnered with pre-trained patrol dogs to begin a fourteen-week certification process. This was an exciting moment for the new handlers, as it meant they would begin bonding with their new dogs.

Scott knew he should feel excited, but felt only a dull readiness to work. Once Scott and his dog were certified, he would be alone with the dog in a car, and that's what Scott wanted. The freedom to be alone. He had plenty of company with Stephanie.

Scott was passing the Hollywood split when his phone rang. The Caller ID showed LAPD, so he answered, thinking it was probably his K-9 Platoon Chief Trainer, Dominick Leland.

"This is Scott."

A male voice spoke, but it wasn't Leland.

"Officer James, I'm Bud Orso, here with Robbery-Homicide. I'm calling to introduce myself. I'm the new lead in charge of your case."

Scott drove on without speaking. He had not spoken with his case investigators in more than three months.

"Officer, you still there? Did I lose you?"

"I'm here."

"I'm the new lead in charge of your case."

"I heard you. What happened to Melon?"

"Detective Melon retired last month. Detective Stengler was reassigned. We got a new team in here on this."

Detective Melon was the former lead, and Stengler was his partner. Scott had not spoken with either man since the day Scott gimped into the Police Administration Building with his walker, and unloaded on Melon in front of the entire Homicide Special squad room because they had been unable to name a suspect or develop new leads after a five-month investigation. Melon had tried to walk away, but Scott grabbed him, fell out of his walker, and pulled Melon down with him. It was an ugly scene Scott regretted, and could have derailed Scott's chance to return to the job. After the incident, Scott's Metro boss, a Captain named Jeff Schmidt, cut a deal with the RHD commander, a Lieutenant named Carol Topping, who buried the incident. An act of compassion for an officer who was shot to shit in the street. Melon had not filed a complaint, but shut Scott out of the investigation and stopped returning his calls.

Scott said, "Okay. Thanks for letting me know."

He didn't know what else to say, but wondered why Orso sounded so friendly.

"Did Melon tell you what happened?"

"Yes, he told me. He said you were an ungrateful prick."

"I am."

Fuckit. Scott hadn't cared what Melon thought of him, and didn't care what the new guy thought, either, but he was surprised when Orso laughed.

"Look, I know you had a problem with him, but I'm the new guy. I'd like to meet you, and go over a couple of things in the file."

Scott felt a flare of hope.

"Did Melon turn any new leads?"

"No, I can't say that. This is just me, trying to get up to speed on what happened that night. Could you roll by sometime to-day?"

The flare of hope faded to a bitter ember. Orso sounded like a nice guy, but Scott had just relived what happened that night, and was fed up with talking about it.

"I'm on shift, then I have plans."

Orso paused. This told Scott Orso knew Scott was giving him the brush.

Orso said, "How about tomorrow, or whenever is convenient?"

"Can I give you a call?"

Orso gave him his direct-dial number, and hung up.

Scott dropped his phone on the seat between his legs. The numbness he felt only moments earlier had been replaced with ir-ritation. Scott wondered what Orso wanted to ask about, and if he should have men-tioned the sideburns even though he didn't know if they were real.

Scott cut across lanes and veered toward the city. He punched in Orso's number as he passed Griffith Park.

"Detective Orso, it's Scott James again. If you're there now, I can swing by."

"I'm here. You remember where we are?"

Scott smiled at that, and wondered if this was Orso's idea of a joke.

"I remember."

59

"Try not to hit anyone when you get here."

Scott didn't laugh, and neither did Orso.

Scott phoned Dominick Leland next, and told him he wouldn't be in to see the new dogs. Leland growled like a German shepherd.

"Why in hell not?"

"I'm on my way to the Boat."

"Fuck the Boat. There is nothing and no one in that damned building more important than these dogs. I did not let you into my K-9 platoon to waste time with those people down there."

Robbery-Homicide housed their special units on the fifth floor of the Police Administration Building. The PAB was a ten-story structure across from City Hall. The side of the PAB facing City Hall was a thin, pointy, triangular glass wedge. This made the PAB look like the prow of a ship, so rank-and-file officers dubbed it the Boat.

"They want me at Robbery-Homicide. It's about the case."

Leland's growl softened.

"Your case?"

"Yes, sir. I'm on my way now."

Leland's voice turned gruff again.

"All right, then, get your ass here as soon as you can."

Scott never wore his uniform to Goodman's office. He kept his uniform in a gym bag and his handgun in a lockbox in the trunk. He dropped off the freeway on First Street, and changed in the Boat's parking garage. He expected more than a few detectives to give him the glare because of his scene with Melon. Scott didn't give a rat's ass, either way. He wanted to remind them he was a police officer.

Scott showed his badge and LAPD ID card to the lobby receptionist, and told her he was there to see Orso. She made a brief call, then gave Scott a different ID card to clip to his shirt.

"He's expecting you. You know where they are?"

"I know."

Scott tried not to limp as he crossed the lobby, which wasn't so easy with all the steel in his leg. The night they wheeled him into the Good Samaritan emergency room, Scott had surgeries on his thigh, shoulder, and lower chest. Three more surgeries followed later that same week, with two additional surgeries six weeks later. The leg wound cost him three pounds of muscle tissue, needed a steel rod and six screws to rebuild his femur, and left him with nerve damage. The shoulder reconstruction required three plates, eight screws, and also left him with nerve damage. The PT after the multiple surgeries had been painful, but he was doing okay. You just had to be tougher than the pain, and eat a few painkillers.

Bud Orso was in his early forties, with a chubby scoutmaster's face topped by a crown of short black hair. He was waiting when Scott stepped off the elevator, which Scott had not expected.

"Bud Orso. Pleasure to meet you, though I'm sorry it's under these circumstances."

Orso had a surprisingly strong grip, but released Scott quickly and led him toward the Homicide Special offices.

"I've been living with this file since they handed me the case. Horrible, what happened that night. How long have you been back on the job?"

"Eleven weeks."

Polite conversation. Scott was already irritated, and wondered what was waiting for him in the Homicide Special squad room.

"I'm surprised they let you."

"Let me what?"

"Come back. You were squared up for a medical."

Scott didn't respond. He was already tired of talking, and sorry he came.

Orso noted the K-9 patch on Scott's shoulder as they walked.

62

"K-9. That should be interesting."

"Better. They do what you say, don't talk back, and it's only a dog."

Orso finally took the hint and fell silent as he led Scott into Homicide Special. Scott felt himself tense when he stepped through the door, but only five detectives were scattered about the room, and none glanced over or acknowledged him in any way. He followed Orso into a small conference room with a rectangular table and five chairs. A large black file box was on the floor at the head of the table. Scott saw his transcribed statements spread across the table, and statements made by the friends and families of the two men who had been inside the Bentley, a real estate developer named Eric Pahlasian, the driver, who had been shot sixteen times, and his cousin from France, a real estate attorney named Georges Beloit, who had been shot eleven times.

Orso went to the head of the table, and told Scott to sit wherever he liked.

Scott braced himself, then averted his face when he sat so Orso couldn't see his grimace. Taking a seat always caused a painful jolt in his side.

"Want a coffee or some water?"

"I'm good. Thanks."

A large drawing of the crime scene leaned

against the wall on the floor. Someone had sketched in the Kenworth, the Bentley, the Gran Torino, and the Adam car. Someone had sketched in Stephanie and Scott. A manila envelope lay on the floor by the poster board. Scott guessed crime scene photos were in the envelope, and glanced away. When he looked up, Orso was watching, and now Orso didn't look like a scoutmaster. There was a focus to his eyes that hardened them to points.

"I understand talking about this might be difficult."

"No sweat. What did you want to know?"

Orso studied him for a moment, then gave him the question.

"Why didn't the big man finish you?"

Scott had asked himself this ten thousand times, but could only guess at the answer.

"Paramedics, is my guess. The sirens were getting closer."

"Did you see him leave?"

If Orso read the interviews, he already knew the answer.

"No. I saw him lift the rifle. The gun came up, I laid back, and maybe I passed out. I don't know."

Later, in the hospital, they told him he had passed out from blood loss.

"Did you hear them leave?"

"No."

"Doors closing?"

"No."

"Were you awake when the paramedics arrived?"

"What did they say?"

"I'm asking you."

"The rifle came up, I put my head back, and then I was in the hospital."

Scott's shoulder was killing him. A deep ache, as if his muscles were turning to stone. The ache spread across his back as if the scar tissue was splitting apart.

Orso slowly nodded, then made a crooked shrug.

"The sirens are a good bet, but you never know. When you slumped back, maybe he thought you were dead. Maybe he was out of ammo. Gun might have jammed. One day we'll ask him."

Orso picked up a slender report, and leaned back.

"Point is, you were hearing just fine until you passed out. Here in your statements, you mentioned you and Officer Anders were talking about how quiet it was. You stated she turned off the car so you could hear the silence."

Scott felt his face flush, and a stab of guilt up through the center of his chest.

65

"Yes, sir. That was on me. I asked her to turn off the vehicle."

"You hear anything?"

"It was quiet."

"I get it was quiet, but how quiet? Were there background sounds?"

"I dunno. Maybe the freeway."

"Don't guess. Voices on the next block? Barking? A noise that stood out?"

Scott wondered what Orso was going for. Neither Melon nor Stengler had asked him about background sounds.

"Nothing I recall."

"A door closing? An engine starting?"

"It was quiet. What are you digging at?"

Orso swiveled toward the crime scene poster. He leaned toward it and touched the side street from which the Kenworth had come. A blue X had been drawn on a storefront three doors from the intersection.

"A store here was burglarized the night you were shot. The owner says it happened after eight, which was when he locked up, but before seven the next morning. We have no reason to think the burglary occurred when you and Anders were at the scene, but you never know. I've been wondering about it."

Scott didn't recall Melon or Stengler mentioning the burglary, which would have

66

been a major element in their investigation.

"Melon never asked me about this."

"Melon didn't know. The place is owned by a Nelson Shin. You know that name?"

"No, sir."

"He distributes candy and herbs and crap he imports from Asia — some of which isn't legal to bring into the U.S. He's been ripped off so many times, he didn't bother to file a report. He went shopping for a weapon instead, and got named in an ATF sting six weeks ago. He shit out when the ATF scooped him, and claimed he needed a full-auto M4 because he's been burglarized so many times. He gave the ATF a list of dates to show how many times his store was cracked. Six times in the past year, if you're curious. One of those dates matched with your shooting."

Scott stared at the blue X that marked the store. When Stephanie shut off the engine, they listened to the silence for only ten or fifteen seconds, then began talking. Then the Bentley appeared, but the Bentley was so quiet he remembered thinking it moved like it was floating.

"I heard the Kenworth rev. Before it came out of the side street, I heard the big diesel rev up."

"That's all?"

Scott wondered how much to say, and how to explain.

"It's a new memory. I only remembered hearing it a couple of weeks ago."

Orso frowned, so Scott went on.

"A lot happened that night in a short period. I remembered the big things, but a lot of small things got lost. They're beginning to come back. The doctor says it happens like that."

"Okay."

Scott hesitated, then decided to tell him about the sideburns.

"I caught a glimpse of the getaway driver. You won't find this in the interviews because I just remembered."

Orso tipped forward.

"You saw him?"

"The side of his face. He raised his mask for a second. He had white sideburns."

Orso pulled his chair closer.

"Could you pick him out of a six-pack?"

A six-pack was a grouping of six photographs of suspects who looked similar.

"All I saw were the sideburns."

"Can I put you together with a sketch artist?"

"I didn't see him well enough."

Now Orso was looking irritated.

"Race?"

68

"All I remember is the sideburns. I might remember more, but I don't know. My doctor says the way it works is, one memory can trigger another. I remembered the Kenworth revving, and now the sideburns, so more things might start coming back to me."

Orso seemed to consider this, and finally settled back in his chair. Everything about him seemed to soften.

"You went through hell, man. I'm sorry this happened."

Scott didn't know what to say. He finally shrugged.

Orso said, "I want you to stay in touch. Anything else you remember, call me. Doesn't matter if you think it's important or not. Don't worry about sounding silly or stupid, okay? I want everything you've got."

Scott nodded. He glanced at the papers spread over the table and the files in the box. It was a larger box and contained more than Scott would have expected, considering the little Melon shared.

Scott studied the box for a moment, then looked back at Orso.

"Could I read through the file?"

Orso followed Scott's eyes to the box.

"You want to go through the file?"

"One memory triggers another. Maybe I'll

see something that helps me remember other things."

Orso considered for a moment, then nodded.

"Not now, but sure. If that's what you want. You'll have to go through it here, but I'm fine with letting you see it. Call in the next couple of days, and we'll set up a time."

Orso stood, and when Scott stood with him, Orso saw his grimace.

"You doing okay?"

"That's scar tissue loosening up. The docs say it'll take about a year for the stiffness to pass."

The same bullshit he told everyone.

Orso said nothing more until they reached the hall and were heading toward the elevator. Then his eyes hardened again.

"One other thing. I'm not Melon. He felt bad for you, but he thought you became a crazy pain in the ass who should've been pushed out on a psycho. You probably think he was a lousy detective. You were both wrong. Whatever you think, those guys busted their asses, but sometimes you can bust your ass and nothing turns up. It sucks, but sometimes that happens."

Scott opened his mouth to say something, but Orso raised a hand, stopping him.

"No one here quits. I'm not going to quit.

I'm going to live out this case one way or another. Are we clear?"

Scott nodded.

"My door is open. Call if you want, but if you call sixteen times a day, I'm not going to return sixteen calls. We clear on that, too?"

"I'm not going to call you sixteen times."

"But if I call *you* sixteen times, you damn well better get back to me asap each and every time, because I will have questions that need answers."

"I'll move in and live with you if it means catching these bastards."

Orso smiled, and looked like the scout-master again.

"You won't have to live with me, but we will catch them."

They said their good-byes at the elevator. Scott waited until Orso returned to his office, then gimped to the men's room. His limp was pronounced when no one was watching.

The pain was so bad he thought he would vomit.

He splashed cold water on his face, and rubbed his temples and eyes. He dried himself, then took two Vicodin from a small plastic bag, swallowed them, then rubbed his face with cold water again.

71

He patted himself dry, then studied himself in the mirror while he let the pills work. He was fifteen pounds thinner than the night he was shot, and half an inch shorter because of the leg. He was lined, and looked older, and wondered what Stephanie would think if she saw him.

He was thinking about Stephanie when a uniformed officer shoved open the door. The officer was young and in a hurry, so he shoved the door hard. Scott lurched sideways, away from the noise, and spun toward the officer. His heart pounded as if trying to beat its way out of his chest, his face tingled as his blood pressure spiked, and his breath caught in his chest. He stood motionless, staring, as his pulse thundered in his ears.

The young officer said, "Dude, hey, I'm sorry I scared you. I have to pee."

He hurried to the urinal.

Scott stared at his back, then clenched his eyes shut. He clenched his eyes hard, but he could not shut out what he was seeing. He saw the masked man with a large belly coming toward him with the AK-47. He saw the man in his dreams, and when he was awake. He saw the man shoot Stephanie first, then turn his gun toward Scott.

"Sir, are you okay?"

Scott opened his eyes, and found the young officer staring.

Scott pushed past him out of the bathroom. He did not limp when he crossed the lobby, or when he reached the training field to claim his first dog.

4.

The K-9 Platoon's primary training facility was a multi-use site located on the east side of the L.A. River only a few minutes northeast of the Boat, in an area where anonymous industrial buildings gave way to small businesses, cheap restaurants, and parks.

Scott turned through a gate, and parked in a narrow parking lot beside a beige cinder-block building, set at the edge of a large green field big enough for softball games or Knights of Columbus barbeques or training police dogs. An obstacle course for the dogs was set up beside the building. The field was circled by a tall chain-link fence, and hidden from public view by thick green hedges.

Scott parked by the building, and saw several officers working their dogs as he got out of his car. A K-9 Sergeant named Mace Styrik was trotting a German shepherd with odd marks on her hindquarters around the

74

field. Scott did not recognize the dog, and wondered if she was Styrik's pet. On the near end of the field, a handler named Cam Francis and his dog, Tony, were approaching a man who wore a thick padded sleeve covering his right arm and hand. The man was a handler named Al Timmons, who was pretending to be a suspect. Tony was a fifty-five-pound Belgian Malinois, a breed that looked like a smaller, slimmer German shepherd. Timmons suddenly turned and ran. Francis waited until Timmons was forty yards away, then released his dog, who sprinted after Timmons like a cheetah running down an antelope. Timmons turned to meet the dog's charge, waving his padded arm. Tony was still six or eight yards away when he launched himself at Timmons, and clamped onto the padded arm. An unsuspecting man would have gone down with the impact, but Timmons had done this hundreds of times, and knew what to expect. He turned with the impact, and kept spinning, swinging Tony around and around in the air. Tony did not let go, and, Scott knew, was enjoying the ride. The Malinois breed bit so hard and well, and showed such bite commitment, they were jokingly called Maligators. Timmons was still spinning the dog when Scott saw Leland standing against the building, watching the officers work their dogs. Leland was standing with his arms crossed, and a coiled leash clipped to his belt. Scott had never seen the man without the leash at his side.

Dominick Leland was a tall, bony African-American with thirty-two years on the job as a K-9 handler, first in the United States Army, then the L.A. County Sheriffs, and finally the LAPD. He was a living legend in the LAPD K-9 corps.

Bald on top, his head was rimmed with short gray hair, and two fingers were missing from his left hand. The fingers were bitten off by a monstrous Rottweiler-mastiff fighting dog on the day Leland earned the first of the seven Medals of Valor he would earn throughout his career. Leland and his first dog, a German shepherd named Maisie Dobkin, had been deployed to search for an Eight-Deuce Crip murder suspect and known drug dealer named Howard Oskari Walcott. Earlier that day, Walcott fired nine shots into a crowd of high school students waiting at a bus stop, wounding three and killing a fourteen-year-old girl named Tashira Johnson. When LAPD ground and air support units trapped Walcott in a nearby neighborhood, Leland and Maisie Dobkin were called out to locate the suspect, who was believed to be armed, dangerous, and hiding somewhere within a group of four neighboring properties. Leland and Maisie cleared the first property easily enough, then moved into the adjoining backyard of a house then occupied by another Crip gangbanger, Eustis Simpson. Unknown to officers at the time, Simpson kept two enormous male Rottweiler-mastiff mixed-breeds on his property, both of which were scarred and vicious veterans of Simpson's illegal dogfighting business.

When Leland and Maisie Dobkin entered Simpson's backyard that day, both dogs charged from beneath the house and attacked Maisie Dobkin. The first dog, which weighed one hundred forty pounds, hit Maisie so hard she rolled upside down. He buried his teeth into Maisie's neck, pinning her down, as the second dog, which weighed almost as much, grabbed her right hind leg and shook it like a terrier shakes a rat. Maisie screamed. Dominick Leland could have done something silly like run for a garden hose or waste time with pepper spray, but Maisie would be dead in seconds, so Leland waded into the fight. He kneed the dog biting her leg to clear a line of fire, pushed his Beretta into the attacker's back, and pulled the trigger. He then grabbed the other dog's face with his free hand to make the dog release Maisie's neck. The overgrown monster bit Leland's hand, and Leland shot the sonofabitch twice, but not before the big dog took his pinky and ring finger. Leland later said he never felt the bite, and never knew the fingers were missing, until he put Maisie into the ambulance and demanded the paramedics rush her to the closest veterinarian. Both Leland and Maisie Dobkin recovered, and worked together for another six years until Maisie Dobkin retired. Leland still kept the official LAPD picture of himself and Maisie Dobkin on the wall of his office. He kept pictures of himself with all the dogs who had been his partners.

Leland scowled when he saw Scott, but Scott didn't take it personally. Leland scowled at everyone and everything except his dogs.

Leland uncrossed his arms, and entered the building.

"C'mon, now, let's see what we have."

The building was divided into two small offices, a general meeting room, and a kennel. The K-9 Platoon used the facility only for training and evaluations, and did not staff the building on a full-time basis.

Scott followed Leland past the offices and

78

into the kennel, Leland talking as they walked. Eight chain-link dog runs with chain-link gates lined the left side of the kennel, with a walkway leading past them to a door at the end of the building. The runs were four feet wide and eight feet deep, with floor-to-ceiling sides. The floor was a concrete slab with built-in drains, so the room could be washed and rinsed with hoses. When the training dogs lived here, Scott and his two classmates, Amy Barber and Seymore Perkins, had begun every morning by scooping up dog shit and washing the floor with disinfectant. This gave the kennel a medicinal smell.

Leland said, "Perkins is getting Jimmy Riggs' dog, Spider. I think they will be a good match. That Spider, I'll tell you something, he has a mind of his own, but he and Seymore will come to terms."

Seymore Perkins was Leland's favorite of the three new handlers. Perkins had grown up with hunting dogs, and possessed a calm confidence with the dogs, who instantly trusted him. Amy Barber had shown an intuitive feel for bonding with the dogs, and a command authority that far surpassed her slight build and higher voice.

Leland stopped between the second and third runs, where the two new dogs were waiting. Both dogs stood when Leland entered, and the near dog barked twice. They were skinny male Belgian Malinois.

Leland beamed as if they were his children.

"Aren't these boys gorgeous? Look at these boys. They are handsome young men."

The barker barked again, and both furiously wagged their tails.

Scott knew both dogs had arrived fully trained by the breeder, in accordance with written guidelines supplied by the K-9 Platoon. This meant Leland, who traveled to breeders all over the world in search of the best available dogs. Leland had spent the past three days personally running the dogs through their paces, evaluating their fitness, and learning each dog's personality and peculiarities. Not every dog sent to the K-9 Platoon measured up to Leland's standards. He downchecked those who did not, and returned them to their breeder.

Leland glanced at the dog in the second run.

"This here is Gutman. Why on earth those fools named him Gutman, I do not know, but that's his name."

Purchased dogs were usually around two years old when they arrived, so they had already been named. Donated dogs were often a year older.

"And this here is Quarlo."

Gutman barked again, and went up on his hind legs, trying to lick Leland through the gate.

Leland said, "Gutman here is kinda high-strung, so I'm gonna put him with Amy. Quarlo here is smart as a whip. He's got a good head on his shoulders, and he's easy to work with, so I think you and Mr. Quarlo here are going to make a fine match."

Scott interpreted "easy to work with" and "smart as a whip" as Leland's way of saying the other dog was too much for Scott to handle. Perkins and Barber were the better handlers, so they were getting the more difficult dogs. Scott was the moron.

Scott heard the door open at the far end of the kennel and saw Mace come in with the German shepherd. He put the shepherd into a run, dragged out a large canine crate, and closed the shepherd's gate.

Scott studied Quarlo. He was a beautiful dog with a dark fawn body, black face, and upright black ears. His eyes were warm and intelligent. His steady demeanor was obvious. Where Gutman frittered and fidgeted, Quarlo stood utterly calm. Leland was probably right. This would be the easiest dog for Scott.

Scott glanced at Leland, but Leland wasn't looking at him. Leland was smiling at the dog.

Scott said, "I'll work harder. I'll work as hard as it takes."

Leland glanced up, and studied Scott for a moment. The only time Scott recalled Leland not scowling was when he looked at the dogs, but now he seemed thoughtful. He touched the leash clipped to his belt with his three-fingered hand.

"This isn't steel and nylon. It's a nerve. You clip one end to you, you clip the other to this animal, it ain't for dragging him down the street. You *feel* him through this nerve, and he feels you, and what flows through here flows both ways — anxiety, fear, discipline, approval — right through this nerve without you and your dog ever even having to look at each other, without you ever having to say a word. He can feel it, and you can feel it, too."

Leland let go of his leash, and glanced back at Quarlo.

"You're gonna work, all right, I know you're a worker, but there's things work can't build. I watched you for eight weeks, and you did everything I asked you to do, but I never saw anything flow through your leash. You understand what I'm saying?"

"I'll work harder."

Scott was trying to figure out what else to say when Cam Francis opened the door behind them, and asked Leland to check Tony's foot. Cam looked worried. Leland told Scott he would be right back, and hurried away, scowling. Scott stared at Quarlo for several seconds, then walked to the other end of the kennel where Mace was now hosing out the crate.

Scott said, "Hey."

Mace said, "Watch you don't get splashed."

The shepherd was lying with her head between her paws on a padded mat at the back of the run. She was a classic black-and-tan German shepherd with a black muzzle giving way to light brown cheeks and mask, a black blaze on the top of her head, and enormous black ears. Her eyebrows bunched as she looked from Scott to Mace, and back again. No other part of her moved. A hard rubber toy lay untouched on the newspaper, as did a leather chew and a fresh bowl of water. A name was written on the side of the crate. Scott cocked his head sideways to read it. Maggie.

Scott guessed she had to go eighty or eighty-five pounds. A lot bigger than the Maligators. She was big through the chest and hips the way shepherds were, but it was the hairless gray lines on her hindquarters that drew him. He squeezed past the crate for a better view, and watched her eyes follow him.

"This Maggie?"

"Yeah."

"She ours?"

"Nah. Donation dog. Family down Oceanside thought we could use her, but Leland's sending her back."

Scott studied the pale lines and decided they were scars.

"What happened to her?"

Mace put aside the hose, and joined Scott at the gate.

"She was wounded in Afghanistan. The scars there are from the surgeries."

"No shit. A military working dog?"

"U.S. Marine, this girl. She healed up okay, but Leland says she's unfit."

"What kind of work did she do?"

"Dual-purpose dog. Patrol and explosives detection."

Scott knew almost nothing about military working dogs, except that the training they received was specialized and excellent.

"Bomb get her?"

"Nope. Her handler was blown up by one of those suicide nuts. The dog here stayed with him, and some asshole sniper tried to kill her."

"No shit."

"For real. Shot her twice, Leland says. Parked herself on her boy, and wouldn't leave. Trying to protect him, I guess. Wouldn't even let other Marines get near him."

Scott stared at the German shepherd, but Mace and the kennel faded, and he heard the gunfire that night — the automatic rifle churning its thunder, the chorus of pistols snapping like whips. Then her brown eyes met his, and he was back in the kennel again.

Scott bit the inside of his mouth, and cleared his throat before speaking.

"She didn't leave."

"That's the story."

Scott noted how she watched them. Her nose worked constantly, sucking in their smells. Even though she had not moved from her prone position, Scott knew she was focused on them.

"If she healed up okay, what's Leland's problem?"

"She's bad with noise, for one. See how she lays back there, all kinda timid? Leland thinks she's got a stress disorder. Dogs get PTSD just like people."

Scott felt himself flush, and opened the gate to hide his irritation. He wondered if Mace and the other handlers spoke about him like this behind his back.

Scott said, "Hey, Maggie, how's it going?"

Maggie stayed on her belly with her ears folded back, which was a sign of submission, but she stared into his eyes, which possibly indicated aggression. Scott slowly approached her. She watched as he came, but her ears stayed down and she issued no warning growl. He held the back of his hand toward her.

"You a good girl, Maggie? My name is Scott. I'm a police officer, so don't give me any trouble, okay?"

Scott squatted a couple of feet from her, and watched her nose work.

"Can I pet you, Maggie? How 'bout I pet you?"

He moved his hand slowly closer, and was six inches from her head when she bit him. She moved insanely fast, snarling and snapping, and caught the top of his hand as he jerked to his feet.

Mace shouted, and charged into the run.

"Jesus! She get you?"

Maggie quit her attack as quickly as she bit him, and once more lay on her belly. Scott had jumped back, and now stood three feet away from her.

"Dude, you're bleeding. Lemme see. She get you deep?"

Scott pressed his handkerchief over the cut.

"It's nothing."

He watched Maggie's eyes move from him to Mace and back, as if she had to watch them both because either might attack.

Scott made his voice soothing.

"You got hurt bad, big girl. Yes, you did."

I'll bet I've been shot more times than you.

He squatted again, and held out his hand again, letting her smell his blood. This time she let him touch her. He spread his fingers through the soft fur between her ears, then slowly stepped away. She stayed on her belly, watching him, as he and Mace backed out of her run.

Mace said, "That's why she's going back. Leland says they get fucked up like this, they're never right again."

"Leland said that?"

"Voice of God."

Scott left Mace washing out Maggie's crate, and walked back through the offices, and outside, where he found Leland on his way back.

Leland said, "You and Quarlo ready to get to work?"

"I want the German shepherd."

"You can't have the shepherd. Perkins is gettin' Spider."

"Not Spider. The one you're shipping back. Maggie. Let me work with her. Give me two weeks."

"That dog's no good."

"Give me two weeks to change your mind."

Leland scowled the Leland scowl, then grew thoughtful again and fingered his leash.

"Okay. Two weeks. You got her."

Scott followed Leland back inside to get his new dog.

5.

DOMINICK LELAND

A few minutes later, Leland resumed his position outside in the spare shade cast by the building, crossed his arms, and watched Scott James work with the dog. Mace stood with him for a while, but grew bored, and went inside to get on with his duties. Leland said little. He watched how the man and the dog related to each other.

Inside, before they came out, Leland walked Scott back to the shepherd.

"Take her out back, and introduce yourself. I'm gonna watch."

Leland walked away without another word, and waited outside. After a while, Officer James came around the far side of the building with the dog on his lead. The dog was on James' left, which was the proper position, and did not try to range from him as they walked, but this proved nothing. The dog had been trained by the

United States Marine Corps. Leland did not doubt the excellence of her training, which he had witnessed himself when he evaluated her.

Officer James called over.

"Anything in particular you want me to do?"

Me. Not us. There was your problem, right there.

Leland answered with a scowl. After a while James withered under Leland's scowl, and went on with it. He made a few ninety-degree left and right turns, and trotted in left and right circles. The dog was always in perfect position except when they stopped. When they stopped, the dog lowered her head, tucked her tail, and hunched herself as if she was trying to hide. Officer James seemed not to notice this, even though he glanced at the dog often.

When Leland was sure James was concentrating on the dog, he slipped a black starter pistol from his pocket, and pulled the trigger. The starter pistol fired a .22-caliber blank cartridge, and was used to test new dogs for their tolerance to loud, unexpected sounds. A dog that freaked out when a gun went off was of little use to the police.

The sound cracked sharply across the training field, and caught both the dog and her handler by surprise.

James and the dog lurched at the same time, but the dog tucked her tail, and tried to hide between James' legs. When James looked over, Leland held up the starter pistol.

"Stress reaction. Can't have a police dog that shits out when a gun goes off."

James said nothing for several seconds. Leland was about to ask what in hell he was looking at when James stooped to touch the dog's head.

"No, sir, we can't. We'll work on it."

"Long strokes. Start at her neck and run your hand back to her tail. They like the long strokes. That's the way her mama did it."

James stroked her, long and slow, but he glared at Leland instead of relating to the dog. This set Leland off into one of his tirades.

"Talk to her, goddamnit. She ain't a stick of furniture. She is one of God's creatures, and she will hear you. I see these goddamned people walkin' dogs, yakking on their phones, makes me wanna kick their sissy asses. What they got a dog for, they want to talk on their phones? That dog there will understand you, Officer James. She will understand what's in your heart. Am I just shouting at the grass and dog shit out here, or are you reading what I am telling you?"

"I'm reading you, Sergeant."

Leland watched him stroke the dog, and talk to her, and then he shouted again.

"Obstacles."

The obstacle course was a series of jumping barriers and climbs. Leland had taken her through the course five times, so he knew what to expect. She was fine with the climbs, made the low jumps easily, but when she reached the last and highest barrier, a five-foot wall, she balked. The first time Leland took her through, he assumed her hips hurt because of her wounds or her strength was gone, but he stroked her and spoke with her, and when they tried again, she clawed her way over, and damn near broke his heart for trying so hard. Officer James brought her to the high barrier three times, and all three times she hit the brakes. The third time she splayed her legs, spun toward James, and snarled. To his credit, James did not jerk her lead, raise his voice, or try to force her. He backed off and talked to her until she calmed. Leland knew of a hundred other things Officer James could have done to help her over, but overall he approved of James' response.

Leland called out another instruction.

"Off the line. Voice commands."

James led her away from the obstacle course, unclipped the lead from her collar, and ran through the basic voice commands. He told her to sit, she sat. He told her to stay, she stayed. Stay, sit, come, heel, down. She would still have to learn the LAPD situational commands, which were different from military commands, but she did these well enough. After fifteen minutes of this, Leland called out again.

"She done good. Reward."

Leland had been through this with her, too, and waited to see what would happen. The best dog training was based on the reward system. You did not punish a dog for doing wrong, you rewarded the dog for doing right. The dog did something you wanted, you reinforced the behavior with a reward — pet'm, tell'm they're a good dog, let'm play with a toy. The standard reward for a K-9 working dog was a hard plastic ball with a hole drilled through it where Leland liked to smear a little peanut butter.

Leland watched James dig the hard plastic ball from his pocket, and wave it in front of the dog's face. She showed no interest. James bounced it in front of her, trying to get her excited, but she moved away, and appeared to get nervous. Leland could hear

James talking to her in the squeaky voice dogs associated with approval.

"Here you go, girl. Want it? Want to go get it?"

James tossed the ball past her, watching it bounce along the ground. The dog circled James' legs, and sat down behind him, facing the opposite direction. Leland had made the mistake of throwing the damned ball way out into center field, and had to go get it.

Leland called out.

"That's enough for today. Pack her up. Take her home. You got two weeks."

Leland returned to his office, where he found Mace Styrik drinking a warm Diet Coke.

Mace frowned, just as Leland expected. He knew his men as well as his dogs.

"Why are you wasting his time and ours, giving him a bad dog like that?"

"That dog ain't bad. She's just not fit for duty. If they gave medals to dogs, she'd have so many, a sissy like you couldn't lift'm."

"I heard the shot. She squirrel up again?"

Leland dropped into his chair, leaned back, and put up his feet. He brooded about what he had seen.

"Wasn't just the dog squirreled up."

"Meaning what?"

Leland decided to think about it. He dug a tin of smokeless tobacco from his pocket, pushed a wad of dip behind his lower lip, and worked it around. He lifted a stained Styrofoam cup from the floor beside his chair, spit into it, then put the cup on his desk and arched his eyebrows at Mace.

"Have a sip of that Coke?"

"Not with that nasty stuff in your mouth."

Leland sighed, then answered Mace's original question.

"His heart isn't in it. He can do the work well enough, else I would not have passed him, but they should have made him take the medical. God knows, he earned it."

Mace shrugged, wordless, and had more of the Coke as Leland went on.

"Everyone has been carrying that young man, and, Lord knows, my heart goes out to him, what happened an' all, but you know as well as I, we were pressured to take him. We passed over far better and more deserving applicants to give him this spot."

"That may be, but we gotta take care of our own. We always have, we always will, and that's the way it should be. He paid dear."

"I'm not arguing that point."

"Sounds like you are."

"Goddamnit, you know me better than

that. There are a thousand jobs they could have given him, but we are K-9. We aren't those other jobs. We are dog men."

Mace grudgingly had to agree.

"This is true. We're dog men."

"He is not."

Mace frowned again.

"Then why'd you give him that dog?"

"He said he wanted her."

"I say I want things all the time, you don't give me squat."

Leland worked the dip around again, and spit, thinking he might have to get up for his own Coke to wash down the taste.

"That poor animal is unfit for this job, and I suspect the same about him. I hope to God in His Glory I am wrong, sincerely I do, but there it is. They are suspect. That dog will help him realize he is not right for this job. Then she'll go back to that family, and he'll retire or transfer to a more suit-able job, and all of us will be happier for it."

Leland dug the remains of the dip from his lip, dropped it into the cup, then stood to go find a drink of his own.

"See if he needs a hand with her crate. Give him the dog's file to take home, and tell him to read it. I want him to see what a fine animal she was. Tell him to be back here

96

at oh-seven-hundred hours tomorrow."

"You going to help him retrain her?"

Dogs suffering from post-traumatic stress disorder shared similar stress reactions with humans, and could sometimes be retrained, but it was slow work that required great patience on the part of the trainer, and enormous trust on the part of the dog.

"No, I am not. He wanted that German shepherd, he got her. I gave him two weeks, and then I will re-evaluate her."

"Two weeks isn't long enough."

"No, it is not."

Leland walked out to search for a Coke, thinking how some days he loved his job, and others he didn't, and this day was one of the sad ones. He looked forward to going home later, and taking a walk with his own dog, a retired Mal named Ginger. They had long talks when they walked, and she always made Leland feel better. No matter how bad the day, she made him feel better.

6.

Scott held the driver's seat forward, and hipped the door open wide to let the dog out.

"Here we go, dog. We're home."

Maggie stuck her head out a few inches, sniffed the air, then slowly jumped down. Scott's Trans Am wasn't a large car. She filled the back seat, but had seemed to enjoy the ride from Glendale to his place in Studio City. Scott had rolled down the windows, and she lay across the seat with her tongue out and eyes narrowed as the wind riffled her fur, looking content and happy.

Scott wondered if her hips ached when she got out as much as his side and shoulder.

Scott rented a one-bedroom guest house from an elderly widow on a quiet residential street not far from the Studio City park, and parked in her front yard under an elm tree. MaryTru Earle was short, thin, and in her early eighties. She lived in a small California ranch-style home at the front of her property, and rented the guest house in the rear to supplement her income. The guest house had once been a pool house and game room, back in the days when she had a pool and children at home, but when her husband retired twenty-odd years ago, they filled the pool, created a flower garden, and converted the pool house into the guest house. Her husband had been gone now for more than ten years, and Scott was her latest tenant. She liked having a police officer close at hand, as she often told him. Having a police officer in the guest house made her feel safe.

Scott clipped the lead to Maggie's collar, and paused beside the car to let her look around. He thought she might have to pee, so he took her on a short walk. Scott let her set the pace, and sniff trees and plants for as long as she wanted. He talked to her as they walked, and when she stopped to worry a smell, he stroked his hand along her back and sides. These were bonding techniques he learned from Leland. Long strokes were soothing and comforting. The dog knows you're talking to her. Most people who walk their dogs take the dog for a people walk instead of a dog walk, drag the little sonofa-bitch along until it squeezes out a peanut, as Leland liked to say, then hurry back home. The dog wants to smell. Their nose is our eyes, Leland had said. You want to show the dog a good time, let her smell. It's *her* walk, not yours.

Scott knew almost nothing about dogs when he applied for the slot at K-9. Perkins had grown up training hunting dogs, and Barber had worked for a veterinarian through high school and raised huge white Samoyed show dogs with her mother, and almost all the veteran K-9 handlers had serious lifetime involvements with dogs. Scott had zip, and sensed resentment on the part of the senior K-9 crew when he was shoved down their throats by the Metro commanders and a couple of sympathetic deputy chiefs. So he had paid attention to Leland, and soaked up the older man's knowledge, but he still felt totally stupid.

Maggie peed twice, so Scott turned around and brought her back to the house.

"Let's get you inside, and I'll come back for your stuff. You gotta meet the old lady."

Scott walked Maggie through a locked side gate and back alongside the house, which is how he got to his guest house. He never went to the front door. Whenever he

100

wanted to speak with Mrs. Earle, he went to her back door, and rapped on the wooden jamb.

"Mrs. Earle. It's Scott. Got someone here to meet you."

He heard her shuffling from her Barcalounger in the den, and then the door opened. She was thin and pale, with wispy hair dyed a dark brown. She gave a toothy false-teeth smile to Maggie.

"Oh, she's so pretty. She looks like Rin Tin Tin."

"This is Maggie. Maggie, this is Mrs. Earle."

Maggie seemed perfectly comfortable. She stood calmly, ears back, tail down, tongue out, panting.

"Does she bite?"

"Only bad guys."

Scott wasn't sure what Maggie would do, so he held her collar tight, but Maggie was fine. She smelled and licked Mrs. Earle's hand, and Mrs. Earle ran her hand over Maggie's head, and scratched the soft spot behind her ear.

"She's so soft. How can big strong dogs like this be so soft? We had a cocker spaniel, but he was always matted and filthy, and meaner than spit. He bit all three of the children. We put him to sleep."

Scott wanted to get going.

"Well, I wanted you to meet her."

"Watch when she makes her pee-pee. A girl dog will kill the grass."

"Yes, ma'am. I'll watch."

"What happened to her hiney?"

"She had surgery. She's all better now."

Scott tugged Maggie away before Mrs. Earle could keep going. The guest house had French doors in front that used to face the pool, and a regular door on the side. Scott used the regular door because the French doors stuck, and it was always a wrestling match to open them. He had a spacious living room behind the French doors, with the back half of the guest house being split into a bedroom, bath, and kitchen. A small dining table with two mismatched chairs and Scott's computer was against the wall by the kitchen, opposite a couch and a wooden rocking chair that were set up to face a forty-inch flat screen TV.

Dr. Charles Goodman would not have liked Scott's apartment. A large drawing of the crime scene intersection was tacked to the living room wall, not unlike the map Scott had seen in Orso's office, but covered with tiny notes. Printouts of eight different stories from the L.A. *Times* about the shooting and subsequent investigation were also tacked to the walls, along with sidebar stories about the Bentley victims and Stephanie Anders. The story about Stephanie ran with her official LAPD portrait. Spiral notebooks of different sizes were scattered on the table and couch and the floor around his couch. The notebooks were filled with descriptions and dreams and details he remembered from the night of the shooting. His floor hadn't been vacuumed in three months. He was behind with his dishes, so he used paper plates. He ate mostly takeout and crap out of cans.

Scott unclipped the lead.

"This is it, dog. *Mi casa, su casa.*"

Maggie glanced up at him, then looked at the closed door, then studied the room as if she was disappointed. Her nose sniffed and twitched.

"Make yourself at home. I'll get your stuff."

Getting her stuff took two trips. He brought in her collapsible crate and sleeping pad first, then the metal food and water bowls, and a twenty-pound bag of kibble. These things were provided by the K-9 Platoon, but Scott figured to pick up some toys and treats on his own. When he got back with the first load, she was lying under

103

the dining table as he had seen her in the LAPD run — on her belly, feet out in front, head on the floor between her feet, watching him.

"How're you doing? You like it under there?"

He was hoping for a tail thump, but all she did was watch him.

Orso called as Scott was heading out the door.

"You want to see what we have, can you get in here tomorrow morning?"

Scott thought about Leland's scowl.

"I'm working the dog in the morning. How about late morning, just before lunch? Eleven or eleven-thirty."

"Shoot for eleven. If we get a call-out, I'll text you."

"Great. Thanks."

Scott figured he could leave the dog in Glendale when he split for the Boat.

When he got back with the food and bowls, Maggie was still under the table. He put her bowls in the kitchen, filled one with water, the other with food, but she showed no interest in either.

Scott had figured he would set up her crate in his bedroom, but he put it beside the table. She seemed to be comfortable there, and now he wondered if she had bothered to cruise through his bedroom and bath. Maybe her nose told her everything she needed to know.

As soon as he had the crate up, she slinked from under the table and into the crate.

"I have to put the pad in. C'mon, get out."

Scott stepped back, and gave her the command.

"Come. Come, Maggie. Here."

She stared at him.

"Come."

Didn't move.

Scott knelt at the crate's mouth, let her smell his hand, and slowly reached for her collar. She growled. Scott pulled back and stepped away.

"Okay. Forget the pad."

He dropped the pad on the floor beside the crate, then went into his bedroom to change. He took off his uniform, grabbed a quick shower, then pulled on jeans and a T-shirt from Henry's Tacos. Even pulling the T-shirt over his head hurt like a sonofabitch, and made his eyes water.

When he was hanging his uniform in the closet, he noticed his old tennis stuff in a faded gym bag, and found an unopened can of bright green tennis balls. He popped the tab on the can, and took a ball so fresh and bright it almost glowed.

Scott went to the door and tossed it into the living room. It bounced across the floor, hit the far wall, and rolled to a stop. Maggie charged from her crate, scrambled to the ball, and touched her nose to it. Her ears were cocked forward and her tail was straight up. Scott thought he had found a toy for her, but then her ears went down and her tail dropped. She seemed to shrink. She looked left, then right, as if looking for something, then went back into her crate.

Scott walked to the ball, and studied the dog. Belly down, feet out in front, head between her feet. Watching him.

He toed the ball to the wall hard enough to bounce it back.

Her eyes followed it briefly, but returned to him without interest.

"Hungry? We'll eat, then go for a walk. Sound good?"

He popped a frozen pizza in the microwave, three minutes, good to go. While the microwave was humming, he searched the fridge, and came out with half a pack of baloney, a white container with two leftover Szechuan dumplings, and a container of leftover Yang Chow fried rice. He stopped the microwave, pulled the pie, and smushed the dumplings on top. He covered it with the fried rice, then set a paper plate over it, and put it back into the microwave. Another two minutes.

While Scott's dinner was heating, he put two scoops of kibble into Maggie's bowl. He tore the baloney into pieces, dropped it into the kibble, then added a little hot water to make a nice gravy. He mixed it together with his hand, then took a piece of the baloney to the crate, and held it out in front of Maggie's nose.

Sniff, sniff.

She ate it.

"I hope this stuff doesn't give you the squirts."

She followed him into the kitchen. Scott took his pizza from the microwave, got a Corona from the fridge, and they ate together on the kitchen floor. He stroked her while she ate, like Leland said. Long smooth strokes. She paid him no attention, but didn't seem to mind. When she finished eating, she returned to the living room. Scott thought she was going back to the crate, but she stopped in the center of the room by the tennis ball, head drooping, nose working, her great tall ears swiveling. Scott thought she was staring at the tennis ball, but couldn't be sure. Then she went into his bedroom. Scott followed, and found her with her face in his tennis bag. She backed out of the bag, looked at him, then walked around his bed, sniffing constantly. She briefly returned to the tennis bag before going into the bathroom. He wondered if she was looking for something, but decided she was exploring, then out came the sound of lapping. Scott thought, crap, he would have to keep the seat down. When the lapping stopped, Maggie returned to her crate, and Scott went to his computer. He had been thinking about the robbery Orso described since he left the Boat.

He used Google Maps to find the site of his shooting, then the satellite-view feature to zoom into the street-level view. He had viewed the intersection this way hundreds of times, as well as the location where the getaway car was found. But this time he directed the map along the side street from which the Kenworth emerged. Three storefronts up from the T-intersection, he found Nelson Shin's shop. He recognized the location by the blocky Korean characters painted on the metal shutter covering the windows, with ASIA EXOTICA painted in English below the Korean. The paint was faded, and virtually covered by gang tags and graffiti.

Scott zoomed out enough to see Shin had the bottom of a four-story building, with

two storefronts on either side. Scott continued past to the next cross street, then realized it was an alley. The street-level feature
wouldn't enter the alley, so Scott zoomed
out until he was in satellite view, and looked
down from overhead. A small service area
branched off the alley behind the row of
storefronts. Dumpsters were lined against
the building, and Scott saw what appeared
to be old fire escapes, though he wasn't sure
because of the poor angle. The roofs appeared to be at differing levels. Some were
cut with skylights, but others weren't. He
zoomed back farther, and saw that if someone had been on the roof that night, they
would have had a hawk's view of everything
that happened below.

Scott printed the image, and pushpinned
it to the wall by his drawing of the crime
scene. Orso had given him a good tip, and
now he wanted to see the alley himself, and
find out if Orso knew anything more about
Nelson Shin.

He was still thinking about this at dusk
when he took Maggie out. They walked
until she pooped. He picked it up with a
plastic bag, and brought her home. This
time, he beat her to the crate, and arranged
the pad. As soon as he backed out of the
crate, she went in, turned twice, then eased

herself down onto her side, and sighed. The way she had settled, he could see the gray lines of her surgery scars. The gray was her skin, where the fur had not grown back. It looked like a large Y laid on its side.

Scott said, "I have scars, too."

He wondered if the sniper had shot her with an AK-47. He wondered if she understood she had been shot, or if the impact and pain had been a sourceless surprise beyond her understanding. Did she know a man had sent the bullet into her? Did she know he was trying to kill her? Did she know she might have died? Did she know she could die?

Scott said, "We die."

He laid his hand gently on the Y, ready to pull back if she growled, but she remained still and silent. He knew she was not sleeping, but she did not stir. The feel of her was comforting. He had not shared his home with another living creature in a very long time.

"Mi casa, su casa."

Later, he studied the picture of Nelson Shin's roof again, and sat on the couch with one of his spiral notebooks. He wrote everything he remembered from his session with Goodman. As he did every time, he described what he remembered of that night from beginning to end, slowly filling this notebook as he had filled the others, but this time he added the white sideburns. He wrote because sometimes the writing helped focus his thoughts. He was still writing when his eyes grew heavy, the notebook fell, and he slept.

7.

MAGGIE

The man's breathing grew shallow and steady, his heartbeat slowed, and when the surge of his pulse grew no slower, Maggie knew he was sleeping. She lifted her head enough to see him, but seeing him was unnecessary. She could smell his sleep by the change in his scent as his body relaxed and cooled.

She sat up, and turned to peer from her crate. His breathing and heartbeat did not change, so she stepped out into the room. She stood for a moment, watching him. Men came, and men left. She was with some men longer than others, but then they were gone, and she never saw them again. None were her pack.

Pete had stayed with her the longest. They were pack. Then Pete was gone, and the people changed and changed and changed, until Maggie was with a man and a woman.

112

The man and the woman and Maggie had become pack, but one day they closed her crate, and now she was here. Maggie remembered the strong sweet smells of the woman and the sour smell of the disease growing in the man, and would always remember their smells, as she remembered Pete's smell. Her scent memory lasted forever.

She quietly approached the sleeping man. She sniffed the hair on his head, and his ears, and mouth, and the breath he exhaled. Each had its own distinct flavor and taste. She sniffed along the length of his body, noting the smells of his T-shirt and watch and belt and pants and socks, and the different living smells of his man-body parts beneath the clothes. And as she smelled, she heard his heart beat and the blood move through his veins and his breathing, and the sounds of his living body.

When she finished learning the man, she quietly walked along the edge of the room, sniffing the base of the walls, and the windows and along the doors where the cool night air leaked through small openings and the smells from outside were strongest. She smelled rats eating oranges in the trees outside, the pungent scent of withered roses, the bright fresh smells of leaves and grass, and the acidic smell of ants marching along the outer wall.

Maggie's long German shepherd nose had more than two hundred twenty-five million scent receptors. This was as many as a beagle, forty-five times more than the man, and was bettered only by a few of her hound cousins. A full eighth of her brain was devoted to her nose, giving her a sense of smell ten thousand times better than the sleeping man's, and more sensitive than any scientific device. If taught the smell of a particular man's urine, she could recognize and identify that same smell if only a single drop were diluted in a full-sized swimming pool.

Continuing around the room, she smelled the bits of leaves and grass the man carried inside after their walk, and followed the trails left by mice across the floor. She recognized the paths left by living roaches, and knew where the bodies of dead roaches and silverfish and beetles lay hidden.

Her nose led her back to the green ball, where she thought of Pete. The chemical smell of this ball was familiar, but Pete's smell was missing. Pete had not touched this ball, or held it, or thrown it, or carried it hidden from her in his pocket. This ball was not Pete's ball, though it reminded her of him, as did other familiar smells.

Maggie followed those smells into the bedroom again, and found the man's gun. She smelled bullets and oil and gunpowder, but Pete's scent was still absent. Pete was not here, and had never been here.

Maggie smelled water in the bathroom, and returned for a drink, but now the big white water bowl was covered, so she padded back to the kitchen. She drank, then returned to the sleeping man.

Maggie knew this was the man's crate because his smell was part of this place. His smell was not a single smell, but many smells. Hair, ears, breath, underarms, hands, crotch, rectum, feet — each part of him had a different smell, and the scents of his many parts were as different and distinct to Maggie as the colors of a rainbow would be to the man. Together they made up this man's smell, and were distinct from the scent of any other human. His smells were part of the walls, the floor, the paint, the rugs, the bed, the towels in his bathroom, the things in his closet, the gun, the furniture, his clothes and belt and watch and shoes. This was his place, but not her place, yet here she was.

Maggie's crate was her home.

The people and places changed, but the

crate remained the same. This place where the man brought her was strange and meaningless, but her crate was here, and she was here, so here was home.

Maggie was bred to guard and protect, so this was what she did. She stood in the still room near the sleeping man, and looked and listened and smelled. She drew in the world through her ears and her nose, and found no threat. All was good. All was safe.

She returned to her crate, but did not enter. She slipped beneath the table, instead. She turned three times until the space felt right, then lowered herself.

The world was quiet, peaceful, and safe. She closed her eyes, and slept.

Then Maggie began to dream.

8.

— the rifle swung toward him, a tiny thing so far away, but different now. Its barrel was gleaming chrome, as long and thin and sharp as a needle. Its glowing tip found him, looking at him as he looked at it, and then the needle exploded toward him, horribly sharp, dangerously sharp, this terrible sharp point reaching for his eyes —

Scott jerked awake as Stephanie's fading voice echoed.

Scotty, come back back back back.

His heart pounded. His neck and chest were tacky with sweat. His body trembled.

Two-sixteen A.M. He was on the couch. The lights were still on in the kitchen and his bedroom, and the lamp above his head at the end of the couch still burned.

He took deep breaths, calming himself, and noticed the dog was not in her crate. Sometime while he slept, she had left the crate and crawled under the table. She was on her side, sleeping, but her paws twitched and moved as if she was running, and as she ran, she whimpered and whined.

Scott thought, that dog is having a nightmare.

Scott stood, cringing at the sharp pain in his side and the stiffness in his leg, and limped to her. He didn't know if he should wake her.

He eased himself to the floor.

Still sleeping, she growled, and made a woofing sound like a bark, and then her entire body convulsed. She jolted awake, upright, snarling and snapping, but not at Scott. He lurched back anyway, but in that moment she realized where she was, and whatever she had been dreaming was gone. She looked at Scott. Her ears folded back, and she breathed as he had breathed. She lowered her head to the floor.

Scott slowly touched her. He ran his hand over her head. Her eyes closed.

Scott said, "You're okay. We're okay."

She sighed so hard her body shivered.

Scott pulled on his shoes, and gathered together his wallet, and gun, and leash. When he picked up the leash, Maggie stood and shook herself. Maybe she could sleep again that night, but he couldn't. He could never go back to sleep.

Scott clipped the lead to her collar, led her out to the Trans Am, and held the door so she could hop into the back seat. That time of night, almost two-thirty, the driving was easy. He hit the Ventura, slid down the Hollywood, and made it downtown in less than twenty minutes. He had made the same drive many times, at hours like this. When he woke hearing Stephanie call for him, he had no other choice.

He parked in the same place they had parked that night, at the little T-intersection where they had stopped to listen to the silence.

Scott said, "Turn off the engine."

He said those same words every time he came, then turned off the engine.

Maggie stood, and leaned forward between the seats. She was so large she filled the car, her head now higher than his.

Scott stared at the empty street before them, but the street wasn't empty. He saw the Kenworth. He saw the Bentley. He saw the men covered in black.

"Don't worry. I'll protect you."

The same words he spoke that night, this time a whisper.

He glanced at Maggie, then back at the street, only now the street was empty. He listened to Maggie pant. He felt her warmth, and smelled her strong dog smell.

"I got my partner killed. It happened right here."

His eyes filled, and the sob racked him so hard he doubled over. He could not stop. He did not try to stop. The pain came in a torrent of jolting sobs that filled his nose and blurred his eyes. He heaved and gasped, and clenched his eyes, and covered his face. Tears and snot and spit dripped in streamers from his chin, as he heard his own voice.

Turn off the engine.

Don't worry. I'll protect you.

Then Stephanie's voice echoed after his own, haunting him.

Scotty, don't leave me.

Don't leave me.

Don't leave.

He finally pulled himself together. He rubbed the blur from his eyes, and found Maggie watching him.

He said, "I wasn't running away. I swear to God I wasn't, but she doesn't —"

Maggie's ears were back and her rich brown eyes were kind. She whimpered as if she felt his anxiety, then licked his face. Scott felt his tears return, and closed his eyes as Maggie licked the tears from his face.

Don't leave me.

Don't leave.

Scott pulled the dog close, and buried his face in her fur.

"You did better than me, dog. You didn't leave your partner. You didn't fail."

Maggie whimpered and tried to pull away, but Scott held on, and didn't let go.

■ ■ ■ ■

Part II

■ ■ ■

■ ■ ■ ■

MAGGIE AND SCOTT

■ ■ ■ ■

9.

Scott and Maggie were due at the training field at seven that morning, but Scott left early and returned to the scene of his shooting. He wanted to see Shin's building during the light.

He drove the same route he took three hours earlier, only this time when he approached the intersection, Maggie stood with her ears tipped forward.

Scott said, "Good memory."

She whined.

"You'll get used to it. I come here a lot."

Maggie stayed between the two front seats, filling the car as she checked their surroundings.

It was five forty-two that morning, light, but still early. A few pedestrians were making their way along the sidewalks, and the streets were busy with trucks making early deliveries. Scott pushed Maggie out of the way so he could see, turned onto the street where the Kenworth had waited, and parked in front of Shin's store.

Scott clipped on Maggie's leash, let her out onto the sidewalk, and examined Asia Exotica. It looked as it had in the Google picture, only with more graffiti. A security shutter was rolled down over the window like a metal garage door. Padlocks secured the shutter to steel rings set into the sidewalk. The door was barred by a heavy steel throw-bolt locked into the wall. Shin's little store looked like Fort Knox, but wasn't unusual. The other shops along the street were similarly protected. The difference was that Shin's locks, shutter, and door were powdered with undisturbed grime, and appeared not to have been opened in a long time.

Scott walked Maggie toward the alley. She went to his left side as she'd been taught, but walked too close, and let her tail and ears droop. When they passed two Latin women walking in the opposite direction, Maggie edged behind Scott, and would have moved to his right if he let her. She glanced at passing cars and buses as if afraid one might jump the curb.

Scott stopped when they reached the alley, and stooped to stroke her back and sides, hearing Leland's lecturing voice:

128

These dogs are not machines, goddamnit. They are alive! They are living, feeling, warm-blooded creatures of God, and they will love you with all their hearts! They will love you when your wives and husbands sneak behind your backs. They will love you when your ungrateful misbegotten children piss on your graves! They will see and witness your greatest shame, and will not judge you! These dogs will be the truest and best partners you can ever hope to have, and they will give their lives for you. And all they ask, all they want or need, all it costs YOU to get ALL of that, is a simple word of kindness. Goddamnit to hell, the ten best men I know aren't worth the worst dog here, and neither are any of you, and I am Dominick Goddamned Leland, and I am never wrong!

Three hours earlier, this living, feeling, warm-blooded creature of God had licked the tears from his face, and now she shivered as a garbage truck rumbled past. Scott scratched her head, stroked her back, and whispered in her ear.

"It's okay, dog. It's okay if you're scared. I'm scared, too."

Words he had never spoken to another living being.

Scott's eyes filled as the words came to him, but he said them again as he stroked her back.

"I'll protect you."

Scott pushed to his feet, wiped his eyes clear, and took a plastic Ziploc bag from his pocket. He had sliced the baloney into squares, and brought them along as treats. Food as a reward was frowned upon, but Scott figured he had to go with what worked.

Maggie looked up even before he opened the bag. Her ears stood strong and straight, and her nostrils flickered and danced.

"You're a good girl, baby. You're a brave dog."

She took a square as if she was starving, and whined for more, but this was a good whine. He fed her a second square, put away the bag, and turned down the alley. Maggie stepped livelier now, and snuck glances at his pocket.

The delivery area behind Shin's building was a place for shopkeepers to load and unload their goods, and toss their trash. A pale blue van with its side panel open was currently parked outside a door. A heavyset young Asian man guided a hand dolly stacked with boxes from the store, and loaded the boxes into the van. The boxes were labeled MarleyWorld Island.

Scott led Maggie around the van to the

rear of Shin's store. The door on this side of the building was as bulletproof as the front, but greasy windows were cut into the back of the four-story building, and a rusted fire escape climbed to the roof. The lowest windows were protected by security bars, but the higher windows were not. The fire escape's retractable ladder was too high to reach from the ground, but a person standing on top of the van could reach it, and climb to the higher windows or break into the upper-floor doors.

Scott was wondering how he could reach the roof when a tall thin man with a Jamaican accent came storming around the van.

"Ahr you de wahn gahnna stop dese crime?"

The man strode past the van directly toward Scott, shaking his finger, and speaking in a loud, demanding voice.

Maggie lunged at him so hard Scott almost lost her leash. Her ears were cocked forward like furry black spikes, her tail was straight back, and the fur along her spine bristled with fury as she barked.

The man stumbled backwards, scrambled into the van, and slammed the door.

Scott said, "Out."

This was the command word to break off the attack, but Maggie ignored him. Her claws raked the asphalt as she snarled and barked, straining against the leash.

Then Leland's voice came to Scott, shouting: *Say it like you mean it, goddamnit! You're the alpha here. She will love and protect her alpha, but you are the boss!*

Scott raised and deepened his voice. The command voice. All authority. Alpha.

"Out, Maggie! Maggie, OUT!"

It was like flipping a switch. Maggie broke off her attack, returned to his left side, and sat, though her eyes never left the man in the van.

Scott was shaken by her sudden ferocity. She did not look at Scott, not even a glance. She watched the man in the van, and Scott knew if he released her she would attack the door and try to chew through the metal to reach him.

Scott scratched her ears.

"Good dog. Atta girl, Maggie."

Leland, screaming again: *The praise voice, you goddamned fool! They like it all high and squeaky! Be her. Listen to her. Let her TEACH you!*

Scott made his voice high and squeaky, as if he was talking to a Chihuahua instead of an eighty-five-pound German shepherd who could tear a man's throat out.

"That's my good girl, Maggie. You're my

132

good girl."

Maggie's tail wagged. She stood when he took out the Ziploc. He gave her another piece of baloney, and told her to sit. She sat.

Scott looked at the man in the van, and made a roll-down-the-window gesture. The man rolled down the window halfway.

"Dat dog hab rabies! I not comeeng out."

"I'm sorry, sir. You scared her. You don't have to get out."

"I abide de law an' be good ceetysen. She wahn to bite sahm one, let her bite de bahstards who steal frahm my bizzyness."

Scott glanced past the van into the man's shop. The kid with the hand dolly peeked out, then ducked away.

"Is this your place of business?"

"Yes. I am Elton Joshua Marley. Doan let dat dog bite my helper. He got deeliveries to make."

"She's not going to bite anyone. What were you asking me?"

"Have you catched dese people who did dis?"

"You were robbed?"

Mr. Marley scowled again, and nervously glanced at the dog.

"Dat be now two weeks ago. De officers, dey come, but dey never come back. Hab you caught dese people or no?"

Scott considered this for a moment, then took out his pad.

"I don't know, sir, but I'll find out. How do you spell your name?"

Scott copied the man's info, along with the date of the burglary. By the time he finished making notes, he had coaxed Marley from the van. Marley kept a wary eye on Maggie as he led Scott past the kid loading boxes, and into his shop.

Marley bought cheap Caribbean-style clothes from manufacturers in Mexico, and resold them under his own label in low-end shops throughout Southern California. The shop was filled with boxes of short-sleeved shirts, T-shirts, and cargo shorts. Marley explained that the burglar or burglars had entered and left through a second-floor window, and made off with two desktop computers, a scanner, two telephones, a printer, and a boom box. Not exactly the crime of the century, but Marley's shop had been burgled four times in the past year.

Scott said, "No alarm?"

"De owner, he put in de alarm last year, but dey break, and he no fix, dat cheep bah-stard. I put de leetle camerah here, but dey take."

Marley had installed a do-it-yourself

134

security camera on the ceiling, but the thief or thieves stole the camera and its hard drive two burglaries ago.

Scott thought of Shin as they left Marley's shop. The old building was a burglar's heaven. A mercury-vapor lamp was mounted overhead, but the little delivery area was hidden from the street. With no security cameras in evidence, a thief would have little fear of being discovered.

Marley went on, still complaining.

"I call you two weeks ago. De police, dey cahm, dey go, an' thas last I heer. Every morneeng I come, I wait for more stealeeng. My insurance, he no pay more. He wahnt charge so much, I cannot pay."

Scott glanced at Shin's again.

"Have all the shops along here been broken into?"

"Ehveebody. Dese assholes, dey break in all de time. Dis block, across de street, on de next block."

"How long has this been going on?"

"Two or tree years. I only be heer wahn year, but thees is waht I heer."

"Is there a way up to the roof besides the fire escape?"

Marley led them inside to a common stairwell, and gave Scott a key to the roof. There was no elevator in the old building.

135

Scott's leg and side ached as he climbed, and the ache grew worse. By the third floor, he stopped, and dry-swallowed a Vicodin. Maggie was engaged and interested as they climbed, but when Scott stopped to let the pain pass, she whimpered. Scott realized she was reading his hurt, and touched her head.

"How about you? Your hips okay?"

He smiled, and she seemed to smile back, so they continued up to the roof and out a metal service door fitted with an industrial security lock. The lock could only be locked and unlocked from the inside. There were no keyholes on the outside, but this hadn't stopped people from trying to break in. The steel frame was scarred with old jimmy marks and dents where people had tried to pry open the door. Most of the marks were painted over or rusted.

Marley's and Shin's building was on the cross street from which the Kenworth appeared. The building next to it overlooked the site of the shooting. The roofs between the two buildings were separated by a low wall.

Marley's roof was poorly maintained like the rest of his building. It was cut with withered tar patches and broken asphalt, and littered with cigarette butts, butane lighters, crushed beer cans, shattered beer bottles, broken crack pipes, and the trash of late-night partiers. Scott figured the partiers probably climbed the fire escape, same as the people who tried to force the door. He wondered if the officers who investigated Marley's burglary had checked out the roof, and what they thought of it.

Careful to avoid the broken glass, Scott led Maggie across Marley's roof to the next building. When they reached the low wall, Maggie stopped. Scott patted the top of the wall.

"Jump. It's only three feet high. Jump."

Maggie looked at him with her tongue hanging out.

Scott swung his legs over the wall, one at a time, wincing at the stitch in his side. He patted his chest.

"I can do it, and I'm a mess. C'mon, dog. You'll have to do better than this for Leland."

Maggie licked her lips, but made no move to follow.

Scott dug out his Ziploc bag, and showed her the baloney.

"Come."

Maggie launched over the wall without hesitation, cleared it easily, and sat at his feet. She stared at the bag. Scott laughed when he saw how easily she cleared the wall.

"You smart ass. You made me beg just to sucker me into a treat. Guess what? I'm a smart ass, too."

He tucked the bag into his pocket without giving her a reward.

"Nothing for you until you jump back."

This building's roof was better maintained, but was also littered with party dregs, a large piece of wall-to-wall carpet, and three cast-off folding lawn chairs. A ripped, dirty sleeping bag was bundled by an air duct, along with several used condoms. Some were only a few days old. Urban romance.

Scott went to the side of the roof that overlooked the kill zone. A short wrought-iron safety fence was bolted to the wall as an extra barrier to keep people from falling. It was so badly rusted, the metal eaten with holes.

Scott peered over the fence, and found an unobstructed view of the crime scene. It was all so easy to see, then and even now. The Bentley floating by on the street below, passing their radio car as the Kenworth roared, the truck and the Bentley spinning to a stop as the Gran Torino raced after them. If someone was partying up here nine months ago, they could have seen everything.

Scott began shaking, and realized he was holding the rusted fence so tight, the rotting metal was cutting into his skin.

"Shit!"

He jumped back, saw his fingers were streaked with rust and blood, and pulled out his handkerchief.

Scott led Maggie back to Shin's building, this time rewarding her when she jumped the wall. He photographed the empties and party debris with his phone, then climbed down the four flights to find Mr. Marley. His helper had finished loading their stock, and the van was now gone. Marley was boxing more shirts in his shop.

When Mr. Marley saw Maggie, he stepped behind his desk, eyeing her nervously.

"You lock de door?"

"Yes, sir."

Scott returned the key.

"One more thing. Do you know Mr. Shin? He has the business two doors down. Asia Exotica."

"He out of bizzyness. He geht robbed too many times."

"How long has he been gone?"

"Months. Eet been a long time."

"You have any idea who's breaking into

these places?"

Marley waved a hand in the general direction of everywhere.

"Drug addeeks and assholes."

"Someone you could point out?"

Marley waved his hand again.

"De assholes 'roun here. If I could name who, I would not need you."

Marley was probably right. The small-time burglaries he described were almost certainly committed by neighborhood regulars who knew when the shops were empty and which had no alarms. It was likely that the same person or persons had committed all the robberies. Scott liked this idea, and found himself nodding. If his theory was right, the thief who broke into Marley's shop could be the same person who broke into Shin's.

Scott said, "I'll find out what's going on with your burglary report, and get back to you later this afternoon. That okay?"

"Daht be good. I tank you. Dese other policemen, dey nevehr call back."

Scott checked his watch, and realized he would be late. He copied Marley's phone number, and trotted back to his car. Maggie trotted along with him, and hopped into his car without effort. This time, she didn't stretch out on the back seat. She straddled the console between the front seats.

"You're too big to stand there. Get in back."

She panted, her tongue as long as a necktie.

"Get in back. You're blocking my view."

Scott tried to push her with his forearm, but she leaned into him and didn't move. Scott pushed harder, but Maggie leaned harder, and held her ground.

Scott stopped pushing, and wondered if she thought this was a game. Whatever she thought, she seemed content and comfortable on the console.

Scott watched her pant, remembering how fiercely she lunged for Marley when she thought they were threatened. Scott roughed the fur on her powerful neck.

"Forget it. Stand wherever you want."

She licked his ear, and Scott drove away. Leland would be furious at the way he indulged her, but Leland didn't know everything.

10.

Maggie whined when they pulled into the training facility's parking lot. Scott thought she seemed anxious, and rested a hand on her shoulder.

"Don't sweat it. You don't live here anymore. You live with me."

They were ten minutes late, but Leland's Toyota pickup wasn't in the lot, so Scott took out his phone. He had been brooding since Leland surprised them with the starter pistol.

Can't have a police dog that shits out when a gun goes off.

Or a police officer.

Scott wondered if Leland noticed Scott had jumped, too, though Scott's reaction was small compared to the dog's. Leland would test her again, and reject her again if she reacted the same, and Scott knew Leland was right to do so. She had to be able to do her job, just as Scott had to do

142

his, only Scott could fake it and Maggie couldn't. *Fake it 'til you make it.*

Scott gripped a handful of her fur, and gently pushed her. Maggie's tongue dripped out, and she leaned into his push.

Scott said, "Maggie."

She glanced at him, and went back to watching the building. He liked the way she responded to him — not like a robot obeying a command, but as if she was trying to figure him out. He liked the warm intelligence in her eyes. He wondered what it was like inside her head, and what she thought about. They had been together for only twenty-four hours, but she seemed more comfortable with him, and he was more comfortable with her. It was weird, but he felt calmer having her with him.

"You're my first dog."

She glanced at him, and glanced away. Scott pushed again. She pushed back, and seemed content with the contact.

"I had to interview with these guys when I asked for the job. The LT and Leland asked me all these questions about why I wanted to join K-9, and what kind of dog I had when I was a kid, and all this stuff. I lied my ass off. We had cats."

Maggie's big head swung his way, and she licked his face. Scott let her for a moment, then pushed her away. She went back to watching the building.

"Before the shooting, I never used to lie, not ever, but I lie to everyone now, pretty much about everything. I don't know what else to do."

Maggie ignored him.

"Jesus, now I'm talking to a dog."

An exaggerated startle response was common in people who suffered from PTSD, particularly combat veterans, police officers, and victims of domestic abuse. Anyone will jump if someone sneaks up behind them and shouts boo!, but PTSD can amp up the startle response to crazy levels. An unexpected loud noise or a sudden movement near the face could trigger an over-the-top reaction that varied from person to person — screaming, raging, ducking for cover, and even throwing punches. Scott had an exaggerated startle response since the shooting, but was seeing improvement with Goodman's help. He still had a long way to go, but had made enough progress to fool the review board. Scott wondered if Goodman could help with the dog.

Dr. Goodman often saw clients early before they went to work, so Scott took a chance, and called. Scott expected Goodman's answering machine, but Goodman answered, which meant he wasn't busy with a client.

"Doc, Scott James. You got a fast minute?"

"As fast or as slow as you like. My seven o'clock canceled. Are you doing okay?"

"Doing good. I want to ask you something about my dog."

"Your dog?"

"I got my dog yesterday. A German shepherd."

Goodman sounded uncertain.

"Congratulations. This must be very exciting."

"Yeah. She's a retired Military Working Dog. She was shot in Afghanistan, and I think she has PTSD."

Goodman answered without hesitation.

"If you're asking if this is possible, yes, it is. Animals can show the same symptoms as humans. Dogs, in particular. There's extensive literature on the subject."

"A big truck goes by, she gets nervous. She hears a gunshot, she wants to hide."

"Mm-hm. The startle response."

Scott and Goodman had discussed these things for hours. There were no medicines or "cures" for PTSD, other than talking. Medicines could relieve symptoms like sleeplessness and anxiety, but you killed the PTSD demon by talking it to death. Goodman was the only person with whom Scott had shared his fears and feelings about that night, but there were some things he had not even told Goodman.

"Yeah, her startle response is off the charts. Is there a fast way to help her?"

"Help her do what?"

"Get over it. Is there something I can do, so she won't jump when a gun goes off?"

Goodman hesitated for several seconds before he responded in a careful, measured tone.

"Scott? Are we talking about a dog now, or you? Is there something you're trying to tell me?"

"My dog. I'm asking about my dog. She can't come talk it out with you, Doc."

"If you're having trouble, we can increase the anxiety medicine."

Scott was wishing he had taken a fistful of anxiety meds that morning when he saw Leland's dark blue pickup pull into the lot. Leland saw him as he got out of his truck, and scowled, no doubt pissed off because Scott was still in his car.

Scott said, "I'm asking about my *dog*. She's an eighty-five-pound German shepherd named Maggie. I'd let you talk to her, but she doesn't talk."

"You seem irritated, Scott. Did yesterday's

regression cause an adverse reaction?"

Scott lowered the phone and took a few breaths. Leland hadn't moved. He was standing beside his truck, scowling at Scott.

"I'm talking about this dog. Maybe I need a dog psychiatrist. Do they make anxiety meds for dogs?"

Goodman hesitated for another several seconds, thinking, but this time he sighed before he answered.

"Probably, but I don't know. I *do* know that dogs suffering from PTSD can be retrained. I would guess that, as with people, the results are varied. You and I have the advantage of medicines that can augment or temporarily alter our brain chemistry. You and I are able to discuss what happened over and over until the event loses much of its emotional potency, and becomes something more manageable."

Goodman had gone into lecture mode, which was his way of thinking out loud, so Scott interrupted.

"Yeah, we bore it to death. Is there a short version of this, Doc? My boss is watching me, and he doesn't look happy."

"She was shot. Like you, her subconscious associates the sound of a gunshot, or any surprising noise, with pain and the fear she felt in that moment."

Leland tapped his watch, and crossed his arms. Scott nodded to acknowledge him and held up a finger. One second.

"She can't talk about it like me, so how do we deal with it?"

"I'll find out if there are canine anxiety medicines, but the therapeutic model will be the same. You can't take the bad experience away from her, so you have to reduce its power. Perhaps you could teach her to associate a loud noise with something pleasurable. Then introduce more noises, until she realizes they have no power to harm her."

Leland had gotten tired of waiting, and was now striding toward him.

Scott watched him approach, but was thinking about the possibilities in Goodman's advice.

"This is going to help, Doc. Thanks. I gotta go."

Scott put away his phone, hooked up Maggie, and got out as Leland arrived.

"Guess you and this dog good to go, you got time to yak with your girlfriends."

"That was Detective Orso at Robbery-Homicide. They want me back downtown, but I put them off until lunch so I can work with Maggie."

Leland's scowl softened as Scott expected.

"Why all of a sudden they want you so much?"

"The lead changed. Orso's new. He's trying to get up to speed."

Leland grunted, then glanced at Maggie.

"How'd you and Miss Maggie here get on last night? She pee on your floor?"

"We walked. We had a long talk."

Leland looked up sharply as if he suspected Scott was being smart, but he softened again when he concluded Scott meant it.

"Good. That would be very good. Now let's you go work with this animal, and see what y'all talked about."

Leland turned away.

"Can I borrow your starter pistol?"

Leland turned back.

Scott said, "Can't have a police dog shit out when a gun goes off."

Leland pooched out his lips, and studied Scott some more.

"You think you can fix that?"

"I won't quit on my partner."

Leland stared at Scott for so long Scott squirmed, but then Leland touched Maggie's head.

"Won't do, you shootin' the gun if you're workin' with her. Might hurt her ears, bein' so close. I'll have Mace help you."

"Thanks, Sergeant."

"No thanks are necessary. Keep talkin' to this dog. Maybe you're already learnin' somethin'."

Leland turned away without another word, and Scott looked down at Maggie.

"I need more baloney."

Scott and Maggie went to the training field.

11.

Mace didn't come out with the starter pistol. Leland came out instead, and brought along a short, wiry trainer named Paulie Budress. Scott had met the man twice during his first week of handler school, but didn't know him. Budress was in his mid-thirties, and sported a peeling sunburn because he had spent the past two weeks fishing with three other cops in Montana. He worked with a male German shepherd named Obi.

Leland said, "Forget that business with the starter pistol for now. You know Paulie Budress?"

Budress gave Scott a big grin and firm handshake, but put most of his grin on Maggie.

Leland said, "Paulie here worked K-9 in the Air Force, which is why I want him to talk to you. These Military Working Dogs

151

are taught to do things different than our dogs."

Budress was still smiling at Maggie. He held out his hand to let her sniff, then squatted to scratch behind her ears.

"She was in Afghanistan?"

Scott said, "Dual purpose. Patrol and explosives detection."

Budress was wiry, but Scott felt a super-calm vibe, and knew Maggie sensed it, too. Her ears were back, her tongue hung out, and she was comfortable letting Budress scratch her. Budress opened her left ear and looked at her tattoo as Leland went on. Both Scott and Leland might as well have been invisible. Budress was all about the dog.

Leland went on to Scott.

"As you know, here in the city of Los Angeles, we train our beautiful animals to hold a suspect in place by barking. Heaven help us she bites some shitbird unless he's trying to kill you, coz our spaghetti-spined, unworthy city council is only too willing to pay liability blackmail to any shyster lawyer who oozes out a shitbird's ass. Is that not correct, Officer Budress?"

"Whatever you say, Sergeant."

Budress wasn't paying attention, but Scott knew the Sergeant was describing the find-

and-bark method that more and more police agencies had adopted to stem the tide of liability lawsuits. So long as the suspect stood perfectly still and showed no aggression, the dogs were trained to stand off and bark. They were trained to bite only if the suspect made an aggressive move or fled, which Leland believed risky to both his dogs and their handlers, and which was one of his unending lecture topics.

"Your military patrol dog, however, is taught to hit her target like a runaway truck, and will take his un-American ass down like a bat out of hell on steroids. You put your military dog on a shitbird, she'll rip him a new asshole, and eat his liver when it slides out. Dogs like our Maggie here are trained to mean business. Is this not correct, Officer Budress?"

"Whatever you say, Sergeant."

Leland nodded toward Budress, who was running his hands down Maggie's legs and tracing the scars on her hips.

"The voice of experience, Officer James. So the first thing you have to do is teach this heroic animal not to bite the murderous, genetically inferior shitbags you will ask her to face. Is that clear?"

Scott mimicked Budress.

"Whatever you say, Sergeant."

"As it should be. I will leave you now with Officer Budress, who knows the military command set, and will help you retrain her to work in our sissified civilian city."

Leland walked away without another word. Budress stood, and painted Scott with a big smile.

"Don't sweat it. She was retrained at Lackland to make her less aggressive, and more people-friendly. It's SOP for dogs they adopt out to civilians. The Sarge there thinks her problem will be the opposite — not aggressive enough."

Scott remembered how Maggie lunged at Marley, but decided not to mention it.

Scott said, "She's smart. She'll have find-and-bark in two days."

Budress smiled even wider.

"You've had her now how long? A day?"

"She was smart enough to soak up everything the Marine Corps wanted her to know. She didn't get shot in the head."

"And how is it you know what the Marines wanted her to know?"

Scott felt himself flush.

"I guess that's why you're here."

"I guess it is. Let's get started."

Budress nodded toward the kennel building.

"Go get an arm protector, a twenty-foot

lead, a six-foot lead, and whatever you use to reward her. I'll wait."

Scott started to the kennel, and Maggie fell in on his left side. He had cut and bagged half a pound of baloney, but now worried if it would be enough, and if Budress would object to his using food as a reward. Then he checked his watch, and wondered how much they could accomplish before he left to see Orso. He wanted to share what he learned about the neighborhood burglaries from Marley, and believed Orso would see the potential. Maybe after nine months of nothing, a new lead was beginning to develop.

Scott picked up his pace, and was thinking about Orso when the gunshot cracked the air behind him. Scott ducked into a crouch, and Maggie almost upended him. She tried to wedge herself beneath him, and was wrapped so tightly between his legs he felt her trembling.

Scott's heart hammered and his breathing was fast and shallow, but he knew what had happened even before he looked back at Budress.

Budress was holding the starter pistol loose at his leg. The smile was gone from his peeling face, and now he looked sad.

He said, "Sorry, man. It's a shame. That

155

poor dog has a problem."

Scott's heart slowed. He laid a hand on Maggie's trembling back, and spoke to her softly.

"Hey, baby girl. That's just a noise. You can stay under me long as you like."

He stroked her back and sides, kneaded her ears, and kept talking in the calm voice. He took out the bag of baloney, stroking her the whole time.

"Check it out, Maggie girl. Look what I have."

She raised her head when he offered the square of baloney, and licked it from his fingers.

Scott made the high-pitched squeaky voice, told her what a good girl she was, and offered another piece. She sat up to eat it.

Budress said, "I've seen this before, y'know, with war dogs. It's a long road back."

Scott stood, and teased her by holding another piece high above her head.

"Stand up, girl. Stand tall and get it."

She raised up onto her hind legs, standing tall for the meat. Scott let her have it, then ruffled her fur as he praised her.

He looked at Budress, and his voice wasn't squeaky.

"Another twenty minutes or so, shoot it again."

Budress nodded.

"You won't know it's coming."

"I don't want to know it's coming. Neither does she."

Budress slowly smiled.

"Get the arm protector and the leads. Let's get this war dog back in business."

Two hours and forty-five minutes later, Scott kenneled Maggie and drove downtown to see Orso. She whined when he left, and pawed at the gate.

12.

Twenty minutes later, Orso and a short, attractive brunette wearing a black pantsuit were waiting when the elevator doors opened at the Boat. Orso stuck out his hand, and introduced the woman.

"Scott, this is Joyce Cowly. Detective Cowly has been reviewing the file, and probably knows it better than me."

Scott nodded, but wasn't sure what to say.

"Okay. Thanks. Good to meet you."

Cowly's handshake was firm and strong, but not mannish. She was in her late thirties, with a relaxed manner and the strong build of a woman who might have been one of those sparkplug gymnasts when she was a teenager. She smiled as she shook Scott's hand, and handed him her card as Orso led them toward the RHD office. Scott wondered if Orso would meet him at the elevator every time he arrived.

Cowly said, "You were at Rampart before

Metro, right? I was Rampart Homicide before here."

Scott checked her face again, but didn't recall her.

"Sorry, I don't remember."

"No reason you should. I've been here for three years."

Orso said, "Three and a half. Joyce spent most of her time here on serial cases with me. I told her about our conversation yesterday, and she has a few questions."

Scott followed them to the same conference room, where he saw the cardboard box was now on the table with the files and materials back in their hangers. A large blue three-ring binder sat on the table beside it. Scott knew this was the murder book, which homicide detectives used to organize and record their investigations.

Orso and Cowly dropped into chairs, but Scott rounded the table to Orso's poster-sized diagram of the crime scene.

"Before we get started, I went to Nelson Shin's store this morning, and met a man who has a business two doors down — here."

Scott found Shin's store on the diagram, then pointed out Elton Marley's location.

"Marley was burglarized two weeks ago. He's been hit four or five times in the past year, and he told me a lot of other businesses in the area have been hit, too. Your diagram here doesn't show a delivery area behind the building that opens off this alley —"

Scott drew an invisible box with his finger to illustrate the area behind the buildings where Marley had been loading his van. Orso and Cowly were watching him.

"A fire escape goes to the roof. There's no security except for window bars on the lowest windows, and the area back here is totally hidden from view. I'm thinking the bad guys use the fire escape to reach the higher windows. They dinged Marley for a computer and a scanner this time. Last time, they grabbed a boom box, another computer, and a few bottles of rum."

Orso glanced at Cowly.

"Small-time breaking and entering, easy-to-carry goods."

Cowly nodded.

"Neighborhood locals."

Scott pushed on with his theory.

"Whoever it is, if the same perp is behind all these jobs, he might be the person who broke into Shin's the night I was shot. Also, I went up to the roof. It's a total party hangout —"

Scott took out his cell phone, found a

good picture of the beer cans and deb
and passed the phone to Orso.

"Maybe the guy who hit Shin's store w
long gone, but if someone else was up he:
when the Kenworth hit the Bentley, the
could have seen everything."

Cowly leaned toward him.

"Did Marley file a report?"

"Two weeks ago. Someone went out, but
Marley hasn't heard back. I told him I'd
check the status and get back to him."

Orso glanced at Cowly.

"That's Central Robbery. Ask them for
the robbery reports and arrests in this area
for the past two years. And whatever they
have on Mr. Marley. I'll want to speak with
the DIC."

DIC was Detective-in-Charge.

Cowly asked Scott to repeat Marley's full
name and the address of his store, and
wrote the information on her pad. As she
wrote, Orso turned back to Scott.

"This is a good find. Good thinking. I like
this."

Scott felt elated, and that something
trapped in his heart for nine months was
beginning to ease.

Orso said, "Okay, now Joyce has something. Come sit. Joyce —"

Scott took a seat as Cowly picked up a

large manila envelope and took out the contents. She dealt out four sheets of heavy gloss paper in front of Scott like playing cards. Each sheet was printed with six sets of color booking photos. The pictures were in pairs, showing each man's full face and profile. The men were of all ages and races, and all had white or gray sideburns of varying shapes and lengths. Cowly explained as she laid out the pictures.

"Identifiers like hair color, hairstyle, length, et cetera, are part of the database. Anyone look familiar?"

Scott went from elated to nauseous in a heartbeat, and in that moment was once more lying in the street, hearing the gunfire. He closed his eyes, drew a slow breath, and imagined himself on a white sandy beach. He was alone, and naked, and his skin was warm from the sun. He pictured himself on a red beach towel. He imagined the sound of the surf. This was a technique Goodman taught him to deal with the flashbacks. Put himself elsewhere, and create the details. Imagining details took concentration, and helped him relax.

Orso said, "Scott?"

Scott felt a flush of embarrassment, and opened his eyes. He studied the pictures, but none of the men were familiar.

"I didn't see enough. I'm sorry."

Cowly pulled the cap off a black Sharpie and handed it to him, still smiling the relaxed, easy smile. She wore no nail polish.

"Don't sweat it. I didn't expect you to recognize a face. I got three thousand, two hundred, and sixty-one hits for gray or white hair. I pulled these because they have different hair types and sideburn styles. That's the purpose of this exercise. As best you can — *if* you can, and no sweat if you can't — circle the style closest to what you saw, or cross out the styles you can definitely rule out."

One of the men had long thin sideburns as sharp as a stiletto. Another had huge muttonchops that covered most of his cheeks. Scott crossed them out along with the other styles he knew were wrong, and circled five men with thick, rectangular sideburns. The shortest stopped mid-ear, and the longest extended about an inch below the man's lobe. Scott pushed the sheets back to Cowly, wondering again if he had seen the sideburns or only imagined them.

"I don't know. I'm not even sure I saw them."

Cowly and Orso shared a glance as she slipped the sheets back into their envelope, and Orso plucked a thin file from the spread on the table.

"This is the criminalist's report on the Gran Torino. After we spoke, I reread it. Five white hairs from the same individual were found on the driver's side."

Scott stared at Orso, then Cowly. Orso smiled. Cowly didn't. She looked like a woman on the hunt, and picked up where Orso left off.

"We can't affirm they're from the man you saw, but a man with white hair was in that vehicle at some point in time. The DNA from the follicles didn't match anything in the CODIS or DOJ data banks, so we don't know his name, but we know he's a Caucasian male. There's an eighty percent chance his hair was brown before it turned white, and we are one hundred percent positive he has blue eyes."

Orso arched his eyebrows, smiled even wider, and looked like a happy scoutmaster.

"Starts adding up, doesn't it? Thought you'd like to know you aren't crazy."

Then the happy scoutmaster face dropped away, and Orso rested his hand on the file box.

"Okay. The case file here is arranged by subject. The murder book contains the case evidence Melon and Stengler thought was the most important, but isn't as complete as the file. You're the man with the questions. What do you want to know?"

Scott wanted something to trigger more memories, but he didn't know what that thing was or what it might be.

Scott looked at Orso.

"Why don't we have a suspect?"

"A suspect was never identified."

"I knew that much from Melon and Stengler."

Orso patted the file box.

"The long version is in here, which you're free to read, but I'll give you the CliffsNotes version."

Orso sketched out the investigation quickly and professionally. Scott knew most of it from Melon and Stengler, but did not interrupt.

The first person suspected when a homicide occurs is the spouse. Always. This is Rule Number One in the Homicide Handbook. Rule Number Two is "follow the money." Melon and Stengler approached their investigation in this way. Did Pahlasian or Beloit owe money? Did either man cheat a business partner? Was either having an affair with another man's wife? Did Pahlasian's wife jilt a lover, who murdered her husband as retaliation, or did his wife have Eric murdered to be with another man?

Melon and Stengler identified only two persons of interest during their investigation. The first was a Russian pornographer in the Valley who had invested in several projects with Pahlasian. His porno enterprise was financed by a Russian Organized Crime element, which put him on their radar, but the man made better than a twenty percent profit with Pahlasian, so Melon and Stengler eventually cleared him. The second person of interest was tied to Beloit. The Robbery-Homicide Division's Robbery Special group informed Melon that Interpol had named Beloit as a known associate of a French diamond fence. This led to a theory Beloit was smuggling diamonds, but the Robbery Special team eventually cleared him of criminal involvement.

All in all, twenty-seven friends and family members, and one hundred eighteen investors, business associates, and possible witnesses were interviewed and investigated, and all of them checked clean. No viable suspect was identified, and the investigation slowly stalled.

When Orso finished, he checked his watch.

"Anything I've said help your memory?"

"No, sir. I knew most of it."

"Then Melon and Stengler weren't holding out on you."

Scott felt his face flush.

"They missed something."

"Maybe so, but this is what they found —"

Orso tipped his head toward the file box as Cowly interrupted.

"— which means this is where Bud and I begin. Just because Melon and Stengler zeroed out, doesn't mean we will. Just because it's in these pages, doesn't mean we accept it as fact."

Orso studied her for a moment, then looked at Scott.

"I have Shin and his burglar, I have you, and I have a dead police officer. I will break this case."

Joyce Cowly nodded to herself, but did not speak.

Orso stood.

"Joyce and I have work to do. You want to look through the files and reports, here they are. You want to go through the murder book, there it is. Where do you want to begin?"

Scott hadn't thought about where to begin. He thought he might read his own statements to see if he had forgotten anything, but then realized there was only one place to begin.

"The crime scene pictures."

Cowly was clearly uncomfortable.

"Are you sure?"

"Yes."

Scott had never seen the crime scene photographs. He knew they existed, but never thought about them. He saw his own version of them every night in his dreams.

Orso said, "Okay, then, let's get you going."

13.

Orso took a hanging file from the box, and placed it on the table.

"These are the pictures. The murder book has copies of the most important shots, but the master file here has everything."

Scott glanced at the file without opening it.

"Okay."

"The pictures are labeled on the back with the relevant report and page numbers. Criminalist, medical examiner, detective bureau, whatever. You want to see what the criminalist said about a particular picture, you look up the report number, then go to the page."

"Okay. Thanks."

Scott was waiting for Orso to leave, but Orso didn't move. His face was grim, as if he wasn't comfortable with what Scott was about to see.

Scott said, "I'm okay."

Orso nodded silently, and passed Cowly coming in. She had stepped out, but now returned with a bottle of water, a yellow legal pad, and a couple of pens.

"Here. If you have any questions or want to make notes, use these. I thought you might like some water, too."

She was staring at him with the same grim concern he'd seen in Orso when her cell phone buzzed with an incoming text. She glanced at the message.

"Central Robbery. You need anything, I'm at my desk."

Scott waited until she was gone, then opened the hanging file. The individual files were labeled AREA, BENTLEY, KEN-WORTH, TORINO, 2A24, PAHLASIAN, BELOIT, ANDERS, JAMES, and MISC. 2A24 had been Scott and Stephanie's patrol car. It felt strange to see his own name, and he wondered what he would find. Then he considered Stephanie's name, and forced himself to stop thinking.

He opened the AREA file first. The photographs within varied in size, and had been taken in the early hours of dawn, after the bodies had been removed. The Kenworth's front bumper hung at a lifeless angle. The Bentley's passenger side was crumpled, and bullet holes pocked its sides and windows.

Firemen, uniformed officers, criminalists, and newspeople were in the background. The white outline of Stephanie's body held Scott's attention like an empty puzzle begging to be filled with missing pieces.

Scott glanced through the pictures of the Bentley next. Its interior was littered with broken glass. So much blood covered the seats and console it looked as if the interior had been splashed with ruby paint. The floorboard in the driver's well was a deep, congealing pond.

The interior of the Kenworth told a different story, as it was undamaged. Brass shell casings from the AK-47 were scattered over the floorboards and seats, and sprinkled the top of the dashboard. The interior was littered with scraps of paper, a crushed Burger King cup, and several empty plastic water bottles. Scott knew from Melon that these things had been removed, examined, and linked to the truck's owner, a man named Felix Hernandez, who had been in jail for beating his wife when his truck was stolen from Buena Park.

Scott didn't bother to look at the Gran Torino. It had been found eight blocks away beneath a freeway overpass, and, like the Kenworth, had been stolen earlier that day for use in the murders.

Scott quickly turned to Pahlasian and Beloit, examining each closely, as if he might see what it was about one or both that had led to their murders.

These pictures had been taken at night, and reminded Scott of the lurid black-and-white photographs he had seen of mobsters machine-gunned in the thirties. Pahlasian was slumped over the console as if he had been trying to crawl into Beloit's lap. His slacks and sport coat were so saturated with blood Scott was unsure of their color. The broken glass Scott had seen in the daytime picture now glittered from the camera's flash.

Beloit was slumped in the passenger seat as if he had melted. The side of his head was missing, and the arm nearest the camera was hanging by ropy red tissue. As with Pahlasian, he had been shot so many times his clothes were saturated with blood.

Scott spoke aloud to himself.

"Man, somebody wanted you *really* dead."

The next folder contained pictures of Stephanie. Scott hesitated, but knew he must look at them, so he opened the folder.

Her legs were together, bent at the knees, and tipped to the left. Her right arm lay perpendicular to her body, palm down, fingers hooked as if she was trying to hold on to the street. Her left hand rested on her belly. Her body was outlined in the predictable manner, though the pool of blood beneath her was so large the outline was broken. Scott flipped through her pictures quickly, and came to a photograph of a large irregular blood smear labeled B1. B2 showed elongated blood smears as if something had been dragged. Scott realized this was his own blood, and just as suddenly realized he had turned from Stephanie's folder to his own. The amount of blood was amazing. There was so much blood he broke into a prickly sweat. He knew he came very close to dying that night, but seeing the amount of blood on the street made his closeness to death visible. How much more blood could he have lost before he would have been in the picture with a white line around his body? A pint? Half a pint? He flipped back to the first picture of Stephanie. Her pool of blood was larger. When the picture blurred, he wiped his eyes and took a picture of Stephanie's body.

Scott closed the photo files, walked around the table to calm himself, and stretched his side and shoulder. He opened the bottle of water, took a long drink, and studied Orso's poster-sized diagram of the crime scene. He snapped a picture of it, checked his picture for clarity, then returned to the file box, feeling uncertain and stupid. He wondered if he was deluding himself by pretending he might remember something to help catch Stephanie's killers and silence her nightly accusations.

He took out random files and spread them on the table. Auto-theft reports on the Kenworth and the Gran Torino. Statements from people who heard the shooting and phoned 911. Autopsy reports.

Scott saw a file labeled SID — COLLECTED EVIDENCE, and paged through it. The file contained reports analyzing the physical evidence collected at the scene, and began with a list of collected items that went on for pages. The work the SID criminalists put into compiling this amount of detail was stunning, but Scott wasn't interested in endless forensics reports. He knew what happened that night was about Pahlasian and Beloit. Someone had wanted them dead, and Stephanie Anders was collateral damage.

Scott found the stack of reports and interviews concerning Eric Pahlasian. There were so many interviews with family members, employees, investors, and others they stacked almost five inches thick. Scott checked his watch, and realized how long

Maggie had been locked in her run. He felt a stab of guilt, and knew he had to get back to the training facility.

Scott went to the door, and found Cowly on the phone in a cubicle against the far wall. She raised a finger, telling him she'd be off in a second, finished her call, then put down the phone.

"How you doing in there?"

"Good. I really appreciate you and Detective Orso letting me see this stuff."

"No sweat. I was just on with Central Robbery about your Mr. Marley. They're working a line on a crew laying off stolen goods at a swap meet. Some of the goods match up with things stolen in the area."

"Great. I'll let him know. Listen, I have to get back to my dog —"

"Don't mention the swap meet."

"What?"

"If you call Marley. You can call him if you want, but don't mention we're working an investigation at the swap meet. Don't say those words. Swap meet."

"I won't."

"Cool. Someone from Central will call him about his burglary. The swap meet thing isn't his business."

"I get it. My lips are sealed."

"You have a picture?"

Scott was confused again.

"Of what?"

"Your dog. I love dogs."

"I just got her yesterday."

"Oh. Well, you get a picture, I want to see her."

"You think it would be all right if I took a few files with me? I'll sign for them, if you want."

Cowly glanced around as if she was hoping to see Orso, but Orso was gone.

Scott said, "It's the Pahlasian stuff. I'd like to read it, but it's a phone book."

"I can't let you take the murder book, but you can borrow the file copies. We have them on disc."

"Okay. Great. Those are the files I'm talking about."

He followed her back into the conference room. She frowned when she saw the files and folders spread across the table.

"Dude. I hope you weren't planning to leave this mess."

"No way. I'll put them back before I leave."

Scott pointed out the towering Pahlasian file.

"This is what I want. The files Detective Orso took from the box."

She grew thoughtful, and Scott worried

she was going to change her mind, but then she nodded.

"It's okay. Orso won't have a problem unless you lose something. The handwritten notes aren't on the disc."

"When do you want them back?"

"If we need something, I'll call you. Just put the rest of this stuff back before you leave, okay?"

"You got it."

Scott returned the folders to their proper file hangers, and was fingering through the hangers when he saw a small manila envelope in the bottom of the box. It was fastened shut by a metal clasp, and had a handwritten note on front: *return to John Chen.*

Scott opened the clasp and upended the envelope. A sealed plastic evidence bag containing what looked like a short brown leather strap slid out, along with a photograph of the strap, a note card, and an SID document. The strap was smeared with what appeared to be a reddish powder. Melon had written a note on the card: *John, thanks. I agree. You can trash it.*

The SID document identified the strap as half of an inexpensive watchband of no identifiable manufacturer, item #307 on the SID collection list. A note was typed across the bottom of the document:

This was collected on the sidewalk north of the shooting (ref item #307) as part of general recovery. Appears to be half of women's or men's size small leather watchband, broken at hinge. The red smears that appear to be dried blood are common iron rust. No blood evidence found. Location, nature, and condition suggest unrelated to crime, but I wanted to check before I dispose.

Scott tensed when he saw the band had been collected on the north side of the street. The Kenworth had come from the north. Shin's building was on the north.

The photograph showed the leather strap with a white number card (#307) beside it on a sidewalk. Scott went back to the master evidence list in the SID file, looked up its reference number, and found the diagram showing where the watchband was found. When Scott saw the diagram, he felt as if his heart was rolling to a slow stop. Item #307 had been collected directly beneath the roof overlooking the crime scene where Scott had stood that morning and touched the wrought-iron bars that striped his hand with rust.

Scott took out his phone and photographed the diagram. He took a second picture to make sure the image was sharp, then returned the remaining files to their proper hangers.

Scott studied the rusty smears, and thought they looked like the rust he'd gotten on his hands. He wondered why Melon hadn't returned the envelope to Chen, and decided it had fallen between the hangers. Melon had probably forgotten about it. After all, if the broken strap was trash, it wasn't worth thinking about.

Scott put everything back into the file box exactly as he had found it except for the watchband. He slipped it back into the envelope, put the envelope in his pocket, and picked up the Pahlasian files. He thanked Cowly on his way out.

14.

It was late afternoon when Scott returned to the training facility. Almost a dozen personal and LAPD K-9 cars crowded the parking lot. He heard barking and shouted commands behind the building, as dogs and handlers trained.

Scott parked opposite the office end of the building, and let himself into the kennel. Maggie was on her feet in the run, watching for him when he opened the door as if she knew it was him before she saw him. She barked twice, then raised up to place her front paws on the gate. Scott smiled when he saw her tail wag.

"Hey, Maggie girl. You miss me? I sure missed you!"

She dropped to all fours as he approached. He stepped inside, scratched her ears, and grabbed the thick fur on the sides of her face. Her tongue lolled out with pleasure, and she tried to play-bite his arm.

"I'm sorry I was gone so long. You think I left you?"

He stroked her sides and back, and down along her legs.

"No way, dog. I'm here to stay."

Budress came along the runs from the office.

"Got all sulky when you left."

"Yeah?"

Budress rotated his right arm.

"Shit, man, I'm gonna be sore. That dog hits like a linebacker."

"She was into it."

They had worked on bite commands and suspect-aggression earlier that morning, with Budress playing the suspect. Leland had come out to watch. Maggie was hesitant at first, but remembered the military command words, and her USMC training had quickly returned. She would focus on Budress at Scott's command, and watch him without moving unless Scott ordered her to attack or Budress moved toward Scott or herself. Then she would charge for his padded arm like a heat-seeking missile. It was the only part of her exercises she seemed to enjoy.

Budress went on, lowering his voice.

"Leland was impressed. These Mals are fast and all teeth and love to bite, but these big shepherds, man, she's thirty pounds heavier and she'll knock you on your ass."

Scott stroked her a last time, and clipped on her lead.

"I'll work her some more."

"She's worked enough."

Budress now blocked the gate. He lowered his voice even more.

"She was limping. After you left, when she was pacing here in the run. I don't know if Leland saw."

Scott stared at the man for a moment, then led Maggie out of the run, watching her.

"She's walking fine."

"It was small. The back legs. She kinda dragged the right rear."

Scott led her in a tight circle, then down past the runs and back, watching her walk.

"Looks good to me."

Budress nodded, but didn't look convinced.

"Okay, well, maybe she tweaked something what with all the running around."

Scott ran his hands over her back legs and feet, and felt her hips. She showed no discomfort.

"She's fine."

"Wanted to let you know. I didn't tell Leland."

Budress rubbed the top of her head, then glanced at Scott.

"Work on her conditioning. But not here, okay? You're done here today. Take her jogging. Throw the ball. We'll work on her startle response more tomorrow."

"Thanks for not telling Leland."

Budress rubbed the top of her head again.

"She's a good dog."

Scott watched Budress walk away, then led Maggie out to his car, checking her gait for the limp. She hopped in when he opened the door, and filled the back seat. Only two days, and it had become automatic. She jumped into the car without hesitation or signs of discomfort.

"He's right. You probably just tweaked a muscle."

Scott slid in behind the wheel, closed his door, and Maggie immediately took her place on the console, blocking his view out the passenger window.

"You're going to get us killed. I can't see."

Her tongue hung free and she panted. Scott dug his elbow into her shoulder and tried to push her back, but she leaned into him and didn't move.

"C'mon. I can't see. Get in back."

She panted louder, and licked his face.

Scott fired up the Trans Am and pulled

out into the street. He wondered if she had ridden in the Hummers this way, standing between the front seats to see what was coming. A bunch of grunts in an armored Humvee could probably see over her, but he had to push her head out of the way.

Scott picked up the freeway and headed home toward the Valley. He was thinking about the rusty brown strap when he remembered his promise to Elton Marley. He called him, reported what he had learned, and told him that a detective from Central Robbery would be in touch.

Marley said, "Ee already hab call. Two weeks, I heer no-teeng, now dey call. T'ank you for helpeeng dis way."

"No problem, sir. You helped me this morning."

"Dey comin' back, dey say. We see. I geeb you free shirt. You look good in Marley-World shirts. De women, dey lub you."

Scott told Marley he would check back to make sure the robbery detectives followed up, then dropped his phone between his legs. He normally kept it on the console, but the console was filled with dog.

Maggie sniffed the pocket where he stowed the baloney, and licked her lips. This reminded Scott he needed baloney and plastic bags, so he dropped off the freeway

in Toluca Lake to find a market. Maggie
nosed at his pocket.

"Okay. Soon. I'm looking."

He bogged down in traffic three blocks
from the freeway. Yet another apartment
building was being framed on a lot intended
for a single-family home. A lumber truck
was blocking the street as it crept off the
site, and a food truck maneuvered to take
its place. Locked in the standstill, Scott
watched the framers perched in the wood
skeleton like spiders, banging away with
their nail guns and hammers. A few climbed
down to the food truck, but most continued
working. The banging ebbed and flowed
around periods of silence; sometimes a
single hammer, sometimes a dozen hammers at once, sometimes nail guns snapping
so fast the construction site sounded like
the Police Academy pistol range.

Scott grabbed the fur behind Maggie's ear
and ruffled her. It was early for dinner, but
Scott had an idea.

"You hungry, big girl? I'm starving."

He parked a block and a half past the
construction site, clipped Maggie's lead,
and walked her back to the food truck.
Maggie grew more anxious the closer they
got, so he stopped every few feet to stroke
her.

185

Three workmen were waiting at the food truck, so Scott lined up with them. Maggie twined around his legs, and shifted from side to side. The nail guns and hammers were loud, and every few minutes a power saw screamed. Scott squatted beside her, and offered the last of the baloney. She didn't take it.

"It's okay, baby. I know it's scary."

The man in front of him gave them a friendly smile.

"You a policeman, he must be a police dog."

"She. Yeah, she's a police dog."

Scott continued to stroke her.

The man said, "She's a beauty. We had a shepherd when I was a kid, but now I got this wife hates dogs. Allergic, she says. I'm gettin' allergic to her."

The food truck didn't have baloney, so Scott bought two turkey sandwiches, two ham sandwiches, and two hot dogs, all plain. He led Maggie to a small trailer serving as the construction office, and asked the foreman if they could sit outside to eat.

The foreman said, "You here to arrest someone?"

"Nope. Just want to sit here with my dog."

"Knock yourself out."

Scott sat on the edge of the building's

foundation, and took up the slack on the lead to keep Maggie close. Whenever a saw screamed or the nail guns banged, she twisted and turned, trying to get away from the sound. Scott felt guilty and conflicted, but stroked her and talked to her, and offered her food. He kept a hand on her the entire time, so they were always connected. This wasn't something Leland told him to do, but Scott sensed his touch was important.

The workmen occasionally stopped to ask questions, and almost all of them asked if they could pet her. Scott held her collar, told them to move slowly, and let them. After a sniff, Maggie seemed fine with it. The men all told her how beautiful she was.

Scott felt her grow calmer. She stopped fidgeting, her muscles relaxed, and after thirty-five minutes, she finally sat. A few minutes later, she took a piece of hot dog, even with a saw screaming above them. He stroked her, told her how wonderful she was, and broke off more pieces. A noise occasionally startled her, and she would lurch to her feet, but Scott noticed it took her less time to relax. She ate the hot dogs and the turkey, but not the ham. Scott ate the ham.

They sat together for well over an hour, but Scott was in no hurry to leave. He enjoyed sitting with her, talking with the workmen about her, and realized he had not felt this calm in weeks. Then he decided he had not felt so peaceful since the shooting. Scott ruffled her fur.

"It flows both ways."

Scott and Maggie went home.

15.

Scott changed into civilian clothes, took Maggie for a short walk, and told her she had to hang out by herself for a few minutes. He raced to a nearby market, bought three pounds of sliced baloney, five boxes of plastic bags, and a roast chicken. He drove home as if he was rolling Code 3. He worried she was barking or ripping apart his apartment, but when he ran inside, Maggie was in her crate, chin down between her front paws, watching him.

"Hey, dog."

Maggie's tail thumped. She stepped out to greet him, and Scott felt an enormous sense of relief.

He put away the groceries, changed Maggie's water, and printed the pictures he had taken in Orso's office. He did not print the picture of Stephanie's body. He pinned the pictures to the wall by his crime scene diagram, then drew in Marley's shop, Shin's shop, the alley, and the loading area and fire escape behind their building. He drew a small X on the sidewalk where the criminalist found the leather strap.

When Scott finished, he studied his diagram, and felt cowardly for leaving out Stephanie. He printed her picture, and pinned it above the map.

"I'm still here."

Scott took the stack of reports and files to the couch. It was a lot to read.

Adrienne Pahlasian, the wife, had been interviewed seven times. Each interview was thirty or forty pages long, so Scott skipped ahead to skim a few shorter interviews. A homeless man named Nathan Ivers told Melon he witnessed the shooting, and stated that the gunfire came from a glowing blue orb that hovered above the street. A woman named Mildred Bitters told Melon several tall thin men wearing black suits and dark glasses were responsible for the shooting.

Scott put these aside and returned to Adrienne Pahlasian's first interview. He knew this interview was the meat, and set the course the investigation eventually followed.

Melon and Stengler had driven to her home in Beverly Hills, where Melon informed her that her husband had been murdered. Melon noted she appeared genuinely shocked, and required several minutes before they could continue. During this first interview, she agreed to speak without the presence of an attorney and signed a document to that effect. She identified Beloit as her husband's cousin, and described him as a "great guy" who stayed at their home when he visited. She stated her husband told her he was going to pick up Beloit at LAX, take him to dinner at a new downtown restaurant called Tyler's, and drive Beloit past two downtown properties Eric hoped to buy. Melon then allowed her to phone her husband's office, where she spoke with a Michael Nathan to obtain the addresses of the two buildings. She grew so emotional when informing Nathan of the murders that Melon took the phone. Nathan was unable to explain why Pahlasian would show Beloit the two buildings at such an unusual hour. The interview ended shortly thereafter when Mrs. Pahlasian's children returned from school. Melon closed the report by stating both he and Stengler found Mrs. Pahlasian credible, sincere, and believable in her grief.

Scott copied the addresses for the two downtown properties and the restaurants, then stared at the ceiling. He felt drained, as if Adrienne Pahlasian's grief had been added to his own.

Maggie yawned. Scott glanced over, and found her watching him. He swung his feet from the couch, and fought back a grimace.

"Let's take a walk. We'll eat when we get back."

Maggie knew the word "walk." She lurched to her feet, and went to her lead.

Scott bagged two slices of baloney, clipped on her lead, then remembered Budress advising him to work on her conditioning. He stuffed the green tennis ball into his pocket along with a poop bag.

Scott was relieved to find the park deserted except for a man and woman jogging around the perimeter. He unclipped Maggie's lead and told her to sit. She watched him expectantly for the next command. Instead of giving a command, Scott grabbed the sides of her head, rubbed his head on her face, and let her escape. She was in full play mode. She dipped her chest to the ground, stuck her butt in the air, and made play growls. Scott decided this was the time for running. He pulled out the green ball, waved it over her nose, and threw it across the field.

"Get it, girl. Get it!"

Maggie broke after the ball, but abruptly stopped. She watched the ball bounce, then returned to Scott with her head and tail sagging.

Scott considered the situation, then clipped her lead.

"Okay. If we don't chase balls, we jog."

A sharp pain tightened Scott's side when he started off, and his leg lit up with the pinpricks of moving scar tissue.

"Next time I'll take a pill."

He remembered Maggie was loping along with a shattered rear end, and wondered if her wounds hurt the same as his. She wasn't limping and showed no discomfort, but maybe she was tougher than him. Maggie had stuck with her partner. He felt a stab of shame and gritted his teeth.

"Okay. No painkillers for you, then none for me."

They chased the ball another eight times before Maggie's right rear leg began to drag. It was slight, but Scott immediately stopped. He probed her hips and flexed the leg. She showed no discomfort, but Scott headed for home. By the time they reached Mrs. Earle's house, the limp was gone, but Scott was worried.

He fed Maggie first, then showered and ate half the roast chicken. When the remains of the chicken were away, he gave her a series of commands, rolled her onto her back, and held her so she had to struggle to get away. Even with all the rough play, she walked normally, so Scott decided to tell Budress the limp had not recurred. He opened a beer, and resumed reading.

In Adrienne Pahlasian's next two interviews, she answered questions about her husband's family and business, and provided the names of friends, family, and business associates. Scott found these interviews boring, so he skipped ahead.

Tyler's manager was named Emile Tanager. Tanager provided precise arrival and departure information based upon the times orders were placed and the tab was closed. The two men arrived together and placed an order for drinks at 12:41. Pahlasian closed their tab on his American Express card at 1:39. Melon had made a handwritten note on Tanager's interview, saying the manager provided a DVD security video, which was booked into evidence as item #H6218A.

Scott sat back when he read Melon's note. The idea of a security video had not occurred to him. He copied the times, and took the notes to his computer.

Scott printed a map of the downtown

area, then located Tyler's and the two commercial buildings. He marked the three locations with red dots, and added a fourth dot where he and Stephanie were shot.

Scott pinned the map to the wall by his diagram, then sat on the floor to study his notes. Maggie came over, sniffed, and lay down beside him. Scott guessed the drive from Tyler's to either building had taken no more than five or six minutes. The drive from the first building to the second probably added another seven or eight. Scott threw in an extra ten minutes at each building for Pahlasian to make his sales pitch, which added twenty minutes to his total. Scott frowned at the times. No matter which building they visited first, there were almost thirty minutes missing when Pahlasian and Beloit reached the kill zone.

Scott stood to look at his map. Maggie stood with him, and shook off a cloud of fur.

Scott touched her head.

"What do you think, Mags? Would two rich dudes in a Bentley walk around in a crappy neighborhood like this, that time of night?"

The four red dots looked like bugs trapped in a spider web.

Scott eased back to the floor like a creaky

old man, and picked up the plastic bag containing the broken watchband. He re-read Chen's note:

No blood evidence.
Common rust.

Maggie sniffed the bag, but Scott nudged her away.

"Not now, baby."

He took the brown band from the bag, and held it close to examine the rust. Maggie leaned in again, and sniffed the strap. This time he didn't push her away.

Common rust. He wondered if SID could tell whether the rust on the watchband came from the wrought-iron rail on the roof.

Maggie sniff-sniff-sniffed the strap, and this time her curiosity made Scott smile.

"What do you think? Some dude on the roof, or am I losing my mind?"

Maggie tentatively licked Scott's face. With her ears folded back, her warm brown eyes looked sad.

"I know. I'm crazy."

Scott put the watchband back into its bag, sealed it, and stretched out on the floor. His shoulder hurt. His side hurt. His leg hurt. His head hurt. His entire body, his past, and his future all hurt.

He looked up at the diagrams and pictures pinned to the wall, seeing them upside down. He stared at Stephanie's picture. The white line surrounding her body was bright against the blood cloverleaf upon which she lay. He pointed at her.

"I'm coming."

He lowered his hand to Maggie's back. Her warmth and the rise and fall as she breathed were comforting.

Scott felt himself drifting, and soon he was with Stephanie again.

Beside him, Maggie's nose drew in his smells, and tasted his changes. After a while, she whimpered, but Scott was far away and did not hear.

16.

MAGGIE

The man loved to chase his green ball. Pete never chased the green ball, which was Maggie's special treat, but this new man threw his ball, chased it, and Maggie trotted along at his side. When he caught up to the ball, he would throw it again, and off they would go. Maggie enjoyed loping along beside him across the quiet grass field.

Maggie did not enjoy the construction site with the loud, frightening sounds and the smell of burned wood, but the man kept her close and comforted her with touches as if they were pack. His scents were calm and assuring. When other men approached, she sniffed them for rage and fear, and watched for signs of aggression, but the man remained calm, and his calm spread to Maggie, and the man shared good smelling things with her to eat.

Maggie was growing comfortable with the

man. He gave her food, water, and play, and they shared the same crate. She watched him constantly, and studied how he stood and his facial expressions and the tone of his voice, and how these things were reflected by subtle changes in his scent. Maggie knew the moods and intentions of dogs and men by their body language and smells. Now she was learning the man. She knew he was in pain by the change in his scent and gait, but as they chased the ball, his pain faded, and he was soon filled with play. Maggie was happy the green ball brought him joy.

After a while the man grew tired, and they started back to the crate. Maggie sniffed for new scents as they walked home, and knew three different dogs and their people had followed much the same path. A male cat had crossed the old woman's front yard, and the old woman was inside the house. A female cat had slept for a time beneath a bush in the backyard but was now gone. She knew the female cat was pregnant, and close to giving birth. As they approached the man's crate, Maggie increased her sniff rate, searching for threats. Before the man opened the door, she already knew no one was inside or had been inside since the man and Maggie left earlier that day.

199

"Okay. Let's get you fed. You're probably thirsty, right, all that running? Jesus, I'm dying."

Maggie followed the man to the kitchen. She watched him fill her water bowl and food bowl, then watched him disappear into his bedroom. She touched her nose to the food, then drank deep from the water. By this time, she heard the man's water running, smelled soap, and knew he was showering. Pete had washed her in the showers when they were in the desert, but she had not liked rain that fell from the ceiling. It beat into her eyes and ears, and confused her nose.

Maggie turned from the food, and walked through the man's crate. She checked the man's bed and the closet and once again circled the living room. Content their crate was as it should be, Maggie returned to the kitchen, ate her food, then curled in her crate. She listened to the man as she drifted near sleep. The running water stopped. She heard him dress, and after a while he came into the living room, but Maggie didn't move. Her eyes were slits, so he probably thought she was sleeping. He moved into the kitchen, where he ate standing up. Chicken. More water ran, then he went to his couch. Maggie was almost asleep when he jumped to his feet, clapping his hands.

"Maggie! C'mon, girl! C'mere!"

He slapped his legs, dropped into a crouch, then sprung tall, smiling and clapping his hands again.

"C'mon, Maggie! Let's play."

She knew the word "play," but the word was unnecessary. His energy, body language, and smile called to her.

Maggie scrambled from her crate, and bounded to him.

He ruffled her fur, pushed her head from side to side, and gave her commands.

She happily obeyed, and felt a rush of pure joy when he squeaked she was a good girl.

He commanded her to sit, she sat, to lay, she dropped to her belly, her eyes intent on his face.

He patted his chest.

"Come up here, girl. Up. Gimme a kiss."

She reared back, front feet on his chest, and licked the taste of chicken from his face.

He wrestled her to the floor, and rolled her over onto her back. She struggled and twisted to escape, but he rolled her onto her back again, where she happily submitted, paws up, belly and throat exposed. His, and happy.

The man released her, smiling, and when

she saw joy in his face, her own joy blossomed. She dropped to her chest, rear in the air, wanting more play, but he stroked her and spoke in his calming voice, and she knew playtime was over.

She nuzzled him as he stroked her, and after a few minutes he lay on the couch. Maggie sniffed a good spot nearby and curled against the wall. She was happy with joy from their play, and sleepy from her long day, but she never fully slept as she sensed a change in the man. Small changes in his scent told her his joy was fading. The scent of fear came with the bright pungent scent of anger as his heart beat faster.

Maggie lifted her head when the man rose, but when he sat at the table she lowered her head and watched him. She took fast, shallow sniffs, noting that the taste of anger left him and was replaced by the sour scent of sadness. Maggie whimpered, and wanted to go to him, but was still learning his ways. She smelled his emotions roll and change like clouds moving across the sky.

After a while he crossed the room, sat on the floor, and picked up a stack of white paper. His tension spiked with the mixed scents of fear and anger and loss. Maggie went to him. She sniffed the man and his paper, and felt him calm with her closeness. She knew this was good. The pack joins together. Closeness brings comfort.

Maggie curled up beside him, and felt a flush of love when he rested his hand upon her. She sighed so deeply she shuddered.

"What do you think, Mags? Would two rich dudes in a Bentley walk around in a crappy neighborhood like this, that time of night?"

She stood at his voice, licked his face, and was rewarded by his smile. She wagged her tail, hungry for more of his attention, but he picked up a plastic bag. Maggie noted the chemical scent of the plastic and the scents of other humans, and how the man focused on it.

He took a piece of brown skin from the plastic, and examined it closely. She watched the man's eyes and the nuanced play of his facial expressions, and sensed the brown skin was important. Maggie leaned closer, nostrils working, sniffing to draw air over a bony shelf in her nose into a special cavity where scent molecules collected. Each sniff drew more molecules until enough collected for Maggie to recognize even the faintest scent.

Dozens of scents registered at once, some more strongly than others — the skin of an animal, organic but lifeless; the vivid strong sweat of a male human, the lesser scents of other male humans; the trace scents of plastic, gasoline, soap, human saliva, chili sauce, vinegar, tar, paint, beer, two different cats, whiskey, vodka, water, orange soda, chocolate, human female sweat, a smear of human semen, human urine — and dozens of scents Maggie could not name, but which were as real and distinct to her as if she was seeing colored blocks laid out on a table.

"What do you think? Some dude on the roof, or am I losing my mind?"

She met the man's eyes, and saw love and approval! The man was pleased with her for sniffing the skin, so Maggie sniffed again.

"I know. I'm crazy."

She filled her nose with the scents. Pleasing the man left her feeling safe and content, so Maggie curled close beside him, and settled for sleep.

A few moments later, he stretched out beside her, and Maggie felt a peace in her heart she had not known in a long while.

The man spoke a final time, then his breath evened, his heart slowed, and he slept.

Maggie listened to the steady beat of his heart, felt his warmth, and took comfort in his closeness. She filled herself with his scent, and sighed. They lived, ate, played, and slept together. They shared comfort and strength and joy.

Maggie slowly pushed to her feet, limped across the room, and picked up the man's green ball. She brought it to him, dropped it, and once more settled for sleep.

The green ball gave the man joy. She wanted to please him.

They were pack.

PART III

■ ■ ■ ■

To Protect
and To Serve

■ ■ ■ ■

17.

Two days later, Scott was dressing for work when Leland called. Leland never phoned him, and seeing his Sergeant's name as an incoming call inspired a twinge of fear.

Leland's voice was as hard as his glare.

"Don't bother coming to work. Those Robbery-Homicide sissies you've been dating want you at the Boat at oh-eight-hundred hours."

Scott glanced at the time. It was a quarter to seven.

"Why?"

"Did I say I know why? The LT got a call from the Metro commander. If the boss knows why, he did not see fit to share. You are to report to a Detective Cowly down there with the geniuses at oh-eight-hundred sharp. Do you have any other questions?"

Scott decided Cowly wanted the files back, and hoped she hadn't gotten in trouble for letting him take them.

"No, sir. This shouldn't take long. We'll see you as soon as we can."

"We."

"Maggie and me."

Leland's voice softened.

"I knew what you meant. Looks like you're learning something, now aren't you?"

Leland hung up, and Scott stared at Maggie. He didn't know what to do with his dog. He didn't want to leave her in the guest house, but he also didn't want to leave her at the training facility. Leland might get it in his head to work with her. If Leland discovered the limp, he wouldn't hesitate to get rid of her.

Scott went to the kitchen, poured a cup of coffee, and sat behind his computer. He tried to think of a friend who could watch her for a few hours, but his friendships had withered since the shooting.

Maggie walked over and put her head on his leg. Scott smiled, and stroked her ears.

"You're going to be fine. Look how screwed up I am, and I made it back."

She closed her eyes, enjoying the ear massage.

Scott wondered if a veterinarian could help with her leg. LAPD had vets under contract to care for their dogs, but they reported to Leland. Scott would have to fly under the radar if he had Maggie checked. If anti-inflammatories or something like cortisone could fix her problem with no one the wiser, Scott would pay for it out of pocket. He had done the same for himself to keep the department from knowing how many painkillers and anti-anxiety meds he took.

He Googled for veterinarians in North Hollywood and Studio City, then skimmed the Yelp, Yahoo!, and Citysearch reviews. He was still reading when he realized it was too late to find someone to dog-sit.

Scott quickly gathered the Pahlasian files, tucked his notes on the missing drive time into his pants, and clipped Maggie's lead.

"Detective Cowly wants to see your picture. We'll do her one better."

The crush-hour drive through the Cahuenga Pass was a forty-five-minute slog, but Scott led Maggie across the PAB lobby with three minutes to spare. They cleared the front desk, and took the elevator to the fifth floor. This time when the doors opened, Cowly was waiting alone. Scott smiled as he led Maggie into the hall.

"I thought the real thing was better than a picture. This is Maggie. Maggie, this is Detective Cowly."

Cowly beamed.

"She's beautiful. Can I pet her?"

Scott ruffled Maggie's head.

"Let her smell the back of your hand first. Tell her she's pretty."

Cowly did as Scott asked, and soon ran her fingers through the soft fur between Maggie's ears.

Scott offered the heavy stack of files.

"I didn't finish. I hope you didn't get into trouble."

Cowly glanced at the files without taking them, and led Scott and Maggie toward her office.

"If you didn't finish, keep them. You didn't have to bring them."

"I thought that's why you wanted to see me."

"Nope, not at all. Some people here want to talk to you."

"People?"

"This thing is developing fast. C'mon. Orso is waiting. He's going to love it you brought your dog."

Scott followed her into the conference room, where Orso was leaning against the wall by his diagram. Two men and a woman were at the table. They turned when Scott and Maggie entered, and Orso pushed away from the wall.

"Scott James, this is Detective Grace Parker from Central Robbery, and Detective Lonnie Parker, Rampart Robbery."

The two Parkers were on the far side of the table, and did not stand. The female Parker made a tight smile, and the male Parker nodded. Grace Parker was tall and wide, with milky skin. She wore a gray dress suit. Lonnie Parker was short, thin, and the color of dark chocolate. He wore an immaculate navy sport coat. Both were in their early forties.

Lonnie Parker said, "Same last name, but we aren't related or married. People get confused."

Grace Parker frowned at him.

"Nobody gets confused. You just like saying it. You say the exact same thing every time."

"People get confused."

Orso cut in to introduce the remaining man. He was large, with a red face, furry forearms, and wiry hair that covered a sun-scorched scalp like cargo netting. He wore a white, short-sleeved shirt with a red-and-blue striped tie, but no sport coat. Scott guessed him to be in his early fifties.

"Detective Ian Mills. Ian's with Robbery Special, down the hall. We've set up a task force to cover these robberies, and Ian's in charge."

Mills was seated on the near side of the table, closest to Scott. He stood and stepped toward Scott to offer his hand, but when he reached out, Maggie growled. Mills jerked back his hand.

"Whoa."

"Maggie, down. Down."

Maggie instantly dropped to her belly, but remained focused on Mills.

"Sorry. It was the sudden move toward me. She's okay."

"Can we try that again? The handshake?"

"Yes, sir. She won't move. Maggie, stay."

Mills slowly offered his hand, this time without standing.

"I'm sorry about your partner. How're you doing?"

Scott felt irritated Mills brought it up, and gave his standard answer.

"Doing great. Thanks."

Orso pointed at an empty chair beside Mills, and took his usual seat beside Cowly.

"Sit. Ian's been involved since the beginning. He and his guys gave us Beloit's French connection, and worked with Interpol. Ian's the reason you're here today."

Mills looked at Scott.

"Not me. You. Bud says you're remembering things."

Scott immediately felt self-conscious, and

tried to downplay it.

"A little. Not much."

"You remembered the driver had white hair. That's pretty big."

Scott nodded, but said nothing. He felt as if Mills was watching him.

"Have you remembered anything else?"

"No, sir."

"You sure?"

"I don't know if there's anything else to remember."

"You seeing a shrink?"

Scott felt a rush of discomfort, and decided to lie.

"They make you see someone if you're involved in a shooting, but I didn't get anything out of it."

Mills studied him for a moment, then pushed a manila envelope forward and rested his hand on it. Scott wondered what was inside.

"You know what we do in Robbery Special?"

"You cover the big bank and armored-car scores. Serial robberies. Things like that."

Mills made a satisfied shrug.

"Close enough. The people who shot you and your partner weren't assholes who blew up a couple of rich guys and police officers for kicks. Your boys had skills. The way they

217

worked together to pull this thing off tight. I'm thinking they were a professional crew — the same people who take down big scores."

Scott frowned.

"I thought the robbery idea was ruled out."

"Robbery as the motive, yeah. We chased bad leads for weeks before we ruled that one out, but we didn't rule out the crews who take scores. Any asshole who will blow up bank tellers and rent-a-cops will do murder for hire. We keep tabs on these people."

Mills opened the envelope, and slid out more pictures.

"Crews are made up of specialists. The alarm guy does alarms, the vault man does vaults, the driver drives."

Mills turned the pictures so Scott could see them. Eight Anglo men with white or light gray hair and blue eyes stared up at him.

"These men are drivers. We believe they were in Los Angeles on or about the night you were shot. Anything?"

Scott stared at the pictures. He looked up, and found Mills, Orso, Cowly, and the two Parkers watching him.

"I saw a sideburn when he turned away. I

didn't see his face."

"What about the other four guys? You remember anything new about them?"

"No."

"Was it four or five?"

Scott didn't like the empty expression in Mills' eyes.

"The driver plus four."

"The driver get out?"

"No."

"So that's four plus the driver makes five, altogether. How many got out of that Kenworth?"

"Two. Two got out of the Torino. Two plus two makes four."

Grace Parker rolled her eyes, but if Mills took offense he didn't show it.

"Four people running around, shooting, is a lot of people. Maybe someone pulled off his mask, or called out a name? Remember anything like that?"

"No. I'm sorry."

Mills studied him a few moments longer, then picked up the pictures and slid them into the envelope.

"These aren't the only drivers in town. Maybe you'll remember something else. Maybe you'll even remember someone else. Lonnie?"

Lonnie Parker leaned forward and placed

yet another booking photo on the table. It showed a thin young man with sunken eyes and cheeks, bad skin, and frizzy black hair that haloed his head in a limp 'fro.

Lonnie Parker tapped the picture.

"Seen this dude before?"

Everyone was watching him again.

"No."

"Skinny guy. Six feet. Take your time. Give him a good look."

Scott felt as if he was being tested and didn't like it. Maggie shifted beside his chair. Scott reached down to touch her.

"No, sir. Who is he?"

Mills stood with his envelope before anyone could answer.

"I'm done here. Thanks for coming in, Scott. You remember anything else — I don't care what — let me know asap. Me and Bud."

Mills glanced at Orso.

"You got it from here?"

"I got it."

Mills told the Parkers to come see him when they finished, and left with his pictures.

Grace Parker rolled her eyes.

"They call him the I-Man. Ian 'the I-Man' Mills. Isn't that precious?"

Orso cleared his throat to quiet her, and

220

looked at Scott.

"Yesterday afternoon, at our request, Rampart and Northeast detectives arrested and questioned fourteen individuals known to resell stolen goods."

Grace Parker said, "Fences."

Orso pushed on.

"Two of these individuals claim to know a thief who laid off Chinese DVDs, Chinese cigarettes, herbs, and the kinds of things Shin carried in his store."

Scott looked from the picture to Orso.

"This man?"

"Marshall Ramon Ishi. Last night, we showed this picture to Mr. Shin. Shin remembers Ishi would loiter in his store, but never buy anything. You put that with the two fences, and, yes, the odds are pretty good Mr. Ishi is the man who burglarized Shin's store the night you were shot."

Scott stared at the picture, and felt a cold prickle over his chest. Maggie sat up, leaned against his legs, and Scott realized Orso was still talking.

"The home he shares with his brother, girlfriend, and two other men is currently under surveillance. Mr. Ishi and the girl are not present. They left —"

Orso checked his watch.

"— forty-two minutes ago. They're being

followed by SIS officers, who tell us Ishi and his friend appear to be selling hits of ice to morning commuters."

Grace Parker said, "Tweakers. They're meth addicts."

Orso nodded happily, and once more resumed.

"They'll go home in a couple of hours. We'll give them a chance to settle in, then arrest them. Joyce will have command. I'd like you to be with her, Scott. Would you go?"

All of them were watching him again.

Scott didn't understand what Orso was asking, then realized he was being handed a ticket into the investigation. He had spent nine months wanting to help catch Stephanie's killers, and now felt unable to breathe.

Maggie rested her chin on his leg and gazed at him. Her ears were folded and her eyes appeared sad.

Grace Parker said, "Damn, that's a big dog. Her poop must be the size of a softball."

Lonnie Parker laughed, and it was the laughter that helped Scott find his voice.

"Yes, sir. Absolutely. I absolutely want to be there. I'll have to clear it with my boss."

"It's cleared. You're mine the rest of the day."

Orso glanced at Maggie.

"Though we only expected one of you."

Cowly said, "He can bring the dog. He's not going to participate."

She grinned at Scott.

"We're management. We watch other people do the work."

Orso stood, ending the meeting, and the other detectives pushed back their chairs and stood with him. Maggie scrambled to her feet, and the two Parkers both stared at her, frowning.

Lonnie said, "What happened to her?"

Scott realized they had not been able to see her hindquarters when they were seated on the other side of the table. Now they saw her scars.

"A sniper shot her. Afghanistan."

"No shit?"

"Twice."

Now Orso and Cowly stared at her, too, and Cowly looked sad.

"You poor baby."

Lonnie's face folded into a grim stack of black plates, and he nudged around the table toward the door.

"I don't wanna hear nuthin' sad 'bout no dog. C'mon. Let's go see the I-Man. We got work to do."

Grace arched her eyebrows at Scott.

"The man has a master's in political science from S.C., and speaks three languages. He puts on the ghetto accent when he gets emotional."

Lonnie looked insulted.

"That's racist and offensive. You know that is not true."

They continued bickering as they left. Scott turned to Orso and Cowly.

"What do you want me to do?"

Cowly answered.

"Stay here or close by. There's a park across the street, if it's easier with Maggie. I'll text you. We have plenty of time. Take the files with you."

When she mentioned the files, Scott remembered the notes in his pocket. He took out his map, showed them the four dots, and pointed out the discrepancy he'd found with Pahlasian's driving time.

"Even if they stopped at both buildings to talk about them, there's no way it should take an hour and ten minutes to get from the restaurant to the kill zone. Seems like there's twenty or thirty minutes missing."

Scott looked up from the map, waiting for their reaction, but Orso only nodded.

"You're missing a stop. Club Red. It's in the files."

224

Scott had no idea what Orso was talking about.

"I read the interviews with Pahlasian's wife and his office assistant. They didn't mention another stop."

Cowly stepped in with the answer.

"They didn't know about it. Club Red is like a strip club. Melon didn't learn about it until Beloit's credit card charges posted. Beloit picked up the tab."

Scott felt deflated and stupid, and even more stupid when Cowly waved at the heavy stack of files.

"It's in there. Melon interviewed the manager and a couple of waitresses. Use my desk or go to the park. I'll text when we have to roll."

Scott tucked the files under his arm, and looked from Cowly to Orso. He wanted to see the security video, but now felt too embarrassed to ask.

"Thanks for letting me tag along. It means a lot."

Orso smiled the scoutmaster smile.

"Sure."

Scott turned away with Maggie at his side. He felt like an idiot for believing he had discovered a glaring discrepancy when top-cop detectives like Orso and Cowly knew the case inside and out.

Scott wasn't an idiot, but three more days would pass before he understood.

18.

Scott took the files to Cowly's cubicle, saw her tiny, cramped space, and decided Maggie would be happier at the park. Then he noticed the framed pictures beside Cowly's computer, and eased into her chair. Maggie wedged herself under the desk.

The first picture showed a younger, uniformed Cowly at her Police Academy graduation with an older man and woman who were probably her parents. The picture next to it showed Cowly and three other young women all glammed up in satin and sequins for a night on the town. Scott studied the four, and decided Cowly was the only one who looked like a cop. This made Scott smile. Stephanie had looked like a cop, too. The next picture showed Cowly and a good-looking young guy on a beach. Cowly was wearing a red one-piece and her friend was wearing baggy swim trunks that hung to his knees. Scott tried to recall if Cowly wore a wedding ring, but couldn't. The last picture showed Cowly on a couch with three little kids. Christmas decorations were on a table behind them, and the oldest kid was wearing a Santa hat. Scott glanced at the pic of Cowly and the man on the beach, and wondered if these were their kids.

"C'mon, Mags. Let's see the park."

Maggie was too big to turn around in the cramped space, so she backed out from under the desk like a horse backing out of a stall.

Scott led her downstairs and across First Street to the City Hall park. The park was small, but a surrounding grove of California Oaks made the space pleasant and shady.

Scott found an unoccupied bench in the shade, and searched through the file for the Club Red interviews. They were short, and mistakenly attached to a document about Georges Beloit.

The three interviews had been conducted twenty-two days after the shooting. Melon described Club Red as "an upscale after-hours lounge featuring what the management calls 'performance erotica,' where semi-nude models pose on small stages above the bar." Melon and Stengler interviewed Richard Levin, the manager on the night of the shooting, and two bartenders.

None of them remembered Pahlasian or Beloit, or recognized their pictures, but Levin provided the times their tab opened and closed from his electronic transaction records. As he did on the interview with Emile Tanager, Melon had handwritten a note on Levin's interview:

R. Levin — deliv sec vid — 2 discs — EV
 # H6218B

Levin had delivered the Club Red security video on two discs, which were logged into the case file.

When Scott finished the interviews, he entered Club Red's address into his phone's map app to find its location, and added a fifth dot to his map. He stared at the fifth dot for a moment, then checked to be sure he entered the correct address. The address was correct, but now the times and routes seemed even more wrong.

Leaving Club Red, both commercial properties were now several blocks beyond the kill zone. If Pahlasian had driven to either property, he would have passed the kill zone and had no reason to turn back. The freeway was in the other direction.

Scott grew frustrated, and decided to see for himself. The kill zone was less than

229

twenty blocks away, and Tyler's and Club Red were closer.

"C'mon, let's take a ride."

They hurried back to the Boat for his car.

Tyler's had been Pahlasian's starting point, so Scott drove to Tyler's.

The restaurant occupied the corner of an older, ornate building at an intersection not far from Bunker Hill. The front was paneled in black glass with its name mounted on the glass in brass letters. Tyler's was closed, but Scott stopped to consider the area. He saw no nearby parking lots, so he assumed valets waited at the corner during business hours. He wondered if the Gran Torino was watching the valet station when Pahlasian arrived, or if it followed him from LAX.

Club Red was only nine blocks away. Scott made the daytime drive in twelve minutes, most of which was spent waiting for pedestrians. At one-thirty in the morning, the travel time would have been four minutes or less.

Club Red was also on the ground floor of an older building. It sat next to a parking lot, and its exposed side bore a faded sign advertising custom machine parts. Jutting from the side of the building into the parking lot was a small vertical neon sign spelling out RED. A red door was cut into the building beneath the sign. Patrons probably passed a couple of oversized bouncers as if entering a clandestine world.

Scott checked his map again. Ignoring Tyler's, the remaining four dots formed a capital Y, with Club Red at the bottom, the kill zone directly above it at the fork, and the two properties Pahlasian wanted to show Beloit at the tips of the arms.

Scott looked at Maggie.

"Everything's wrong."

Maggie sniffed his ear, and blew dog breath in his face. Scott tried to push her off the console, but she held firm.

Two attendants were on duty in the parking lot. Scott parked across their entrance, and got out. The older attendant was a Latin man in his fifties with short black hair and a red vest. He hurried over when he saw Scott block their drive, but pulled up short when he saw Scott's uniform. This was the cop effect.

He said, "You wan' to park?"

Scott let Maggie out. The man saw her, and took a step back. This was the German shepherd effect.

Scott pointed at the building.

"The club here, Club Red? What time do they close?"

"Really late, man. They don't open 'til nine. They close at four."

"Four in the morning."

"Yeah, four in the morning."

Scott thanked the man, let Maggie back into the car, and climbed in behind the wheel. He thought he had it figured.

"There's no mystery here. They were coming back. They saw the buildings, and decided they wanted another drink. That's all there is to it."

Maggie panted, but this time Scott was out of range. Then he glanced at the map again and realized his latest theory was also wrong.

"Shit."

The Bentley's direction.

The Bentley wasn't driving toward Club Red when it passed in front of his radio car. Pahlasian was driving in the opposite direction. Toward the freeway.

Scott was still staring at the map when Cowly texted him.

WE'RE ROLLING. CALL ME

Scott immediately called.

"I'm only a few blocks away. Give me five minutes."

"Take ten, but don't come to the Boat.

232

We're staging at MacArthur Park. Can you be there in ten?"

"Absolutely."

"On the east side between Seventh and Wilshire. You'll see us."

Scott put down his phone, wondering why Pahlasian was going to the freeway when he entered the kill zone. Time was still missing, and it hadn't been filled by looking at buildings.

MacArthur Park was four square blocks split down the middle by Wilshire Boulevard. A soccer field, playgrounds, and a concert pavilion occupied the area north of Wilshire. MacArthur Park Lake took up the south side. The lake was once known for paddleboats until gang violence, drug dealing, and murders drove away the people who rented the boats. Then LAPD and the local business community rolled in, the lake and the park were rebuilt, serious surveillance systems were installed, and the gang-banging drug dealers were rolled out. The paddleboats tried to make a comeback, but the lake's reputation for 'bangers and violence had polluted the water. So had the tools of their trade. When the lake was drained for repair, more than a hundred handguns were found on the bottom.

Scott followed Wilshire to the park, and saw the staging area. Six LAPD radio cars, a SWAT van, and three unmarked but obvious police sedans were parked near the old paddleboat concession. A uniformed police officer blocked the entrance when he saw a Trans Am turning in, but he stepped aside when he saw Scott's uniform. Scott rolled down the window.

"I'm looking for Detective Cowly."

The officer leaned closer to grin at Maggie.

"With the SWAT team. Man, I love having these dogs with us. He's a beauty."

Maybe the officer leaned too close or spoke too loudly. Maggie's ears spiked forward, and Scott knew what was coming even before she growled.

The officer stepped back and laughed.

"Jesus, I love these dogs. Good luck finding a place to park. Maybe put it on the grass over there."

Scott raised the window, and ruffled Maggie's fur as he pushed her out of the way.

"He, my ass. How can he think a beautiful girl like you is a he?"

Maggie licked Scott's ear, and watched the officer until they were parked.

Scott clipped her lead, got out, and watered her with a squirt bottle. After she drank, he let her pee, and spotted Cowly beside the SWAT unit's tactical van. She was huddled with the SWAT commander, a uniformed lieutenant, and three detectives, none of whom Scott recognized. The SWAT team was lounging by the boathouse, as relaxed as if they were on a fishing trip. Scott felt the kiss of a passing dream, then looked down at Maggie, and found her watching him, tongue hanging loose, ears back and happy. He petted her head.

"No limping. Either of us."

Maggie wagged her tail and fell in beside him.

Cowly saw him approaching, and held up a finger, signaling him to wait. She spoke with her group a few minutes longer, then they broke up and went in different directions, and Cowly came over to meet him.

"We'll take my car. Ishi is only five minutes away."

Scott was doubtful.

"You don't mind? She's going to leave hair."

"All I care is she doesn't throw up. She gets carsick, you have to clean it."

"She doesn't get carsick."

"She's never ridden with me."

Cowly led them to an unmarked tan Impala that wasn't in much better shape than Scott's ratty Trans Am. He loaded Maggie in back, and climbed into the shotgun seat as Cowly fired the engine. She popped it in gear, and backed up to leave.

"This won't take long. You see the man-power we got? The I-Man wanted to roll the Bomb Squad, forchrissake. Orso said, these idiots *use* meth, they don't *cook* it."

Scott nodded, not knowing how to respond.

"Thanks again for asking me along. I appreciate it."

"You're doing your part."

"By keeping you company?"

Cowly gave him a glance he couldn't read.

"By eyeballing Ishi. If you see him, maybe you'll remember him."

Scott immediately tensed. Maggie paced from side to side in the back seat, whining. Scott reached back to touch her.

"I didn't see him."

"You don't remember seeing him."

Scott felt as if he was being tested again, and didn't like it. His stomach knotted, and he flashed on the shooting — bright yellow bursts from the rifle, the big man walking closer, the impact as the bullet slammed through his shoulder. Scott closed his eyes, and visualized himself on a beach. Then Cowly and her boyfriend appeared on the sand, and he opened his eyes.

"This is bullshit. I'm not a lab monkey."

"You're what we have. You don't want to be here, I'll let you out."

"We don't even know if this is the guy."

"He laid off Chinese goods three different occasions before Shin closed. He lives fourteen blocks from the kill zone. You see him up close, maybe something will come back to you."

Scott fell silent and stared out the window. He desperately hoped Ishi had witnessed the shootings, but didn't want to believe he had seen the man and forgotten. That was too crazy. Seeing a man and forgetting you've seen him was way more screwed up than recalling white hair. Cowly and Orso seemed to think this was possible, which left Scott feeling they doubted his sanity.

Cowly guided the D-ride onto a narrow residential street past two idling black-and-whites, turned at the first cross street, and stopped in the center of the street. A pale green unmarked sedan exactly like hers faced them at the next cross street. Scott saw no other police presence.

Cowly said, "Fourth house from the corner, left side. See the van covered with graffiti? It's parked in front."

A battered Econoline van covered with Krylon graffiti was parked in front of a pale green house. A broken sidewalk led up a withered yard to a narrow cinder-block porch.

Scott said, "Who's inside?"

Ishi shared the house with two male friends who were also meth addicts, a girlfriend named Estelle "Ganj" Rolley, who worked as a part-time prostitute to support their meth addiction, and his younger brother, Daryl, a nineteen-year-old dropout with several misdemeanor arrests to his credit.

Cowly said, "Ishi, the girl, and one of the males. The other guy left earlier, so we picked him up. The brother hasn't been home since yesterday. You see our guys?"

The street and the houses appeared deserted.

"Nobody."

Cowly nodded.

"A team from Fugitive Section will make the pop. Two guys are on either side of the house right now, and two more have the rear. Plus, we have people from Rampart Robbery to handle the evidence. Watch close. These people are the best."

Cowly lifted her phone and spoke softly.

"Showtime, my lovelies."

The van's driver's-side door popped open. A thin African-American woman slipped out, rounded the van to the sidewalk, and walked toward the house. She wore frayed jean shorts, a white halter top, and cheap flip-flop sandals. Her hair hung in braids dotted with beads.

Cowly said, "Angela Sims. Fugitive detective."

The woman knocked when she reached the door. She waited with the nervous anxiety of an impatient tweaker. When no one opened the door, she knocked again. This time the door opened, but Scott did not see who opened it. Angela Sims stepped into the doorway, and stopped, preventing the door from being closed. Two male Fugitive dicks charged from each side of the house at a dead sprint, converging on the door as Angela Sims shoved her way into the house. The four male officers slammed inside behind her. As the Fugitive detectives made their entry, a male and a female detective jumped from the van and raced up the sidewalk.

Cowly said, "Wallace and Isbecki. Rampart Robbery."

Wallace and Isbecki were still on the sidewalk when two radio cars screeched to a stop behind Cowly's sedan and two more stopped behind the sedan at the far end of the street. Four uniformed officers deployed from each car to seal the street.

240

Ishi's house was quiet and still, but Scott knew all hell was breaking loose inside. Maggie fidgeted from his anxiety.

Five seconds later, two of the male Fugitive detectives emerged with an Anglo male handcuffed between them. Cowly visibly relaxed.

"That's it, baby. Done deal."

Cowly drove forward, parked alongside the van, and shoved open her door.

"C'mon. Let's see what we've got."

Scott let Maggie out the rear, clipped her lead, and hurried to catch up as Sims and another Fugitive dick brought out Estelle Rolley. Rolley looked like a walking skeleton. Street officers called this "the meth diet."

Cowly motioned Scott to join her in the yard.

The remaining Fugitive Section detective brought out Marshall Ishi last. Ishi's hands were cuffed behind his back. He was maybe five eleven, and had the same hollow eyes and cheeks as in his booking photo. He stared at the ground, and wore baggy cargo shorts, sneakers without socks, and a discolored T-shirt that draped him like a parachute.

Scott studied the man. Nothing about him was familiar, but Scott couldn't turn away.

241

He felt as if he was falling into the man.

Cowly nudged close.

"What do you think?"

She sounded lost in a tunnel.

The arresting detective steered Ishi off the porch down two short steps to the sidewalk.

Scott saw the Kenworth slam into the Bentley. He saw the Bentley roll, and the flare of the AK-47. He saw Marshall Ishi on the roof, peering down at the carnage, and running away. Scott saw these things as if they were happening in front of him, but he knew this was only a fantasy. He saw Stephanie die, and heard her beg him to come back.

Ishi glanced up, met Scott's eyes, and Maggie growled deep in her chest.

Scott turned away, hating Cowly for dragging him here.

"This was stupid."

"Man, you should've seen your face. Are you okay?"

"I was thinking about that night, is all. Like a flashback. I'm fine."

"Did seeing him help?"

"Does it look like it helped?"

Scott's voice was sharp, and he immediately regretted it.

Cowly showed her palms and took a step back.

"Okay. Just because you didn't see him doesn't mean he wasn't there. He could be our guy. We just have to roll with it."

Scott thought, *Fuck you and your roll with it.*

Scott followed her into a small, dirty house permeated with a burnt-plastic and chemical odor so strong it made his eyes water. Cowly fanned the air, making a face.

"That's the crystal. Soaks into the paint, the floors, everything."

The living room contained a futon piled with rumpled sheets, a threadbare couch, and an elaborate blue glass bong almost three feet tall. Rock pipes dotted the futon and couch, and a square mirror smeared with powder sat on the floor. Maggie strained against her lead. Her nostrils flickered independently as she tested the air, then the floor, then the air again, and her anxiety flowed up the leash. She glanced at Scott as if checking his reaction, and barked.

"Take it easy. We're not here for that."

Scott tightened her lead to keep her close. Maggie had been trained to detect explosives, and explosives-detection dogs were never trained to alert to drugs. Scott decided the combined chemical smells of crystal and rock were confusing her. He tightened her

243

lead even more, and stroked her flanks.

"Settle, baby. Settle. We don't want it."

The male Rampart detective appeared in the hall, and grinned at Cowly.

"We own this dude, boss. Come see."

Cowly introduced Scott to Bill Wallace, who worked Rampart Robbery. Claudia Isbecki was in the first of two tiny bedrooms, photographing dime bags of rock cocaine, a large pill bottle filled with crystal meth, a glass jar filled with weed, and assorted plastic bags containing Adderall, Vyvanse, Dexedrine, and other amphetamines. Wallace then led them to a second bedroom, where he pointed out a tattered black gym bag, and grinned like a man who won the lottery.

"Found this under the bed. Check it out."

The bag contained a pry bar, two screwdrivers, a bolt cutter, a hacksaw, a lock pick set with tension wrenches, a bottle of graphite, and a battery-powered lock pick gun.

Wallace stepped back, beaming.

"We call this a do-it-yourself burglary kit as defined under Penal Code four-forty-six. Also known as a one-way ticket to conviction."

Cowly nodded.

"Pictures. Log everything, and email the

244

pix to me asap. They'll save time with his lawyer."

Cowly glanced at Scott, then turned away.

"Let's go. We're finished here."

"What happens now?"

"I'll bring you to your car. Then I'm going back to the Boat, and you should probably go wherever you dog guys go."

"I meant with Ishi."

"We'll question him. We'll use the charges we have to press him about Shin. If he didn't rob Shin, maybe he knows who did. We work the case."

Her phone rang when they reached the living room. She glanced at the Caller ID.

"That's Orso. I'll be out in a minute."

She moved away to take the call. Scott wondered if he should wait, then decided to get Maggie out of the stink, and took her outside.

A small crowd of neighborhood residents was gathered across the street and in the surrounding yards to watch the action. Scott was watching them when two senior officers came up the walk with a thin young male in his early twenties. He sported a mop of curly black hair, gaunt cheeks, and nervous eyes. Then Scott saw the resemblance, and realized this was Marshall Ishi's younger brother, Daryl. He was not handcuffed, which meant he was not under arrest.

Scott was stepping off the sidewalk to let them pass when Maggie alerted, and lunged toward Daryl. She caught Scott by surprise, and almost pulled him off his feet. She pulled so hard, she raised up onto her hind legs.

Daryl and the closest officer both lurched sideways, and the officer shouted.

"Jesus Christ!"

Scott reacted immediately.

"Out, Maggie. Out!"

Maggie retreated, but kept barking.

The officer who shouted was bright red with anger.

"Christ, man, control your dog. That thing almost bit me!"

"Maggie, out! Out! Come!"

Maggie followed Scott away. She didn't seem frightened or angry. Her tail wagged, and she glanced from Daryl Ishi to the pocket with the hidden baloney to Daryl Ishi again.

Daryl said, "That dog bites me, I'll sue your ass."

Cowly stepped from the house and came down the steps. The flushed uniform introduced Daryl as Marshall's brother.

"Says he lives here and wants to know what's going on."

Cowly nodded, and seemed to consider Daryl with a remote detachment.

"Your brother has been arrested on suspicion of burglary, theft, possession of stolen goods, possession of narcotics, and possession of narcotics with the intent to distribute."

Daryl waited for her to continue. When she didn't, he leaned sideways, trying to see inside through the open front door.

"Where's Ganj?"

"Everyone within the house has been arrested. Your brother is being processed at the Rampart Community Police Station, and will then be transferred to the Police Administration Building."

"Uh-huh. Okay. I got things in there. Can I go inside?"

"Not at this time. When the officers are finished, you'll be allowed to enter."

"I can leave?"

"Yes."

Daryl Ishi slouched away without looking back. Maggie watched him, whimpering as she looked from Daryl to Scott.

Cowly said, "What's wrong with her?"

"He probably smells like the house. She didn't like that chemical odor."

"Who in their right mind would?"

Cowly watched Daryl disappear down the

street, and shook her head.

"How'd you like Marshall as your resident adult? That boy is following in his brother's footprints right into his brother's shitty life."

She turned to Scott, and her professional face was softer.

"If this was unpleasant for you, I'm sorry. We should have explained why we wanted you here. Bud made it sound like we were doing you a favor."

Scott's head flooded with things to say, but they all sounded like apologies or excuses. He finally managed a shrug.

"Don't sweat it."

Scott said nothing more as they drove back to MacArthur Park. The SWAT van was gone, and only two radio cars and his Trans Am remained.

When Cowly stopped behind his car, he remembered the security videos and asked her about them.

"Melon got the security videos from Tyler's and Club Red. Okay if I see them?"

She seemed surprised.

"Fine by me. All you'll see is whatever the bartenders and waitresses said. They don't show anything else."

Scott tried to figure out how to explain.

"I've never seen Pahlasian and Beloit. Still pictures, yeah, but not alive."

She gave a slow nod.

"Okay. I can make that happen."

"They weren't in the box."

"Physical evidence is in the evidence room. I'll dig them out for you. It probably won't be today. I'll be busy with Ishi."

"I understand. Whenever is fine. Thanks."

Scott got out, and opened the back door for Maggie. He clipped her lead, let her hop out, then looked at Cowly.

"I'm not crazy. It's not like I have big holes in my head."

Cowly looked embarrassed.

"I know you're not crazy."

Scott nodded, but didn't feel any better. He was turning away when she called.

"Scott?"

He waited.

"I'd want to see them, too."

Scott nodded again, and watched as she drove away. He checked the time. It was only ten minutes after eleven. He still had most of the day to work with his dog.

"You don't think I'm crazy, do you?"

Maggie stared up at him and wagged her tail.

Scott scratched her ears, stroked her back, and gave her two pieces of baloney.

"You're a good girl. A really good girl. I

shouldn't have taken you into that damned house."

He drove to the training field, hoping the chemicals in the house hadn't hurt Maggie's nose. A dog man would know. A dog man would keep his dog safe.

20.

The sun beat down hot and hard on the training field, frying the grass and the men and the dogs.

Budress said, "No peeking."

Sweat and sunblock dripped into Scott's eyes.

"No one is peeking."

Scott was crouched beside Maggie behind an orange nylon screen. The screen was pulled taut between two tent poles stuck into the ground. Its purpose was to prevent Maggie from seeing a K-9 officer named Bret Downing hide in one of four orange tents scattered at far points on the field. The tents were tall and narrow like folded beach umbrellas, and big enough to conceal a man. Once Downing was hidden, Maggie would have to use her nose to find him, and alert Scott by barking.

Scott was scratching her chest and praising her when a sharp explosion behind him

251

caught them off guard. Budress had surprised them with the starter pistol.

Scott and Maggie cringed at the shot, but Maggie instantly recovered, licked her lips, and wagged.

Scott rewarded her with a chunk of baloney, squeaked what a good girl she was, and ruffled her fur.

Budress put away the gun.

"Somebody oughta feed you that baloney. You jump pretty good."

"Could you step back a couple of feet next time? I'm going deaf."

Budress surprised them three or four times during each session. He would fire the gun, and Scott would give Maggie a treat. They were trying to teach her to associate unexpected sounds with a positive experience.

Budress waved at Downing to continue.

"Stop whining and get her ready. I like to watch her hunt."

They had already run the exercise eight times, with five different officers posing as "bad guys" to vary the scent. Maggie had been flawless. Scott was relieved to see Maggie's sense of smell was unharmed by the chemical odors in Ishi's house.

Earlier, Leland had watched for almost an hour, and was so impressed he took a turn

252

playing the bad guy. Scott instantly saw why. Leland rubbed himself on all four tents, then climbed a tree at the end of the field. His trick confused her for all of twenty seconds, then she whiffed his track leading from the tents, and narrowed the cone until she found him.

Leland had trotted back from the tree without his usual scowl.

"That dog may be the best air dog I've seen. I do believe she could follow a fly fart in a hurricane."

Air dogs excelled at tracking scent in the air. Ground dogs like bloodhounds and beagles worked best tracking scent particles close to or on the ground.

Scott was pleased with Leland's enthusiasm, but relieved when Leland was called inside for a call. He worried Maggie's limp would return with all the running, and Leland would see.

Now, with Leland gone, Scott felt more at ease, and enjoyed the work. Maggie knew what he expected of her, and Scott was confident with her performance.

When Downing disappeared inside the third tent, which was eighty yards across the field and slightly upwind, Budress gave Scott the nod.

"Turn her loose."

253

Scott jiggled Downing's old T-shirt in Maggie's face, and released her.

"Smell it, girl. Smell it — seek, seek, seek!"

Maggie charged from behind the screen, head high, tail back, ears up. She slowed to test the air for Downing's scent, then ran in a slow curve downwind of the tents. Thirty yards from the screen, Scott saw her catch the edge of Downing's scent cone. She veered into the breeze, broke his ground scent, and powered hard for the third tent. Watching her dig in and stretch out when she accelerated was like watching a Top Fuel dragster explode off the line.

Scott smiled.

"Got him."

Budress said, "She's a hunter, all right."

Maggie covered the distance to the tent in two seconds, jammed on the brakes, and barked. Downing eased out until he was in full view. Maggie stood her ground, barking, but did not approach him, as Scott and Budress had taught her.

Budress grunted his approval.

"Bring her in."

"Out, Maggie. Out."

Maggie broke away from the tent and loped back, pleased with herself. Her joy showed in her bouncy stride and happy, open-mouth grin. Scott rewarded her with another chunk of baloney and praised her in the high squeaky voice.

Budress shouted for Downing to take five, then turned to Scott.

"Tell you what, dog with her nose, she saved a lot of grunts finding IEDs. That's a masterful fact. You can't fool her."

Scott ran his hand over Maggie's back, and stood to ask Budress a question. Budress had worked with explosives-detection dogs in the Air Force, and knew almost as much about dogs as Leland.

"The house we were in reeked of crystal, that nasty chemical stink?"

Budress grunted, knowing the stink. Leland had the scowl, Budress the grunt.

"We go in, and right away she was whining and trying to search. You think she confused the ether with explosives?"

Budress spit.

"Smells don't confuse these dogs. If she wanted a smell, it was a smell she knew."

"When we were leaving, she alerted on this guy who lives there, same way."

Budress thought for a moment.

"Were they making or using?"

"Does it matter?"

"We taught our dogs to alert to explosives like RDX and Semtex and whatnot, but we also taught'm the main components insurgents use for homemade explosives. Remember — the 'I' in IED stands for 'improvised.' "

"These people were users. They weren't cooking."

Budress worked his lips as he thought about it some more, then shrugged and shook his head.

"Probably wouldn't matter anyway. A couple of your typical meth lab components could be used to improvise an explosive, but the ingredients are too common. We never taught our dogs to alert to common materials. If we did, we'd have dogs alerting every time we passed a gas station or a hardware store."

"So ether or starter fluid wouldn't confuse her?"

Budress smiled at Maggie, and offered his hand. She sniffed, then lay down at Scott's feet.

"Not this nose. If I asked you to point out the orange tents, would the green hedges or blue sky or the tree bark confuse you?"

" 'Course not."

"She smells like we see. Just laying here, she's picking up thousands of scents, just like we're seeing a thousand shades of green and blue and whatever. I say, show me the orange, you instantly spot the orange, and

256

don't think twice about all those other colors. It's the same way for her with scents. If she was trained to alert to dynamite, you can wrap dynamite in plastic, bury it under two feet of horseshit, and douse the whole thing with whiskey, and she'll still smell the dynamite. Ain't she amazing?"

Scott studied Budress for a moment, and realized how much the man loved these dogs. Budress was a dog man.

Scott said, "Why do you think she alerted?"

"Dunno. Maybe you oughta tell your detective friends to search that house for IEDs."

Budress burst out laughing, pleased with himself, then shouted for Downing to find a new tent.

"She's looking real good. Give her some water, and we'll do one more."

Scott was clipping up Maggie for the tenth run when Leland stormed out of his office.

"Officer James!"

Scott turned, and heard Budress mumble. "Now what?"

Leland covered the ground in long, angry strides.

"Tell me I'm wrong. Tell me you did not DARE to participate in a police action this morning without my permission."

"I watched an arrest with the Robbery-Homicide detectives. I didn't participate."

Leland stomped closer until his nose was in Scott's face.

"I know for a FACT you and your dog took part in an ARREST. My ASS was just reamed for that little FACT."

Maggie growled — a low guttering warning, but Leland did not move.

"Call your dog out."

"Out, Maggie. Down."

Maggie didn't obey. Her eyes were locked on Leland. Her muzzle wrinkled to show her fangs.

"Down."

Maggie growled louder, and Scott knew he was losing more ground with Leland by the second.

Behind him, Budress spoke softly.

"You're the alpha. Be alpha."

Scott made his voice commanding.

"Down. Maggie, down."

Maggie eased to her belly, but did not leave Scott's side. She was totally focused on Leland, who was still totally focused on Scott.

Scott wet his lips.

"We did not take part in the arrest. We were not there as a K-9 team. I didn't know there was going to be an arrest until I got to

258

the Boat. I thought they wanted files back. That's why I took Maggie with me. I assumed I would drop the files off, then come here. That's it, Sergeant."

Scott wondered who complained, and why. He flashed on the senior officer who crapped his pants when Maggie lunged; the officer who turned so red he looked like he was going to stroke.

Scott sensed Leland was trying to decide whether to believe him.

"We were out here for an hour, and you didn't mention it. This makes me think you didn't want me to know."

Scott hesitated.

"The Homicide people thought my seeing the guy they arrested would trigger my memory. It didn't. I don't. It feels like I'm letting my partner down."

Leland was silent for several seconds, but his scowl remained firm.

"It was reported you could not control your dog, and your dog attacked a civilian."

Scott felt himself flush. *As red as the asshole who jumped.*

"I controlled Maggie and the situation, and no one was harmed. Kinda like now. With you."

Budress spoke softly again, but this time to Leland.

259

"Looks like Scott has Maggie well in hand to me, Top. Even though she's all set to rip out your throat."

Leland's scowl flicked to Budress, and Scott knew Budress had saved him.

Leland's scowling eyes grew thoughtful.

"Do you want to remain in my K-9 platoon, Officer James?"

"You know I do."

"And you still hope to convince me this dog should be approved by me as fit for duty?"

"I'm going to convince you."

"Way it works is, my boss reams me about you, I get your back. I tell him my officer is an outstanding young officer who has surprised the hell out of me by the progress he has made with his dog, and I do not for one goddamn second believe he cannot control his dog, and anyone says otherwise better come over here and say it to my face."

Scott didn't know what to say. This was as close to a compliment as Leland had come.

Leland let it soak in, then continued.

"When all the back-gettin' is done, I then ream you. We clear on this principle?"

"Yes, sir. We're clear."

"Fact is, this dog is not part of my K-9 platoon until I certify her, which I have not. If she had bitten this fool, and the vic's money-chiseling lawyer found out YOU — a member of THIS platoon — exposed the public to an uncertified animal, they could and would sue the blue off our asses. I like my blue ass. Don't you?"

"Yes, sir. I'm liking your blue ass just fine."

"You lock this dog in her crate next time or you leave her with me. We clear?"

"Clear, Sergeant."

A bead of sweat leaked down the side of Leland's face. He wiped it slowly away using the hand with the missing fingers, and let the hand linger. Scott sensed Leland did this on purpose.

"Are you a dog man, Officer James?"

"You bet your blue ass."

"It's not my blue ass on the line."

Leland stared into Scott's eyes a moment longer, then took one step back and looked down at Maggie. She growled, low and deep in her big shepherd's chest.

Leland smiled.

"Good dog. You're a damned good dog."

He looked up at Scott again.

"Dogs do what they do to please us or save us. They don't have anything else. We owe them no less."

He turned and stalked away.

Scott didn't breathe until Leland disappeared into the building, then he turned to Budress.

"Thanks, man. You saved me."

"Maggie saved you. He likes her. Doesn't mean he won't get rid of her, but he likes her. You should've left her here this morning."

"I was scared he'd see her limp."

Budress studied Maggie for a moment.

"She didn't limp. Not once. Has she been limping at home?"

"Not once."

Budress glanced up, and Scott could tell Budress knew he was lying.

"Then let's not press it. Stow the gear. We're done for today."

Budress shouted for Downing to come in, and the two senior officers left Scott to clean up. Scott let Maggie off her leash, and was pleased when she stayed beside him. He broke down the screen, rolled it, and collected the four tents with Maggie beside him.

Scott rolled the last tent, and was carrying them toward the kennel when he glanced down and saw Maggie limping. Same as before, her right rear leg dragged half a heartbeat behind the left.

Scott stopped so Maggie would stop, and looked at the kennel. Leland's window was empty. The door was closed. No one was watching.

Scott put down the tents, clipped Maggie's lead, and hoisted the tents. He made her walk behind him so he was between Maggie and the building.

No one was inside when he stowed the tents. Budress, Downing, and the others were probably in the offices, or gone. Scott made sure the parking lot was empty before he led her to his car. Her limp had grown more and more obvious.

Scott fired the engine and backed away.

Maggie stepped forward on the console. Her tongue was out, her ears were folded, and she looked like the happiest dog in the world.

Scott laced his fingers in her fur. She looked at him and panted, content.

Scott said, "You bet your blue ass."

He pulled out of the lot and headed for home.

21.

An overturned big rig on the northbound 5 turned the freeway into a parking lot. Scott worked his way to an exit when they reached North Hollywood, and found a condo complex being framed in Valley Village. Feeding Maggie at construction sites had become their pattern. He watched her carefully when they left the car. Her leg dragged so slightly now, Scott wasn't sure if she was limping or this was her natural gait, but he was relieved by the improvement.

He bought roast chicken and hot dogs for Maggie, a pork carnitas burrito for himself, and sat with her among snapping nail guns and curious construction workers. Maggie cringed when the first bang surprised her, but Scott decided her startle response was less exaggerated than at the beginning. Once she accepted a piece of hot dog, she focused on Scott and ignored the unpredictable sounds.

They ate and socialized with the construction crew for almost an hour. Scott saved the remains of his baloney stash for a treat, and gave it to her when they returned to the car. By then, her limp was gone.

Twenty minutes later, the sun was behind trees and the sky was purple when Scott parked in MaryTru Earle's front yard. Her shades were down as always, keeping her safe from the outside world.

Scott took Maggie for a short walk to do her business, then through the gate, and along the side of Mrs. Earle's house toward his guest house. The light was gloomy fading to dark, and Mrs. Earle's television provided its usual sound track. Scott had made this same walk hundreds of times, and this time was no different until Maggie stopped. There was no mistaking her expression. She lowered her head, spiked her ears, and stared into the darkness. Her nostrils flickered as she sampled the air.

Scott looked from Maggie to the guest house to the surrounding shrubs and fruit trees.

"Really?"

The light above his side door had been out for months. The drapes covering the French doors were partially open as he had left them, and the kitchen lights were on.

He saw Maggie's crate, the dining table, and part of the kitchen. His guest house looked fine, and nothing appeared different. Scott had never felt unsafe in this neighborhood, but he trusted his dog, and Maggie clearly whiffed something she didn't like. Scott wondered if a cat or a raccoon was in the bushes.

"What do you smell?"

He realized after the fact he had whispered.

Scott considered letting her off the leash, but thought better of it. He didn't want an eighty-five-pound attack dog blindsiding a cat or a kid in the agapanthus. He gave her six feet of lead instead.

" 'kay, baby, let's see what you have."

Maggie hoovered up ground scent as she pulled him forward. She led him directly to the side door, then to the French doors. She returned to the side door, sniffed hard at the lock, then once more rounded the guest house to the French doors, where she pawed at the glass.

Scott opened the French doors, but did not enter. He listened for a moment, heard nothing, then unclipped Maggie and spoke in a loud, clear voice.

"Police. I'm going to release this German

shepherd. Speak up, or this dog will rip you open."

No one answered.

Scott released her.

Maggie did not charge inside, so Scott knew if anyone had been in his home, they were now gone.

Instead, Maggie quickly circled the living room, cruised through the kitchen, then trotted into the bedroom and returned. She crisscrossed the living room, checked her crate and the table and the couch, and again disappeared into the bedroom. When she returned, her anxiety was gone. She wagged her tail, went into the kitchen, and Scott heard her drinking. He stepped inside, and pulled the door closed.

"My turn."

Scott walked through the guest house. He checked the windows and doors first, and found them secure. None were broken or jimmied. His computer, printer, and papers on the table were fine, as were his TV equipment and cordless phone. Its red message light was blinking. The papers on the floor by his couch and the maps and diagrams pinned to his wall seemed undisturbed. His checkbook, his dad's old watch, and the three hundred in cash he kept in an envelope under the clock radio beside his bed were untouched. His gun cleaning kit, two boxes of ammo, and an old .32 snub-nose were still in the LAPD gym bag stowed in his closet. His anxiety meds and pain pills were in their usual places on the bathroom counter.

Scott returned to the living room. Maggie was on the floor beside her crate. She rolled onto her side when she saw him, and lifted her hind leg. Scott smiled.

"Good girl."

Everything appeared normal, but Scott trusted Maggie's nose, and Maggie had smelled something. Mrs. Earle had a key, and would open the guest house for repairmen and the pest service that sprayed for ants. She always warned Scott in advance, but she might have forgotten.

"I'll be right back."

Mrs. Earle answered the door wearing a sweatshirt, shorts, and fluffy pink slippers. The roar of the television was behind her.

"Hey, Mrs. Earle. Did you let anyone in the guest house today?"

She glanced past Scott as if she expected to see the guest house in ruins.

"I didn't let anyone in. You know I always tell you."

"I know, but Maggie smelled something that kinda upset her. I thought maybe you let the plumber or pest people in."

She looked past him again.

"Are you having a problem with that toilet again?"

"No, ma'am. That was just an example."

"Well, I didn't let anyone in. I hope you weren't robbed."

"It's just the way Maggie acted. The windows and doors look okay, so I thought you might have opened the door. She smelled something new. She doesn't like new smells."

Mrs. Earle frowned past him again.

"I hope she didn't smell a rat. You might have a rat in there. I hear them in these trees at night, eating all my fruit. Those nasty things can chew right through a wall."

Scott glanced at the guest house.

Mrs. Earle said, "If you hear it or see poop, you let me know. I'll have the pest people come out."

Scott wondered if she was right, but wasn't convinced.

"I will. Thanks, Mrs. Earle."

"Don't let her pee-pee on the grass. These girl dogs kill a lawn faster than gasoline."

"Yes, ma'am. I know."

Scott went back to the guest house. He locked the French doors, and drew the curtains. Maggie was on her side in front of

269

her crate, halfway to dreamland.

"She thinks we have rats."

Maggie's tail thumped the floor. Thump.

Scott went to his phone, and found a message from Joyce Cowly.

"Scott, Joyce Cowly. I pulled the DVDs. No rush. You can come see them anytime, just call first to make sure one of us is here."

Scott put down the phone.

"Thanks, Cowly."

Scott grabbed a Corona from the fridge, drank some, then took off his uniform. He showered, and pulled on a T-shirt and shorts. He finished the first beer, grabbed a second, and brought it to the pictures on his wall.

He touched Stephanie.

"Still here."

Scott took his beer to the couch. Maggie pushed herself up, gimped over as if she was a hundred years old, and lay on her side by his feet. Her body shuddered when she sighed.

Scott eased onto the floor beside her. He sat with his legs straight out because crossing them hurt. He rested his hand on her side. Maggie's tail thumped the floor. Thump thump thump.

Scott said, "Man, we're a pair, aren't we?"

Thump thump.

"Maybe a doctor can help you. They shot me up with cortisone. It hurt, but it works."

Thump thump thump.

File folders, diagrams, and the mass of newspaper clippings he compiled on the shootings spread from the couch to the wall in neat little stacks. Scott sipped more beer, and decided he looked like a nut case trying to prove aliens worked for the CIA, raving about lost memories, recovered memories, imagined memories, and memories that may not even exist — a flash of white hair, forchrissake — as if some miraculous miracle memory only HE could provide would solve the case and bring Stephanie Anders back to life. And now he even had the best detectives at Robbery-Homicide buying into it, as if he could provide the missing piece to their puzzle.

Scott ran his fingers through Maggie's fur.

Thump thump.

"Maybe it's time to move on. What do you think?"

Thump.

"That's what I thought."

He stared at the stacks with their corners all squared off and neat, and their neatness began to bother him. Scott wasn't neat. His car, his apartment, and his life were a mess. If rats were in his apartment, they had made

271

an effort to make his papers appear undisturbed, and overdid it. If someone had the tools in Marshall Ishi's burglary kit, they wouldn't need Mrs. Earle to get inside without breaking a window.

Scott got his Maglite from the bedroom, and went out. Maggie followed him, sniffing at the French doors as he shined his light on the lock.

"You're in the way. Move."

The lock was weathered and scratched, but Scott found no new scratches on the keyhole or faceplate to indicate the lock had been picked.

He checked the side door next. The French doors had a single lock, but the side door had a knob lock and a deadbolt. Scott knelt close with the light. No fresh cuts showed on either lock, but he noticed a black smudge on the deadbolt's faceplate. It might have been dirt or grease, but it gave a metallic shimmer when he adjusted the light.

Scott touched it with his pinky, and it came away on his skin. The substance appeared to be a silvery powder, and Scott wondered if it was graphite — a dry lubricant used to make locks open more easily. A bottle of graphite had been in Marshall Ishi's burglary kit. Squirt in some graphite, insert a lock pick gun, and the lock would open in seconds. No key was necessary.

Scott suddenly laughed and turned off the light. Nothing had been stolen, and his place hadn't been vandalized. Sometimes a smudge was just a smudge.

"See a burglary kit, and now you're imagining burglars."

Scott went back inside, locked up, and pulled the curtains. He went to Stephanie's picture.

"I'm not moving on, and I'm not going to quit. I did not leave you behind, and I'm not leaving now."

He sat on the floor beneath her picture, and looked over the files and documents. Maggie lay down beside him.

Melon and Stengler had gotten nowhere, but it hadn't been from lack of effort. He now understood their effort had been enormous, but they needed the ATF to bust Shin, and Shin wasn't arrested until they were both off the case. Shin changed everything.

Scott fingered through the clutter, and found the evidence bag containing the cheap leather watchband. Rust, Chen had said. Scott wondered again if the rust on the band had come from the roof. Not that this would prove anything even if it had.

Scott unzipped the bag. Maggie lurched to her feet when he took out the leather strap.

Scott said, "You need to pee?"

She nosed so close she almost stood in his lap. She looked at Scott, wagged her tail, and sniffed the cheap leather. The first time he opened the bag to examine the band, she had been in his face, and now she was trying to reach the strap as if she wanted to play.

She was behaving like she had at Marshall Ishi's house.

Scott moved the band to the right, and she followed the band. He hid it behind his back, and she danced happily from foot to foot as she tried to get behind him.

Play.

Dogs do what they do to please us or save us. They don't have anything else.

Maggie was with him the first time he took the band from the bag. They had been playing a few minutes earlier, and she had nosed at the band when he examined it. She had come so close he pushed her away, so maybe she associated the band with play. He tried thinking about it the way he imagined Maggie would think.

Scott and Maggie play.

Scott picks up the band.

The band is a toy.

Maggie wants to play with Scott and his toy.

Find the band when you smell the band, Scott and Maggie will play.

Welcome to Dogland.

Scott dropped the band back into the evidence bag. He originally thought Maggie alerted to the chemicals fumed off the crystal because she confused them with explosives. Budress had convinced him this wasn't the case, which meant there must be another scent on the band she recognized.

Marshall and Daryl would both carry the chemical crystal scent, but Maggie had not alerted to Marshall. She had alerted inside the house, she alerted on Daryl, and now she had alerted on the watchband. Scott stared at Maggie, and slowly smiled.

"Really? I mean, REALLY?"

Thump thump thump.

The thin leather strap had been in the bag for almost nine months. Scott knew scent particles degraded over time, but it seemed logical a person's sweat and skin oils would soak deep into a leather band.

He reached for his phone, and called Budress.

"Hey, man, it's Scott. Hope this isn't too late."

"No, I'm good. What's up?"

Scott heard TV voices in the background.

"How long can a scent last?"

"What kind of scent?"

"Human."

"I need more than that, bro. A ground scent? An air scent? An air scent is gone with the wind. A ground scent, you get maybe twenty-four to forty-eight. Depends on the elements and environment."

"A leather watchband in an evidence bag."

"Shit, that's different. One of those plastic bags?"

"Yeah."

"Why you want to know something like this? You got a sample you want to hunt?"

"One of the detectives asked. It's a piece of evidence from one of their cases."

"Depends. A glass container is best because it's nonporous and non-reactive, but those heavy-duty evidence bags are pretty good. Has the bag been sealed? If it wasn't sealed, you get air migration and the oils break down."

"No, it was sealed. It's been in a box."

"How long?"

Scott felt uneasy with all the questions, but he knew Budress was trying to help.

"They made it sound like a pretty long time. Six months? Call it six months. They

276

were just asking in general."

"Okay. In one of those sealed bags, air-tight, no sunlight, I'm thinking they'd have good scent for three months easy, but I've seen dogs work off clothes sealed for more than a year."

"Okay, man, thanks. I'll pass it along."

Scott was ending the call when Budress stopped him.

"Hey, I forgot. Leland told me he likes the way you're working with Maggie. He thinks we're making progress with her startle response."

"Great."

Scott didn't want to talk about Leland.

"Don't tell him I told you, okay?"

"Never."

Scott hung up, and fingered the band through the bag.

He's following in his brother's footsteps.

Daryl lived in his brother's house, so Daryl's scent was in the house. Maggie alerted on Daryl and on the band. Could the watch have been Daryl's?

Scott touched Maggie's nose. She licked his fingers.

"No effin' way."

Maybe both brothers robbed Shin's store. Maybe Daryl was his brother's lookout, up on the roof to watch for the police. Maybe

Daryl was the witness, and not Marshall.

Scott studied the shabby brown piece of leather in the plastic evidence bag.

Scott put the bag aside, and thought about Daryl as he petted his dog.

22.

Scott woke the next morning, feeling anxious and agitated. He had dreamed about Marshall and Daryl. In the dream, they stood calmly in the street as the shooting unfolded around them. In the dream, Marshall told Orso and Cowly the five men removed their masks after the shooting, and called each other by name. In the dream, Marshall knew their names and addresses, and had close-up photos of each man on his cell phone. Scott just wanted to know if the man had been there.

He took Maggie out, then showered, and ate cereal at the kitchen sink. He brooded over whether to tell Cowly and Orso about the watchband. He decided they already thought he was crazy enough. He didn't want to make things worse by floating a theory based on a dog.

At six-thirty, he was fed up with waiting, and phoned Cowly on her cell.

"Hey, Joyce, it's Scott James. Okay if I pick up the discs?"

"You know it's only six-thirty?"

"I didn't mean now. Whenever you say."

She was silent for a moment, and Scott worried she was still in bed.

"Sorry if I woke you."

"I just finished a five-mile run. Let me think. Can you roll by about eleven?"

"Eleven would be great. Ah, listen, what's happening with Ishi? Did he see anything?"

"As of last night, he wasn't talking. He's got a pretty good P.D. Orso has a D.A. coming down, first thing. They're trying to work out a deal."

Scott reconsidered whether to mention Daryl, but again decided against it.

"Okay, I'll see you around eleven."

Scott worked with Maggie at the training facility from seven-fifteen until ten-thirty, then left her and rolled for the Boat. Her confused expression when he closed her run filled him with guilt. He felt even worse when she barked as he walked away. Her steady bark-bark-bark plea hurt so badly he clenched his eyes. He walked faster when he realized he had heard it before.

Scotty, don't leave me.

The Trans Am felt empty without Maggie beside him. Maggie cut the car in half like a black-and-tan wall when she straddled the console, but now the car felt strange. This was only the second time he had been alone in the car since he brought Maggie home. They were together twenty-four hours a day. They ate together, played together, trained together, and lived together. Having Maggie was like having a three-year-old, only better. When he told her to sit, she sat. Scott glanced at the empty console, and hoped she wasn't still barking.

He pushed on the gas, then realized, here he was, a grown man, a cop, and he was speeding because he was worried his dog was lonely. He laughed at himself.

"Relax, moron. You're all spooled up like she was a human being. She's a dog."

He pushed the gas harder.

"You're talking to yourself way too much. This can't be right."

Scott parked at the Boat twelve minutes later, went up to the fifth floor, and was surprised when he found Orso waiting with Cowly. She held out a manila envelope.

"You can keep them. I burned copies."

Scott felt the discs shift when he took the envelope, but only managed a nod. Orso looked like a funeral director.

"You have a few minutes? Could we see you inside?"

A bitter heat filled Scott's belly.

"Was it Ishi? He was there?"

"Let's talk inside. I'm sorry you didn't bring Maggie. It was fun having her here."

Scott heard only mumbles. He was preparing to relive the shooting through Marshall Ishi's eyes, even as he disappeared in his own nightmare. The Bentley rolling over, the big man raising his rifle, Stephanie reaching out with red hands. Scott was vaguely aware Orso expected a response, but walked on in silence.

None of them spoke again until they were seated in the conference room, and Orso explained.

"Mr. Ishi confessed this morning. He remembered three of the items he stole that night — a set of carved ivory pipes."

Cowly said, "Not ivory. Rhinoceros horn. Inlaid with tiger teeth. Illegal in the United States."

"Whatever. The pipes were among the things Mr. Shin listed stolen."

Scott didn't care what was stolen.

"Did he see the shooters?"

Orso shifted as if he was uncomfortable. His face softened and turned sad.

"No. I'm sorry, Scott. No. He can't help us."

Cowly leaned forward.

282

"He broke into Shin's almost three hours before the hit. He was back home and loaded by the time you rolled up."

Scott looked from Cowly to Orso.

"That's it?"

"We took our shot. It looked really good, here's this burglary fifty feet from the shooting, on the same night, what are the odds? But he didn't see it. He can't help us."

"He's lying. He saw these guys murder a police officer and two other people. A fucking asshole with a machine gun."

Cowly said, "Scott —"

"He's scared they'll kill him."

Orso shook his head.

"He's telling the truth."

"A meth-addict? A drug-dealing burglar?"

"Between witness testimony and evidence, we had the man cold on nine separate felony and misdemeanor charges. He already has a felony strike, so two more would put him over the three strike mandatory."

"That doesn't mean he told the truth. It means he was scared."

Orso kept going.

"He confessed to four burglaries including Shin's. Everything he told us about time, place, how he got in, what he stole, all the details — everything checked. His statements about the Shin burglary — checked.

He was required to take a polygraph. He passed. When we asked him what time he broke into Shin's, and what time he left, and what he saw, he passed."

Orso leaned back and laced his fingers.

"We believe him, Scott. He wasn't lying. He didn't see anything. He can't help us."

Scott felt as if he had lost something. He thought he should ask more questions, but nothing occurred to him, and he didn't know what to say.

"Did you release him?"

Orso looked surprised.

"Ishi? God, no. He's in Men's Central Jail until the sentencing. He's going to prison."

"What about the girl and the roommates?"

"Flipped like three burgers. They helped with our leverage, so we let them walk."

Scott nodded.

"Okay. So now what?"

Orso touched his hair.

"White hair. Ian has sources. Maybe one of them knows of a driver with white hair."

Scott looked at Cowly. She was staring at the table as if she was about to nod out. Scott felt the urge to ask her about the man on the beach, and wondered again if he should mention the watchband.

Cowly suddenly straightened as if she felt his stare, and looked at him.

"This really sucks, man. I'm sorry."

Scott nodded. The connection between the watchband and Daryl was lame. If he tried to explain, they would think he sounded pathetic or crazy. He didn't want Cowly to see him that way.

He absently reached down to touch Maggie, but felt only air. Scott glanced at Cowly, embarrassed, but she seemed not to have noticed. Orso was still talking.

"And we have you, Scott. The investigation didn't end with Marshall Ishi."

Orso stood, ending the meeting.

Scott stood with Cowly. He picked up the manila envelope, shook their hands, and thanked them for their hard work. He respected them the way he now knew he should have respected Melon and Stengler.

Scott believed Orso was right. The investigation didn't end with Marshall Ishi. There was Daryl, only Orso and Cowly didn't know it.

Scott wondered if Maggie was still barking. He was careful not to limp when he hurried out.

23.

Maggie was barking when Scott entered the kennel, but now her bark was pure joy. She jumped onto the gate, standing tall and wagging her tail. Scott let her out and ruffled her fur as he spoke in the squeaky voice.

"Told you I'd be back. Told you I wouldn't be long. I'm happy to see you, too."

Maggie wagged her tail so hard her entire body wiggled.

Paul Budress and his black shepherd, Obi, were at the end of the hall. Dana Flynn was in a run with her Malinois, Gator, checking his razor-sharp teeth. Scott smiled. All these tough K-9 handlers, a lot of them ex-military, and nobody thought twice about grown men and women talking to dogs in a high-pitched, little girl's voice.

Scott clipped Maggie's lead as Leland appeared behind him.

"Good of you to rejoin us, Officer James.

We hope you'll stick around."

Maggie's joy became a soft, low growl. Scott took up the play in her leash and held her close to his leg. If Leland liked the way Scott worked with Maggie and thought they were making progress, then Scott would give him more. But not by sticking around.

"Just coming to see you, Sergeant. I'd like to do some crowd work with her. That okay with you?"

Leland's scowl deepened.

"And what would 'crowd work' be?"

Scott quoted from sessions with Goodman.

"She gets nervous with people because of anxiety that comes with the PTSD. The anxiety makes her think something bad is going to happen, like when she's surprised by a gunshot. It's the same anxiety. I want her to spend time in crowded places so she learns nothing bad will happen. If she gets comfortable with crowds, I think it might help her with gunfire. You see?"

Leland was slow to respond.

"Where'd you get all this?"

"A book."

Leland slowly considered it.

"Crowd work."

"If it's okay with you. They say it's good therapy."

Leland was just as slow to nod.

"I think we should try this, Officer James. Crowd work. All right, then. Go find some crowds."

Scott loaded Maggie into his car, and drove to Marshall Ishi's house. He wanted to put Maggie in a crowd, but not to treat her anxiety. He wanted to test her nose, and his theory about Daryl Ishi.

Scott studied the house. He didn't care if the girl and the two roommates were inside, but he didn't want Maggie to see Daryl. He also didn't want to hang around for hours if no one was home.

Scott drove to the first cross street, turned around, and parked three houses away where grass lined the sidewalk. He let Maggie out, watered her with the squirt bottle, then pointed at the grass.

"Pee."

Maggie sniffed out a spot and peed. A trick she learned in the Marine Corps. Pee on command.

When she finished, Scott dropped her leash.

"Maggie. Down."

Maggie immediately dropped to her belly.

"Stay."

Scott walked away. He did not look back, but he worried. At the park by his house and the training facility, he could drop her, plant her, and she stayed while he crossed the field and back. She even stayed when he walked around the building, and couldn't see him. The Marine K-9 instructors had done an outstanding job with her basic skill set, and she was an outstanding dog.

He went to Ishi's door, and glanced at Maggie. She was rooted in place, watching him, her head high with her ears spiked like two black horns.

Scott faced the door, rang the bell, and knocked. He counted to ten, and knocked harder.

Estelle "Ganj" Rolley opened the door. First thing she did when she saw Scott's uniform was fan the air. Scott wondered how long it had taken her to score crystal once she was released. He ignored the smell, and smiled.

"Ms. Rolley, I'm Officer James. The Los Angeles Police Department wants you to know your rights."

Her face knotted with confusion. She looked even more emaciated, and stood in a hunch as if she wasn't strong enough to stand erect.

"I just got released. Please don't arrest me again."

"No, ma'am, not those rights. We want

you to know you have the right to complain. If you feel you were mistreated, or possessions not booked into evidence were illegally taken, you have the right to complain to the city, and possibly recover damages. Do you understand these rights as I have explained them?"

Her face screwed up even more.

"No."

Daryl Ishi walked up behind her. He squinted at Scott, but gave no indication of recognition.

"What's going on?"

Estelle crossed her arms over nonexistent breasts.

"He wants to know if we were arrested okay."

Scott interrupted. He now knew Daryl was home, and that's all he needed. He wanted to leave.

"Are you Mr. Danowski or Mr. Pantelli?"

"Uh-uh. They ain't here."

"They have the right to file a complaint if they feel they were unfairly or illegally treated. It's a new policy we have. Letting people know they can sue us. Will you tell them?"

"No shit? They sent you to tell us we can sue you?"

"No shit. You folks have a good day."

Scott smiled pleasantly, stepped back as if he was going to leave, then stopped and dropped the smile. Estelle Rolley was closing the door, but Scott suddenly stepped close and held it. He stared at Daryl with cold, dangerous street-cop eyes.

"You're Marshall's brother, Daryl. You're the one we didn't arrest."

Daryl fidgeted.

"I didn't do anything."

"Marshall's been saying some things. We'll be back to talk to you. Stay put."

Scott stared at him for another ten seconds, then he stepped back.

"You can close the door now."

Estelle Rolley closed the door.

Scott's heart was pounding as he walked back to his car. His hands trembled as he ruffled Maggie's fur and praised her for staying put.

He loaded Maggie into the car, drove to the next block, parked again, and waited. He didn't wait long.

Daryl left the house eight minutes later, walking fast. He picked up speed until he was trotting, then turned up the next cross street toward Alvarado, which was the nearest and busiest large street.

Scott followed, hoping he wasn't crazy. And hoping he wasn't wrong.

24.

Scott served in two-person, black-and-white Adam cars as a uniformed patrol officer. He had never worked a plainclothes assignment or driven an unmarked car. When Scott followed someone in a black-and-white, he turned on the lights and drove fast. Following Daryl was a pain in the ass.

Scott thought Daryl might catch a bus when he reached Alvarado, but Daryl turned south and kept walking.

The slow pace on a busy street made following Daryl in a car difficult, but following on foot would have been worse. Maggie drew attention, and if Daryl hopped a ride when Scott was on foot, Scott would lose him.

Scott pulled over, watched until Daryl was almost out of sight, then tightened the gap and pulled over again. Maggie didn't mind. She enjoyed straddling the console and checking the sights.

Daryl went into a mini-market, and stayed so long Scott worried he had ducked out the back, but Daryl emerged with a super-size drink and continued hoofing it south. Five minutes later, Daryl crossed Sixth Street and entered MacArthur Park one block from where the arrest team staged to bag Marshall.

"Small world."

Scott frowned into the mirror.

"Stop talking to yourself."

Scott parked at the first open meter across from the park, cracked the door, and stepped out for a better view. Scott liked what he saw.

MacArthur Park above Wilshire contained a soccer field, a bandstand, and bright green lawns dotted with picnic tables, palm trees, and gray, weathered oaks. Paved walkways curved through the grass, inviting women with strollers, skateboard rats, and slow-motion homeless people pushing overloaded shopping carts stolen from local markets. Women with babies clustered at two or three tables, young Latin dudes with nothing to do hung out at two or three more, and homeless people used others as beds. People were catching sun on the grass, sitting in circles with friends, and reading books under trees. Latin and Middle Eastern men raced back and forth on the soccer field, while replacement players waited on the sidelines. Two girls strummed guitars at the base of a palm. Three kids with dyed hair passed a joint. A schizophrenic stumbled wildly across the park, passing three 'bangers with neck ink and teardrops who laughed at his flailing.

Daryl circled the 'bangers and cut across the grass, passed the three stoners, and made his way along the length of the soccer field toward the far side of the park. Scott lost sight of him, but that was the plan.

"C'mon, big girl. Let's see what you got."

Scott clipped Maggie's twenty-foot tracking lead, but held it short as he led her to the spot where Daryl entered the park. Scott knew she was anxious. She brushed his leg as they walked, and nervously glanced at the unfamiliar people and noisy traffic. Her nostrils rippled in triple-time to suck in their surroundings.

"Sit."

She sat, still glancing around, but mostly staring up at him.

He took the watchband from the evidence bag, and held it to her nose.

"Smell it. Smell."

Maggie's nostrils flickered and twitched. Her breathing pattern changed when she sniffed for a scent. Sniffing wasn't breathing. The air she drew for sniffing did not enter her lungs. Sniffs were small sips she took in groups called trains. A train could be from three to seven sniffs, and Maggie always sniffed in threes. Sniff-sniff-sniff, pause, sniff-sniff-sniff. Budress' dog, Obi, sniffed in trains of five. Always five. No one knew why, but each dog was different.

Scott touched her nose with the band, waved it playfully around her head, and let her sniff it some more.

"Find it for me, baby. Do it for me. Let's see if we're right."

Scott stepped back and gave the command.

"Seek, seek, seek."

Maggie surged to her feet with her ears spiked forward and her face black with focus. She turned to her right, checked the air, and dipped to the ground. She hesitated, then trotted a few steps in the opposite direction. She tasted more air scent, and stared into the park. This was her first alert. Scott knew she caught a taste, but did not have the trail. She sniffed the sidewalk from side to side as she moved farther away, then abruptly reversed course. She stared into the park again, and Scott knew she had it. Maggie took off, hit the end of her lead, and pulled like a sled dog. The three 'bangers saw them, and ran.

Maggie followed Daryl's path between the picnic tables and along the north side of the soccer field. The players stopped playing to watch the cop and his German shepherd.

Scott saw Daryl Ishi when they reached the end of the soccer field. He was standing behind the concert pavilion with two young women and a guy about Daryl's age. One of the girls saw Scott first, then the others looked. Daryl stared for maybe a second, then bolted away in the opposite direction. His friend broke past the back of the building and ran for the street.

"Down."

Maggie dropped to her belly. Scott caught up fast, unclipped her lead, and immediately released her.

"Hold'm."

Maggie powered forward in a ground-eating sprint. She ignored the other man and everyone else in the park. Her world was the scent cone, and the cone narrowed to Daryl. Scott knew she saw him, but following his scent to the end of the cone was like following a light that grew brighter as she got closer. Maggie could be blindfolded, and she would still find him.

Scott ran after her, and felt little pain, as

if the knotted scars beneath his skin were in another man's body.

Maggie covered the distance in seconds. Daryl ran past the pavilion into a small stand of trees, glanced over his shoulder, and saw a black-and-tan nightmare. He skidded to a halt at the nearest tree, pressed his back to the trunk, and covered his crotch with his hands. Maggie braked at his feet, sat as Scott taught her, and barked. Find and bark, bark to hold.

When Scott arrived, he stopped ten feet away and took a minute to catch his breath before calling her out.

"Out."

Maggie broke off, trotted to Scott, and sat by his left foot.

"Guard'm."

Marine command. She dropped into a sphinx position, head up and alert, eyes locked on Daryl.

Scott walked over to Daryl.

"Relax. I'm not going to arrest you. Just don't move. You run, she'll take you down."

"I'm not gonna run."

"Cool. Heel."

Maggie trotted up, planted her butt by his left foot, and stared at Daryl. She licked her lips.

Daryl inched to his toes, trying to get as

far from her as possible.

"Dude, what is this? C'mon."

"She's friendly. Look. Maggie, shake hands. Shake."

Maggie raised her right paw, but Daryl didn't move.

"You don't want to shake hands?"

"No fuckin' way. Dude, c'mon."

Scott shook her paw, praised her, and rewarded her with a chunk of baloney. When he put the baloney away, he took out the evidence bag. He studied Daryl for a moment, deciding how to proceed.

"First, what just happened here, I shouldn't have done this. I'm not going to arrest you. I just wanted to talk to you away from Estelle."

"You were at the house when Marsh was busted. You and the dog."

"That's right."

"He tried to bite me."

"She. And, no, she didn't try to bite you, or she would have bitten you. What she did is called an alert."

Scott held up the evidence bag so Daryl could see the broken band. Daryl glanced at it without recognition, then looked again. Scott saw the flash of memory play over Daryl's face as he recognized the familiar band.

"Recognize it?"

"What is it? It looks like a brown Band-Aid."

"It's half your old watchband. It kinda looks like the one you're wearing now, but you caught this one on a fence, the band broke, and this half landed on the sidewalk. You know how I know it's yours?"

"It ain't mine."

"It smells like you. I let her smell it, and she tracked your scent across the park. All these people in the park, and she followed this watchband to you. Isn't she amazing?"

Daryl glanced past Scott, looking for a way out, then glanced at Maggie again. Running was not an option.

"I don't care what it smells like. I never seen it before."

"Your brother confessed to burglarizing a Chinese import store nine months ago. A place called Asia Exotica."

"His lawyer told me. So what?"

"You help him do it?"

"No fucking way."

"That's where you lost the watch. Up on the roof. Were you his lookout?"

Daryl's eyes flickered.

"Are you kidding me?"

"You guys hang out up there after, party a little, kick back?"

"Ask Marshall."

"Daryl, did you and Marshall see the murders?"

Daryl sagged like a leaking balloon. He stared past Scott for a moment, swallowed once, then wet his lips. His answer was slow and deliberate.

"I have no idea what you are talking about."

"Three people were murdered, including a police officer. If you saw anything, or know anything, you can help your brother. Maybe even buy him a get-out-of-jail card."

Daryl wet his lips again.

"I want to talk to my brother's lawyer."

Scott knew he had hit the end of his lead. He couldn't think of anything else, so he stepped back.

"I told you I wasn't going to arrest you. We were just talking."

Daryl glanced at Maggie.

"Is he gonna bite me?"

"She. No, she isn't going to bite you. You can go. But think about what I said, Daryl, okay? You can help Marshall."

Daryl edged away, and walked backwards to keep an eye on Maggie until he was out of the trees. Then he turned, stumbled, and ran.

Scott watched him go, and imagined

300

Daryl and his brother peering down from the roof, their faces lit by flashes from guns.

"He was there. I know that kid was there."

Scott looked at Maggie. She was staring at him, mouth open in a big grin, tongue hanging out over a ridge of sharp, white enamel.

Scott touched her head.

"You're the best girl ever. You really are."

Maggie yawned.

Scott clipped Maggie's lead and walked back across the park to their car. He texted Joyce Cowly as they walked.

25.

Orso's eyes were flat as a frying pan heating on the stove. Scott had kenneled Maggie with Budress, and now sat at the conference table with Cowly and Orso. His news had not been received in the way he expected.

Orso stared at the evidence bag as if it was filled with dog crap.

"Where was it?"

"Bottom of the box under the files. It was in a manila envelope. One of the small envelopes, not the big size. Melon was sending it back to Chen."

Cowly glanced at her boss.

"SID bagged it because the smears look like blood. Turned out to be rust, so they sent it to Melon for permission to dispose. Melon wrote a card, giving his okay. I guess he didn't get around to sending it."

Orso tossed the bag onto the table.

"I didn't see it. Did you see this envelope when you went through the material?"

"No."

Scott said, "I have it — their notes and the envelope. Down in my car. You want, I'll go get it."

Orso shifted position. He had been shifting and adjusting himself for the past ten minutes.

"Oh, I want, but not now. What made you think you could take *anything* from this office without asking?"

"The note said it was trash. Melon told him to toss it."

Orso closed his eyes, but his face rippled with tension. His voice was calm, but his eyes remained closed.

"Okay. So you gave yourself permission to take it because you thought it was trash, but now you believe it's evidence."

"I took it because of the rust."

Orso opened his eyes. He didn't say anything, so Scott kept going.

"They collected this thing on the sidewalk directly below the roof above the kill zone. This is the roof I told you about. When I was there, I got rust on my hands. I thought there might be a connection. I wanted to think about it."

"So you hoped it was evidence when you took it."

"I don't know what I hoped. I wanted to

think about it."

"I'll take that for a yes. Either way, 'cause I don't give a shit if you thought it was evidence or trash, here's the problem. If it's evidence, by taking it home like you have, you not being an investigating officer on this case, only an asshole we were courteous to, you've broken the chain of custody."

Cowly's voice was soft.

"Boss."

Scott did not respond, and did not care if Orso thought he was an asshole. The cast-off brown leather strip had led to Daryl, and Daryl might lead to the shooters.

Tension played on Orso's face until a tic developed beneath his left eye. Then the ripples settled, and his face softened.

"I apologize, Scott. I should not have said that. I'm sorry."

"I fucked up. I'm sorry, too. But the band was at the scene, and Daryl Ishi was wearing it. Guaranteed. My dog isn't wrong."

Cowly said, "Daryl denies it's his, and denies being at the scene. Okay, we can swab him and comp the DNA. Then we'll know."

Orso considered the evidence bag, then rolled his chair to the door.

"Jerry! Petievich! Would you see if Ian's here? Ask him to come see me."

The I-Man joined them a few minutes later. His face was more red than Scott remembered. A surprised smile split Ian Mills' face when he saw Scott.

"You get a news flash from the memory bank? That white sideburn turn into a big ol' pocked nose?"

The stupid joke was irritating, but Orso got down to business before Scott responded.

"Scott believes Marshall Ishi's younger brother, Daryl, was present when Marshall robbed Shin's store, and may have witnessed the shootings."

Mills frowned.

"I didn't know he had a brother."

"No reason you should. Until now, we had no reason to think he was involved."

Mills crossed his arms. He peered at Scott, then turned to Orso.

"He passed the poly. We established Marshall left before the shootings went down."

"He also claimed he was alone. If Scott's right, maybe Marshall is just a good liar."

The I-Man's gaze clicked back to Scott.

"You remember this kid? He saw the shootings?"

"This isn't a memory. I'm saying he was at the scene, and I believe he was on the roof. I don't know when he was there, and I don't know what he saw."

Orso slid the evidence bag to Mills, who glanced at the bag but did not touch it.

"Scott found this in the case file. It's half a leather watchband SID collected at the scene. Scott believes he's linked it to Daryl Ishi, which would put Daryl at the scene. Before we go further, you need to know we have a chain-of-custody issue."

Orso described Scott's mistake without passion or inflection, but Mills' face grew darker. Scott felt like a twelve-year-old in the principal's office when Mills unloaded.

"Are you fucking kidding me? What the fuck were you thinking?"

"That no one had done a goddamned thing for nine months and the case was still open."

Orso held up a hand for Mills to stop, and glanced at Scott.

"Tell Ian about the dog. Like you explained it to me."

Scott began with Maggie's first exposure to the scent sample, and walked the I-Man through his test at MacArthur Park, where Maggie tracked the scent across the width of the park directly to Daryl Ishi.

Scott gestured at the evidence bag, which was still on the table by Mills.

"This was his. He was there the night we

were shot."

Mills had listened in silence, frowning across his bristling forearms. When Scott finished, his frown deepened.

"This sounds like bullshit."

Orso shrugged.

"Easy enough to find out. The dog might have something."

Scott knew Mills would listen to Orso, so he pressed his case harder.

"She has Daryl Ishi. See these red streaks? There's a rusty iron safety fence on the roof. SID says these little red smears are rust. His watch got caught on the fence, the band broke, and this piece landed on the side-walk. That's where SID found it."

Orso leaned toward Mills.

"Here's what I'm thinking. We pick the kid up, swab him, run the DNA. Then we'll know if it's his. After that, we can worry about whether he saw anything."

Mills paced to the door, but didn't leave, as if he had needed motion to contain him-self.

"I don't know whether to hope the thing is good or garbage. You screwed us, kid. I can't fucking believe you walked out with a piece of evidence, which, by the way, even the stupidest defense attorney will point out you contaminated."

Orso leaned back.

"Ian, it's done. Let it go."

"Really? After nine fucking months with nothing to show?"

"Pray it's good. If we get a match, we'll know he's a liar, we'll know he's hiding something, and we'll find a thousand work-arounds. We've danced this dance before, man."

If a future judge excluded the watchband, he or she might also exclude all downstream evidence derived from the band. The downstream evidence was called "fruits of the poisonous tree," under the principle that evidence derived from bad evidence was also bad. If investigators knew they had a piece of bad fruit, they tried to find a path around the bad fruit by using unrelated evidence to reach the same result. This was called a work-around.

Mills stood in the door, shaking his head.

"I'm too old. The stress is killing me."

He seemed thoughtful for a moment, then turned back to Scott.

"Okay. So when you and the Hound of the Baskervilles ran down this kid, I suppose you questioned him?"

"He denied everything."

"Uh-huh, and you being the trained interrogator you are, did you ask if he saw the shootings?"

"He said he wasn't there."

"Of course he did. So what you actually accomplished here was, you gave the kid a big heads-up that we're coming for him, and what it is we want to know. Now he'll have plenty of time to think up good answers. Way to go, Sherlock."

The I-Man walked out.

Scott looked at Orso and Cowly. He mostly looked at Cowly.

"I know it's worth nothing, but I'm sorry."

Orso shrugged.

"Shit happens."

Orso pushed back from the table and walked away.

Cowly stood last.

"Come on. I'll walk you to the elevator."

Scott followed her, not knowing what to say. When he found the small leather strap in the manila envelope, the sidewalk where it was found and the smears of rust gave him a sense the band and he somehow shared the events of that night. It had been a physical link to Stephanie and the shooting and the memories he could not recall, and he had hoped it would help him see the night more clearly.

When they reached the elevator, Cowly touched his arm. She looked sad.

"These things happen. Nobody died."

"Not today."

Cowly flushed, and Scott realized his comment had made her feel awkward and embarrassed.

"Jesus, I'm batting a thousand. I didn't mean it the way it sounded. You were being nice."

Her flush faded as she relaxed.

"I was being nice, but I meant it. Exclusions aren't automatic. Issues like this are argued every day, so don't sweat it until it's time to start sweating."

Scott was feeling a little better.

"Whatever you say."

"I say. And if the DNA matches Daryl to the band, we have something to chase, which is all thanks to you."

The elevator opened. Scott caught the doors with a hand, but didn't go in.

"The picture of you and a man on the beach. Is he your husband?"

Cowly was so still, Scott thought he had offended her, but she smiled as she turned away.

"Don't even think about it, Officer."

"Too late. I'm thinking."

She kept walking.

"Turn off your brain."

"My dog likes me."

When she reached the Homicide Special door, Cowly stopped.

"He's my brother. The kids are my niece and nephews."

"Thank you, Detective."

"Have a good day, Officer."

Scott boarded the elevator and rode down to his car.

26.

Scott spent the rest of the afternoon working with Maggie on advanced vehicle exercises. These included exiting the car through an open window, entering a car through an open window to engage a suspect, and obeying off-leash commands while outside the vehicle when Scott remained inside the vehicle. Their K-9 vehicle was a standard police patrol sedan with a heavy wire screen separating the front and back seats, and a remote door-release system that opened the rear doors from as far as one hundred feet away. The remote system allowed Scott to release Maggie without exiting the car, or exit the vehicle without her, and release her from a distance by pushing a button on his belt.

Maggie hated the K-9 car. She hopped into the back seat willingly enough, but as soon as Scott got in behind the wheel, she whined and pawed at the screen that kept them apart. She stopped when he gave her commands to lie down or sit, but a few seconds later she would try even harder to reach him. She bit and pulled the mesh so hard, Scott thought her teeth would break. He moved on to other exercises as quickly as possible.

Leland watched them work on and off throughout the afternoon, but was absent most of the time. Scott wasn't sure if this was a good sign, but with Maggie jumping in and out of the car, the less Leland was around, the better. He was relieved when Maggie reached the end of the day without limping.

Scott stowed the training gear, cleaned up, and was leading Maggie out of the kennel when the office door opened behind them and Leland appeared.

"Officer James."

Scott tugged the leash to stop Maggie's growl.

"Hey, Sergeant. Heading for home."

"I won't keep you."

Leland came out, so Scott walked back to meet him.

"I am assigning our beautiful young man, Quarlo, to another handler. Because I first offered Quarlo to you, I thought you should hear this from me."

Scott wasn't sure why Leland was telling him, or what his assigning Quarlo to another handler meant.

"Okay. Thanks for telling me."

"There is one more thing. When we began our work with Miss Maggie here, you asked for two weeks before I re-evaluated her. You may have three. Enjoy your evening, Officer James."

Scott decided a treat was in order. They celebrated at a construction site in Burbank with fried chicken, beef brisket, and two turkey drumsticks. The women who worked in the food truck fell in love with Maggie, and asked if they could take each other's picture, posing with Scott and the dog. Scott said sure, and the construction workers lined up for pictures, too. Maggie growled only once.

Scott walked her when they reached home, then showered and brought the envelope containing the discs to his table. The idea of watching two dead men enjoying themselves creeped him out, but Scott hoped this would help him deal with the crazy, innocent-bystander nature of the shooting and Stephanie's violent loss. He hoped he wasn't deluding himself. Maybe he only wanted a better target for his rage.

Scott found two discs when he opened the

envelope, one labeled Tyler's, the other Club Red. Something about the number of discs bothered him, and then he recalled Melon had logged two discs from Club Red. He wondered why Cowly gave him only one of the Club Red discs, but decided it didn't matter.

Scott fed the Club Red disc into his computer. While it loaded, Maggie went into the kitchen, slurped up what sounded like gallons of water, then curled into a huge black-and-tan ball at his feet. She did not sleep in her crate anymore. He reached down to touch her.

"Good girl."

Thump thump.

The Club Red video had been recorded using a stationary, black-and-white ceiling camera. There was no sound. The high angle covered a room crowded with upscale men and couples in booths or at tables, watching costumed women pose while servers moved between the tables. Thirty seconds into the video, Beloit and Pahlasian were shown to a table for two. Scott felt nothing as he watched them. A couple of minutes later, a waitress approached to take their order. Scott grew bored, and hit the fast-forward. Drinks were delivered by the high-speed, herky-jerky waitress, Beloit yukked it up,

Pahlasian stared at the dancers. At one point, Beloit stopped a passing waitress, who pointed to the rear of the room. Beloit followed her finger at triple-time speed, and returned just as quickly two minutes later. Pit stop. More fast-forward minutes passed, Beloit paid, they left, off to meet the Wizard, and the image froze.

End of recording.

Other than staff, the two men had interacted with no one. No one approached them. Neither man approached or spoke to another customer. Neither had used his cell phone.

Scott ejected the disc.

Beloit and Pahlasian were no more real now than before — two middle-aged men about to get whacked for reasons unknown. Scott hated them. He wished he had a video of them being shot to death. He wished he had shot them as they left the club, stopped the bastards cold right there before they got Stephanie killed and him shot to pieces, and put Scott James on a path that led to him, here, now, crying.

Thump thump thump.

Maggie was beside him, watching. With her folded ears and caring eyes, she looked as soft and sleek as a seal. He stroked her head.

"I'm okay."

Scott drank some water, took a pee, and loaded the Tyler's disc. The high angle included the reception station, an incomplete view of the bar, and three blurry tables. When Pahlasian and Beloit entered from the bottom left corner of the frame, their faces were hidden by the bad angle.

A host and hostess in dark suits greeted them. After a brief conversation, the woman showed them to their table. This was the last Scott saw of Pahlasian and Beloit until they departed.

Scott ejected the disc.

The Club Red disc was by far the superior, which left Scott wondering what the missing disc showed. He dug out Melon's interview with Richard Levin to make sure he had it right, and reread the handwritten note:

R. Levin — deliv sec vid — 2 discs — EV
 # H6218B

Scott decided to phone Cowly.

"Joyce? Hey, it's Scott James. Hope you don't mind. I have a question about these discs."

"Sure. What's up?"

"I was wondering why you gave me only

one of the Club Red discs and not both."

Cowly was silent for a moment.

"I gave you two discs."

"Yeah, you did. One from Tyler's and one from Club Red, but there are supposed to be two from Club Red. Melon has a note here saying two discs were logged."

Cowly was silent some more.

"I don't know what to tell you. There was only the one disc from Club Red. We have the LAX stuff, the disc from Tyler's, and the disc from Club Red."

"Melon's note says there were two."

"I hear you. Those things were screened, you know? All we got was a confirmation of arrival and departure times. Nobody saw anything unusual."

"Why is it missing?"

She sounded exasperated.

"Shit happens. Things get lost, misplaced, people take stuff and forget they have it. I'll check, okay? These things happen, Scott. Is there anything else?"

"No. Thanks."

Scott felt miserable. He hung up, put away the discs, and stretched out on the couch.

Maggie came over, sniffed for a spot, and lay down beside the couch. He rested his hand on her back.

"You're the only good part of this."

Thump thump.

27.

MAGGIE

Maggie roamed a drowsy green field, content and at peace. Belly full. Thirst quenched. Scott's hand a warm comfort. The man was Scott. She was Maggie. This place was their crate, and their crate was safe.

Dogs notice everything. Maggie knew Scott was Scott because he looked at other humans when they used the word. This was how she learned Pete was Pete, and she was Maggie. People looked at her when they said it. Maggie understood come, stay, out, crate, walk, ball, pee, bunk, seek, rat, MRE, chow, good girl, drink, sit, down, fucker, roll over, treat, sit up, guard'm, eat up, find'm, get'm, and many other words. She learned words easily if she associated them with food, joy, play, or pleasing her alpha. This was important. Pleasing her alpha made the pack strong.

Maggie opened her eyes when Scott moved his hand. Their crate was quiet and safe, so Maggie did not rise. She listened to Scott move through the crate. She heard him urinating a few seconds before she smelled his urine, which was followed by the familiar rush of water. A moment later, she smelled the sweet green foam Scott made in his mouth. When the water stopped, Scott returned, smelling brightly of the green foam, water, and soap.

He squatted beside her, stroked her, and made words she did not understand. This did not matter. She understood the love and kindness in his tone.

Maggie lifted her hind leg to expose her belly.

Alpha happy, pack happy.

I am yours.

Scott lay down on the couch in the darkness. Maggie smelled the growing cool of his body, and knew when he slept. When Scott slept, she sighed, and let herself drift into sleep.

A sound new to their crate roused her.

Their crate was defined by its scents and sounds — the carpet; the paint; Scott; the scent of the mice in the walls, and the squeak when they mated; the elderly female who lived with only her voice for pack; the rats clawing their way up the orange trees for fruit; the scent of the two cats who hunted them. Maggie began learning their crate when Scott brought her home, and learned more with each breath, like a computer downloading a never-ending file. As the information compiled in her memory, the pattern of scents and sounds grew familiar.

Familiar was good. Unfamiliar was bad.

A soft scuffing came from beyond the old female's crate.

Maggie instantly lifted her head, and cocked her ears toward the sound. She recognized human footsteps, and understood two people were coming up the drive.

Maggie hurried to the French doors and pushed her nose under the curtain. She heard a twig snap, brittle leaves being crushed, and the scuffing grow louder. Tree rats stopped moving to hide in their stillness.

Maggie walked quickly to the side of the curtains, stuck her head under, and sampled more air. The footsteps stopped.

She cocked her head, listening. She sniffed. She heard the soft metal-to-metal clack of the gate latch, caught their scent, and recognized the intruders. The strangers who had entered their crate had returned.

Maggie erupted in a thunder of barking. She lunged against the glass, the fur on her back bristling from her tail to her shoulders.

Crate in danger.

Pack threatened.

Her fury was a warning. She would drive off or kill whatever threatened her pack.

She heard them running.

"Maggie! Mags!"

Scott came off the couch behind her, but she paid him no mind. She drove them harder, warning them.

"What are you barking at?"

The scuffing faded. Car doors slammed. An engine grew softer until it was gone.

Scott pushed aside the curtains, and joined her.

The threat was gone.

Crate safe.

Pack safe.

Alpha safe.

Her job was done.

"Is someone out there?"

Maggie gazed up at Scott with love and joy. She folded her ears and wagged her tail. She knew he was seeking danger in the darkness, but would find nothing.

Maggie trotted to her water, and drank. When she returned, Scott was back on his couch. She was so happy to see him, she laid her face in his lap. He scratched her ears and stroked her, and Maggie wiggled with happiness.

She sniffed the floor, turned until she found exactly the best position, and lay down beside him.

Alpha safe.

Crate safe.

Pack safe.

Her eyes closed, but Maggie lay awake as the man's heart slowed, his breathing evened, and the hundred scents that made him Scott changed with his cooling skin. She heard a living night familiar with squeaking mice and freeway traffic; tasted air rich with the expected scent of rats, oranges, earth, and beetles; and patrolled their world from her place on the floor as if she was an eighty-five-pound spirit with magical eyes. Maggie sighed. When Scott was at peace, she let herself sleep.

28.

The next morning, after he walked Maggie and showered, Scott decided to check on the missing disc himself. Richard Levin's contact information was on the first page of his interview.

Club Red would be deserted at this hour, so he phoned Levin's personal number. The voice mail message was male, but offered no identifying information. Scott identified himself as a detective working on the Pahlasian murder, said he had questions regarding the discs, and asked Levin to phone as soon as possible.

At seven-twenty, Scott was tying his boots while Maggie bounced between the door and her lead. He got a kick out of how she knew the signs. Whenever he tied his boots, she knew they were going out.

Scott said, "You one smart dog."

His phone rang at seven twenty-one. Scott thought he had lucked out, and Levin was returning his call. Then he saw LAPD in the incoming-call window.

"Morning. Scott James."

He tucked the phone under his chin, and finished tying as he listened.

"Detective Anson, Rampart Detectives. I'm in front of your house with my partner, Detective Shankman. We'd like to speak with you."

Scott went to the French doors, wondering why two Rampart detectives had come to his home.

"I'm in the guest house. See the wood gate in front of you? It's not locked. Come through the gate."

"We understand you have a K-9 police dog on the premises. We don't want a problem with the dog. Will you secure her?"

"She won't be a problem."

"Will you secure the dog?"

Scott didn't want to lock her in her crate, and if he put her in the bedroom, she would shred the door trying to get out.

"Hang on. I'll come out."

Scott nudged Maggie aside, and opened the door.

"Do *not* come out. Please secure the dog."

"Listen, man, I don't have anywhere to secure her. So come meet the dog or I'll come to you. Your choice."

"Secure the dog."

Scott tossed the phone onto the couch, slipped past Maggie, and went out to meet them.

A gray Crown Vic was parked in the street across the mouth of the drive. Two men in sport coats and ties had come up partway, and stood in the drive. The taller was in his early fifties, with dusty blond hair and too many lines. The shorter detective was in his late thirties, and broader, with a shiny face and a bald head ringed with brown hair. Neither looked friendly, and neither pretended.

The older man flashed a badge case showing his ID card and gold detective shield.

"Bob Anson. This is Kurt Shankman."

Anson put away the badge.

"I asked you to secure the dog."

"I don't have a place to secure her. So it's out here or inside with the dog. She's harmless. She'll sniff your hands, you'll love her."

Shankman looked at the gate as if he was worried.

"You latch the gate? She can't get out, can she?"

"She's not in the yard. She's in my house. It's fine, Shankman. Really."

Shankman hooked his thumbs in his belt,

opening the sport coat enough to flash a holster.

"You've been warned. That dog comes charging out here, I'll put her down."

The hair on Scott's neck prickled.

"What's wrong with you, man? You pull on my dog, you better pop me first."

Anson calmly interrupted.

"Do you know a Daryl Ishi?"

There it was. Daryl had probably filed a complaint, and these two were here to investigate.

"I know who he is, yes."

"Would Mr. Ishi think your dog is harmless?"

"Ask him."

Shankman smiled without humor.

"We're asking you. When was the last time you saw him?"

Scott hesitated. If Daryl filed a complaint, he would have been asked if there were witnesses. Anson and Shankman might have spoken with Estelle Rolley and Daryl's friends from the park. Scott answered carefully. He wasn't sure where they would take this, but he did not want to be caught in a lie.

"I saw him yesterday. What is this, Anson? You guys work for IAG? Should I call a PPL rep?"

"Rampart Detectives. We're not with Internal Affairs."

Shankman didn't wait for Scott to respond.

"How'd that come about, you seeing him yesterday?"

"Daryl's brother was recently arrested on multiple burglary counts —"

Shankman interrupted.

"His brother being?"

"Marshall Ishi. Marshall copped to four burglaries, but there's evidence Daryl worked with him. I went to his home to speak with him. I was told he was meeting friends at MacArthur Park."

Shankman interrupted again.

"By who?"

"Marshall's girlfriend, a woman named Estelle Rolley. She's a tweaker, hard-core like Marshall. She lives in their house."

Anson gave a vague nod, which seemed to confirm he had gotten a full report, and was now considering the differences between what he had been told and what Scott was telling him.

"Okay. So you went to MacArthur Park."

"Daryl ran when he saw me approaching. My dog stopped him. Neither my dog nor myself touched him at any time, nor was he placed under arrest. I asked for his co-

329

operation. He refused. I told him he was free to leave."

Shankman arched his eyebrows at Anson.

"Listen to this dude, Bobby, out questioning people. When did K-9 officers start carrying detective shields?"

Anson never looked at his partner, nor changed his expression.

"Scott, let me ask you — did Daryl threaten you during this conversation?"

Scott found Anson's question odd, and wondered where he was going.

"No, sir. He didn't threaten me. We talked."

"Did you see Daryl a second time yesterday, after the park?"

Scott found this question even more odd.

"No. Did he say I did?"

Shankman interrupted again.

"You buy drugs from Daryl?"

The drug question came out of nowhere, and caused a sick chill to flash up Scott's spine.

"Oxy? Vicodin?"

Shankman made jazz hands, as if taunting Scott for an answer he already knew.

"No? Yes? Both?"

Both painkillers had been prescribed by Scott's surgeon, and legally purchased from a pharmacy two blocks away. Shankman had used brand names, not generic names. He specifically named the two painkillers prescribed for Scott.

Shankman dropped the hands, and turned serious as death.

"No answer? Are you medicated now, Scott? Do the anxiety meds make it difficult to think?"

The chill spread across his shoulders and out to his fingers. Scott flashed on Maggie's intruder alert when they returned home the other night.

Scott took a step back.

"Until and unless I'm ordered otherwise by my boss, this Q&A is over. You assholes can fuck off."

Anson remained calm and casual, and made no move to leave.

"Do you blame Marshall Ishi for Stephanie's murder?"

The question froze Scott like the click of a shutter.

Anson kept going, voice reasonable and understanding.

"You got shot up, your partner was murdered, these two assholes maybe saw it, and never came forward. You must carry a lot of anger, man. Who could blame you, with the shooters still running around? Marshall and Daryl are letting them skate. I can see how

331

a man would be angry."

Shankman nodded agreeably, his unblinking eyes like tarnished dimes.

"Me, too, Bobby. I'd want to punish them. Oh, yeah. I'd want to get mine."

The two detectives stared at him. Waiting.

Scott's head throbbed. He now understood they were investigating something worse than a harassment complaint.

"Why are you people here?"

Anson seemed genuinely friendly for the first time.

"To ask about Daryl. We did."

Anson turned, and walked to their car.

Shankman said, "Thanks for your cooperation."

Shankman followed his boss.

Scott spoke to their backs.

"What happened? Anson, is Daryl dead?"

Anson climbed into the passenger side.

"If we have further questions, we'll call."

Shankman trotted around the front end, and dropped in behind the wheel.

Scott called out as the Crown Vic started.

"Am I a suspect? Tell me what happened."

Anson glanced back as the car rolled away.

"You have a good day."

Scott watched them leave. His hands trembled. His shirt grew damp with sweat. He told himself to breathe, but he couldn't make it happen.

Barking.

He heard Maggie barking. Him here, Maggie trapped in the guest house, she didn't like it and wanted him back.

Scotty, don't leave me.

"I'm coming."

Maggie bounced up and down when he opened the door, and spun in happy circles.

"I'm here. Hang on, baby. I'm happy, too."

Scott wasn't happy. He was confused and scared, and stood numb by the door as Maggie swirled around him until he noticed the phone's message light was blinking. The counter showed he had received two calls in the minutes he was outside with Anson and Shankman.

Scott touched the playback button.

"Hello, Scott, this is Doctor Charles Goodman. Something rather important has come up. Please call me as soon as possible. This is very important."

This is Doctor Charles Goodman.

As if Scott wouldn't recognize the man's voice after seeing him for seven months.

Scott deleted the message, and moved on. Paul Budress was next.

"Dude, it's Paul. Call me before you come in. Call right now, man. Do *not* come in until we talk."

Scott didn't like the strain in Budress' voice. Paulie Budress was one of the calmest people he'd ever met.

Scott took a deep breath, blew out, and called him.

Budress said, "What the fuck, man? What's going on?"

Scott prayed he wouldn't throw up. He could tell Budress knew something from his tone.

"What are you talking about?"

"Some IAG rats are here waiting for you. Fucking Leland is gonna explode."

Scott took deep breaths, one after another. First Anson and Shankman, and now Internal Affairs.

"What do they want with me?"

"Shit, man, you don't know?"

Fake it 'til you make it.

"Paul, c'mon. What did they say?"

"Mace heard them in there with Leland. They're hauling you downtown, and you won't be coming back here."

Scott felt as if Budress was talking about someone else.

"I'm being suspended?"

"Full on. No badge. No pay. You're going home, pending whatever the fuck investigation."

"This is crazy."

"Call the union. Hook up with a rep and a lawyer before you come in. And for Christ's sake, don't tell them I called you."

"What about Maggie?"

"Dude, you don't own her. I'll find out what I can. I'll call you back."

Budress hung up.

Scott felt woozy and off balance. He clenched his eyes, and imagined himself alone on a beach the way Goodman taught him. Distraction came with focusing on the details. The sand was hot from the sun, and gritty, and smelled of dead seaweed and fish and salt. The sun beat down until his skin crinkled with its terrible heat. Scott's heart slowed as he calmed, and his head cleared. He had to be calm to think clearly. Clarity was everything.

Internal Affairs was investigating, but Anson and Shankman hadn't arrested him. This meant no arrest warrant had been issued. Scott had room to move, but he needed more facts.

He called Joyce Cowly's cell, and prayed his call wouldn't go to her voice mail.

She answered on the third ring.

"It's Scott. Joyce, what's happening? What's going on?"

She didn't answer.

"Joyce?"

"Where are you?"

"Home. Two Rampart detectives just left. They made it sound like Daryl Ishi was dead, and I was the suspect."

She hesitated again as if she was deciding whether to answer, and he grew frightened she would hang up. She didn't.

"The Parkers went to pick him up for a swab last night. They found him shot to death. Daryl, Estelle Rolley, and one of the roommates."

Scott lowered himself to the couch.

"They think I killed three people?"

"Scott —"

"It sounds like a drug killing. These people deal drugs. They're addicts."

"Ruled out. They had a new stash, and they hadn't been robbed."

She paused again.

"There's this talk about you being unstable —"

"Bullshit."

"— the way you blew up at Melon and Stengler, the stress you've been under, all these medications you take."

"The Rampart dicks knew my prescriptions. They specifically knew which meds I take. How could they know, Joyce?"

"I don't know. No one here should know."

"Who's saying this stuff?"

"Everyone's talking about you. Top floor. Division brass. It could have come from anyone."

"But how can they know?"

"It's a big deal. They don't like the way you inserted yourself into the case."

"I didn't kill these people."

"I'm just telling you what's being said. You're a suspect. Lawyer up. I can give you some names."

He went back to the beach. Slow deep breaths in, slow exhales out.

Maggie rested her chin on his knee. He stroked her seal-sleek head and wondered if she would like to run on the beach.

"Why would I kill him? I wanted to know if he saw something. Maybe he didn't. Now we won't know."

"Maybe you tried to make him talk, and got carried away."

"Is that what they're saying?"

"It's been mentioned. I have to go."

"You think I did this?"

Cowly was silent.

"Do you think I killed them?"

"No."

Joyce Cowly was gone.

Scott lowered his phone.

Maggie's soft brown eyes watched him.

He stroked her head, wondering if Daryl

had died with anything worth knowing.

"Now we'll never know."

Nine months was a long time to keep secrets. If Daryl saw something, Scott doubted he could keep quiet, and wondered who Daryl would tell. Marshall might know, but Marshall was currently in Men's Central Jail.

Scott thought for a moment, then went to his computer. He opened the Sheriff's Department website for Marshall's booking number and the phone for the MCJ Liaison Desk.

"This is Detective Bud Orso, LAPD Robbery-Homicide. I need to see a prisoner named Marshall — M, A, R, S, H, A, double-L — Ishi, I, S, H, I."

Scott read off Marshall's booking number, and continued his request.

"I'm coming with information regarding his brother, so this is a courtesy visit. He won't need his attorney."

When the meeting was arranged, Scott clipped up Maggie and left the guest house as quickly as possible. He needed to move, and keep moving, or he wouldn't go through with it.

Scott picked up the freeway in Studio City, and made for downtown Los Angeles and Men's Central Jail. He rolled down the windows. Maggie straddled the console in her usual spot, watching the scenery and enjoying the wind. She looked awkward with the poor footing, but happy and content. Scott leaned into her the way he did when he tried to move her. He felt better when she leaned back.

Once he walked into jail, he hoped they would let him out.

PART IV

■ ■ ■ ■

PACK

■ ■ ■ ■

29.

Scott was passing Universal Studios at the Hollywood split when his phone rang. He hoped it was Cowly or Budress, with more information, but it was Goodman. The last person he wanted to speak with, but he answered the call.

"This is Charles Goodman, Scott. I've been trying to reach you."

"I was going to call. I have to cancel our session tomorrow."

Scott's regular appointment was the following day.

"I was phoning to cancel, as well. Something happened here at the office. Personally embarrassing for me, and I'm afraid this will be upsetting for you."

Scott had never heard Goodman so strained.

"Are you okay, Doc?"

"The privacy of my clients and their trust is of paramount importance to me —"

"I trust you. What happened?"

"My office was broken into two nights ago. Scott, some things were stolen, your file among them. I'm terribly sorry —"

Scott flashed on Shankman and Anson, and the top-floor brass knowing things about him they had no way to know.

"Doc, wait. My file was stolen? *My* file?"

"Not only yours, but yours was among them. Apparently they grabbed a handful of files at random — current and past clients whose last names begin with the letters G through K. I've been calling to —"

"Did you call the police?"

"Two detectives came out. They sent a man to look for fingerprints. He left black powder on the door and the windows and my cabinet. I don't know whether I'm supposed to leave it or if I can clean it."

"You can clean up, Doc. They're finished. What did the detectives say?"

"They didn't tell me whether to leave it or clean it."

"Not about the fingerprint powder. What about the burglary?"

"Scott, I want you to know I did not give them your name. They asked for a list of the clients whose files were stolen, but that would violate our confidence. The State of California protects you in this. I did not and will not identify you."

Scott had the sick feeling his confidence had already been violated.

"What did they say about the burglary?"

"The door and the windows weren't broken, so whoever broke in apparently had a key. The detectives said burglaries like this are usually committed by someone known to the cleaning crew. They have a key made, and grab the first thing they see."

"What would a janitor want with files?"

"The files have your personal and billing information. The detectives said I should warn you — not you specifically, but all of you — to alert your credit card companies and banks. I can't tell you how sorry I am. These people are out there with my notes on your sessions, and now you have to deal with this credit card nonsense."

Scott's mind raced from Anson and Shankman to Cowly to Goodman's break-in, all of it coming together.

"When did this happen?"

"Two nights ago. I came to the office yesterday morning, and, well, my heart sank when I saw what had happened."

Three nights ago, Maggie alerted to an intruder. Scott recalled a powdery substance on his locks, but had written it off.

Scott steered for the next off-ramp, and

left the freeway in the Cahuenga Pass. He stopped in the first parking lot he saw.

"Doc? Who were the detectives who came out?"

"Ah, well, I have their — yes, here we are. Detective Warren Broder and a Detective Deborah Kurland."

Scott jotted the names, told Goodman he would phone in a few days, and immediately called the North Hollywood Community Police Station. When he reached the Detective Bureau, he identified himself, and asked to speak with Broder or Kurland.

"Kurland's here. Hold on."

A few seconds later, Kurland picked up. Her smart professional voice reminded him of Cowly.

"Detective Kurland speaking."

Scott repeated his name, adding his badge number and station.

Kurland said, "Okey-doke, Officer. How can I help?"

"You and Detective Broder are handling the burglary of a Doctor Charles Goodman. His office in Studio City?"

"You bet. May I ask your interest?"

"Doctor Goodman is a friend. This call is unofficial."

"I get it. Ask whatever you like. I'll answer or I won't."

"How'd the perp get in?"

"Door."

"Funny. You guys told Goodman the guy used a passkey?"

"No, that was me, and what I said was, you see entries this clean, more often than not the perp bought a key from someone who works at the building. My partner thinks the locks were bump-keyed. Personally, I think the dude used a pick gun. Up on that second-floor walkway with your butt in the air, you want the locks open fast. A pick gun is easier."

The ache in Scott's side crept up his back.

"Why either one instead of the passkey?"

"I wanted to check the locks, so I borrowed the doctor's keys. They felt slippery. I wiped them, worked the locks, the keys were slippery again. Both locks were blown full of graphite."

The Trans Am's doors and top bulged toward him, as if the car was being crushed by an outside pressure.

Kurland said, "Anything else?"

Scott started to say no, then remembered.

"The prints?"

"Nothing. Gloves."

Scott thanked her, and lowered his phone. He stared at the passing traffic, and grew more frightened with each passing car.

Someone had invaded his life, and was using his life to frame him for Daryl Ishi's murder. Someone wanted to know what he knew, and thought, and suspected about Stephanie's killers. Someone didn't want Stephanie's killers found.

Scott turned around and drove back to his guest house. He went to his bedroom, and found his old dive bag in his closet. It was a huge nylon duffel, currently packed with fins, a buoyancy compensator, and other diving gear. Scott dumped the contents while Maggie sniffed from the door. He had not opened the bag in almost three years. He wondered if she smelled the ocean and fish, or if time had killed their scent.

Scott filled the bag with his spare pistol and ammo, his dad's old watch, the cash under the clock radio, the shoe box filled with credit card receipts and billing statements, two changes of clothes, and his personal items. He cleaned out his meds from the bathroom. Goodman's name was on the labels, and now Scott had no doubt there was a connection. Three nights ago, someone entered his home, went through his things, and saw Goodman's name. Two nights ago, someone broke into Goodman's office, and made off with Scott's therapeutic history.

Scott carried his bag to the living room. He gathered the material he amassed on the shooting into a single large stack, and packed it into the bag. The empty floor looked larger.

Maggie stuck her head into the bag, looked at Scott as if she was bored, and walked into the kitchen for water.

Scott studied the room, thinking what else should he take? He added his laptop computer, and took down his diagrams and pictures. He considered leaving Stephanie's picture on the wall, but she had been with him at the beginning, and he wanted her with him at the end. Her picture was the last thing he put in the bag.

He clipped Maggie's lead, and braced himself as he slung the dive bag over his shoulder. He expected his side to scream, but he felt almost normal.

"C'mon, big girl. Let's get this done."

Scott told Mrs. Earle he would be away for a few days, stowed the dive bag in his trunk, and headed back to the freeway.

Going to jail.

Driving fast.

30.

JOYCE COWLY

Elton Joshua Marley frowned at their surroundings as she stepped onto the roof.

"Look how fil'ty, all dis mess. You ruin dese nice clothes you hab."

"I'll be fine, Mr. Marley. Thanks."

The roof was littered with wine bottles, broken rock pipes, and condoms, as she had seen in Scott James' pictures. She moved away from the stairwell to get her bearings. She was looking for the roof above the kill zone.

Mr. Marley stayed at the door.

"Leh me do dis, sabe you nice clothes? Come down de stairs. I gib you beach pants an' a beautiful MarleyWorld shirt, de rayahn so soft it keess your skeen."

"Thank you, but I'm good like this."

Cowly determined the direction of the intersection, and picked her way across the roof.

"Watch for de needles. Dey be nahsty tings up here."

His concern was cute, but annoying as hell. Cowly was glad he stayed by the door.

She climbed over a low wall onto the corner building, and moved to the edge of the roof. A low, wrought-iron safety barrier ran along the parapet just as Scott described. It was dirty, rusted, and eaten by corrosion. Cowly was careful not to touch it when she leaned forward to look between the bars. She saw a perfectly normal street four floors below, bustling with normal activity, but nine months ago, three people were murdered here, Scott James was bleeding to death, and the street glittered with cartridge casings.

Cowly walked along the fence. The little remaining black paint had faded to a soft gray. Most of the metal was scabbed with fine, reddish-brown rust. Cowly touched it, and examined the rust on her finger. More brown than red, but enough red to look like dried blood.

She stood on her toes, trying to see the sidewalk, but wasn't tall enough. She was directly above the spot where SID collected the watchband, thinking the red smears were blood.

Cowly took the evidence bag from her

purse. She unsealed the bag and maneu-vered the leather strap until it was exposed, being careful not to touch it with her fingers. She held it using the plastic like a glove.

Cowly pressed her free thumb to the fence, and compared the rust on her thumb to the streaks on the leather. They looked alike. Cowly pressed her thumb to the fence again, and grinded it to pick up more rust. The streaks on the band and on her thumb now looked identical. Cowly was encour-aged, but knew their appearance proved little or nothing.

She resealed the evidence bag, tucked it into her purse, and took out a white enve-lope and pen. Using the pen, she scraped a generous amount of rust into the envelope. When she felt she had enough, she sealed the envelope, thanked Mr. Marley for being so helpful, and took her samples to SID.

31.

Men's Central Jail was a low, sleek, concrete building wedged between Chinatown and the Los Angeles River. Built stern and foreboding, it could have passed for the science center at a well-endowed university except for the chain-link fence rimming its perimeter and the five thousand inmates between its walls.

Scott parked in a public parking lot across the street, but stayed in his car, his hand on Maggie's back to keep them both calm. Twenty-five minutes later Maggie sniffed, and her ears went up on alert. Scott clipped her lead and waited. When Paul Budress appeared, they got out.

"She had you forty seconds before I saw you."

Budress was clearly uncomfortable. His mouth was an unhappy line and his eyes were narrowed to slits.

"The rats left. They decided you weren't

coming in."

"I didn't do it."

"Hell, man, I know, else I wouldn't be here."

Scott hadn't been able to figure out what to do with Maggie while he was in jail, so he called Budress from the freeway. Budress thought he was crazy, but here he was.

Scott held out the lead. Budress frowned for a moment, but took it. He let Maggie sniff his hand, and ruffled her head.

"We'll take a walk. Text me when you're out."

"If they take her, find her a good home, okay?"

"She has a home. Go."

Scott walked quickly away and did not look back. They knew Maggie would try to follow him, and she did. In her world, they were a pack, and the pack stayed together.

Maggie whined and barked, and he heard her claws scrape the tarmac like files. Budress had cautioned him not to look back or wave bye-bye or any of the silly things people did. Dogs weren't people. Eye contact would make her struggle harder to reach him. A dog could see your heart in your eyes, Budress told him, and dogs were drawn to our hearts.

Scott dodged cars to cross the street, and

entered the main entrance. During his seven years as a patrol officer, he had visited MCJ less than two dozen times. Most of these had been to transport suspects or prisoners from his area station, and deliveries were made up a ramp in the back.

Scott took a moment to orient himself, then told a Sheriff's Deputy he was scheduled to see a prisoner, and gave Marshall's name. Standing there in his dark navy uniform with his badge pinned to his chest, Scott looked nothing like a Robbery-Homicide detective. He took a breath, and identified himself as Bud Orso.

The dep made a call without comment, and a female deputy appeared a few minutes later.

"You Orso?"

"Yes, ma'am."

"We're bringing him up. I'll take you back."

Scott felt little relief. He followed her past a security station to a room where she asked for his handcuffs and weapon. She gave him a receipt, locked both in a gun safe, and showed him to an interview room. Scott was pleased with the room. Civilian visitors and attorneys were brought to booths where they talked to prisoners on phones while separated by a heavy glass screen. Law-enforcement personnel required an interview environment with greater flexibility. The room contained an ancient Formica-topped table and three plastic chairs. The table jutted from a wall, and was fitted with a steel rod for securing prisoners. Scott took a chair facing the door.

The deputy said, "Here he comes. You need anything?"

"No, thanks. I'm good."

"I'm at the end of the hall when you finish. Out this door, turn right. We'll get you your things."

An athletic young dep fresh from the Academy guided Marshall into the room. Marshall wore a bright blue jumpsuit, sneakers, and manacles on his pencil-thin wrists. He appeared even more frail than Scott remembered, which was probably from the withdrawal. Marshall glanced at Scott, and stared at the floor. Same as when he was led from his house.

The young dep seated Marshall in the chair facing Scott, and hooked the manacles to the steel rod.

Scott said, "You don't need to do that. We're fine."

"Got to. Marshall, you okay?"

"Uh-huh."

The deputy closed the door on his way out.

Scott studied Marshall, and realized he didn't have a plan. He didn't know anything about Marshall Ishi other than he was a wasted-away tweaker with a brother and a girlfriend who were murdered the day before. Marshall probably learned about it this morning. The red eyes were probably from crying.

"You love your brother?"

Marshall glanced up before glancing away. Scott caught a flash of anger in the red eyes.

"What kind of question is that?"

"I'm sorry. I don't know what kind of relationship you had. Some brothers, you know how it is, they hate each other. Others . . ."

Scott let it trail. The welling in Marshall's eyes gave the answer.

"I raised him since he was nine."

"I'm sorry. About Daryl, and Estelle, too. I know how it hurts."

Marshall's eyes flashed angry again.

"Oh, that's right, for sure. Spare me, partner, how could you? Let's get down to business here. Who killed my brother?"

Scott pushed his chair back, stood, and unbuttoned his shirt.

Marshall leaned back, clearly surprised.

He didn't understand what was happening, and shook his head.

"No, don't do that. Stop, dude, I'll call the sheriffs."

Scott dropped his shirt on the chair, took off his undershirt, and watched Marshall's expression change when he saw the gray lines across Scott's left shoulder and the large, knobby Y that wrapped around his right side.

Scott let him take a good look.

"This is how I know."

Marshall glanced at Scott, then went back to the scars. He couldn't stop looking at the scars.

"What happened?"

Scott pulled on the undershirt, and buttoned his shirt.

"When you cut your plea, you told detectives about a Chinese import store you hit nine months ago. They asked if you saw a shooting. Three people were murdered. One left for dead."

Marshall nodded as he answered.

"Yes, sir, they asked. I did commit that burglary, but I didn't see the shooting. My understanding is all that happened after I left."

He glanced at Scott's shoulder, but the scars were hidden.

"Was that you, left for dead?"

Marshall was so genuine and natural, Scott knew he was telling the truth. The poly wasn't necessary.

"I lost someone close that night. Last night, you lost your brother. The same people who did this to me killed Daryl."

Marshall sat there, staring, his face pinched as he struggled to get his head around it. His eyes shimmered, and Scott thought, if Budress was right, if a dog saw a person's heart through their eyes, Maggie would see a heart broken in Marshall.

"Help me out here, 'cause —"

"Was Daryl with you that night?"

Marshall leaned back again, and seemed irritated.

"What the fuck? I don't take Daryl with me to do burglary. What are you talkin' about?"

"Up on the roof. Your lookout."

"No fuckin' way."

He meant it. Marshall was telling the truth.

"Daryl was there."

"Bullshit. I'm telling you, he wasn't."

"What if I told you I could prove it?"

"I'd call you a liar."

Scott decided to leave Maggie out of it, and tell Marshall they had a DNA match.

But as he took out his phone for a picture of the watchband, it occurred to him Marshall might remember his brother's watch.

He held out his phone so Marshall could see.

"Did Daryl have a watch with a band like this?"

Marshall slowly sat taller. He reached for the phone, but the manacles stopped him.

"I got that watch for him. I gave it to him."

Scott thought carefully. Marshall was with him now, and Marshall would help. Luck was better than DNA.

"This was found on the sidewalk the morning I was shot. These little smears are from a fence on the roof. I don't know when he was up there that night, or why, or what he saw, but Daryl was there."

Marshall shook his head slow, trying to remember and asking himself questions.

"Are you saying he saw those murders?"

"I don't know. He never mentioned it to you?"

"No, 'course not. Not ever. Jesus, don't you think I'd remember?"

"I don't know if he saw them or not, but I think the shooters were scared he had seen them."

Marshall's gaze shifted, searching the little room for answers.

362

"Y'all thought I saw the shootings, and I didn't. Maybe Daryl was long gone like me, and didn't see shit."

"Then they killed him for nothing, and he's still dead."

Marshall wiped his eyes on his shoulders, leaving dark spots on the blue.

"Goddamnit, this is bullshit. Fuckin' bullshit."

"I want them, Marshall. For me and my friend, and for Daryl. I need your help to get this done."

"What the fuck, if he saw something, he didn't tell me. Shit, even if he *didn't* see anything, he didn't tell me. Probably scared I'd kick his ass!"

"Something crazy and exciting like this? Let's say he saw it. Let's pretend."

Because if Daryl left the roof having seen nothing, Scott had no place to go.

"It's a big thing to hold. Who would he tell? His best friend. A person he might tell even if he was too scared to tell anyone else."

Marshall's head bobbed.

"Amelia. His baby mama."

"Daryl has a child?"

Marshall's gaze flicked around the room as he sorted through memories.

"Be about two, a girl. Don't *really* know it's Daryl's, but she says it is. He loves her."

Then Marshall realized what he'd said. "Loved."

Her name was Amelia Goyta. The baby's name was Gina. Marshall didn't know the address, but told Scott where to find her building. Marshall hadn't seen the baby in almost a year, and wanted to know if she looked like Daryl.

Scott promised to let Marshall know, and was leaving to find the deputy when Marshall twisted around in his chair and asked a question Scott had been asking himself.

"All this time later, why they all of a sudden get scared Daryl seen'm? How'd they know Daryl was up there?"

Scott thought he knew, but didn't share the answer.

"Marshall, the detectives will probably come see you. Don't tell them about this. Don't tell anyone unless you hear that I'm dead."

Marshall's red eyes grew scared.

"I won't."

"Not even the detectives. Especially not the detectives."

Scott took a right turn out the door, collected his handcuffs and gun, and left the jail as quickly as he could.

He waited on the sidewalk by the parking lot for almost ten minutes before Budress and Maggie rounded the corner. Maggie bounced and yelped and strained at her lead, so Budress let her go. She raced toward Scott with her ears back and tongue out, looking like the happiest dog in the world. Scott opened his arms, and caught her when she plowed into him. Eighty-five pounds of black-and-tan love.

Budress didn't look as happy as Maggie.

"What happened in there?"

"I'm still in the game."

Budress grunted.

"Okay, then. Okay. I'll see you later."

Budress turned to leave.

"Paul. Marshall recognized the watch-band. It was Daryl's. Maggie pinned him, man."

Budress glanced at the dog, then the man.

"Never doubt."

"I didn't."

Scott and Maggie climbed into their car.

32.

Scott found Amelia Goyta's prewar apartment house on a shabby run-down street north of the freeway in Echo Park. The old building had three floors, four units per floor, an interior central stair, no air-conditioning, and was pretty much identical to every building on the block except for the Crying Virgin. A towering Virgin Mary crying tears of blood was painted on the front of her building. Marshall told Scott the painting looked more like an anorexic Smurf, but he couldn't miss it. Marshall had told it true. The Virgin Smurf was three stories tall.

Marshall didn't remember which was Amelia's apartment, so Scott checked with the manager. Wearing his uniform helped. Top floor in back, 304.

Scott wondered if news of Daryl's death had reached Amelia. When he and Maggie reached the third floor, he heard crying and knew it had. He paused outside her door to listen, and Maggie sniffed at the floor jamb. Inside, a child wailed between whooping breaths, as a sobbing woman alternated pleas to stop crying with reassurances they were going to be okay.

Scott rapped on the door.

The child kept wailing, but the sobbing stopped. A moment later, the wailing stopped, too, but no one came to the door.

Scott rapped again, and gave her his patrol officer's voice.

"Police officer. Please open the door."

Twenty seconds passed without a response, so Scott knocked again.

"Police officer. Open the door or I'll have the manager let me in."

The wailing began again, and now the woman's sob came from the other side of the door.

"Go away. Go AWAY! You're not the police."

She sounded afraid, so Scott softened his voice.

"Amelia? I'm a police officer. I'm here about Daryl Ishi."

"What's your name? WHAT IS YOUR NAME?"

"Scott James."

Her voice rose to a frantic scream.

"TELL ME YOUR NAME."

"Scott. James. My name is SCOTT. Police officer. Open the door, Amelia. Is Gina safe? I'm not leaving until I see that she's safe."

When he finally heard the deadbolt slide, Scott stepped away to appear less threatening. Maggie automatically stood by his left leg as she'd been trained, and faced the door.

A girl not more than twenty peeked out when the door opened. She had long, straw-colored hair and pale, freckled skin. Her eyes and nose were red, and her lips quivered between gasps, but nothing about her expression suggested a broken heart or mourning.

Scott had seen her expression on the faces of women who were punching bags for their husbands, hookers on the run from pimps out to cut them, and the shell-shocked faces of rape victims. He had seen it on mothers with missing children — an expectation that something worse was coming. Scott knew the face of fear. He saw it on Amelia Goyta, and instantly knew Daryl had witnessed the shooting, and told her he would be killed if the shooters found out.

She wiped away snot, and asked him again.

"What's your name?"

"I'm Scott. This is Maggie. Are you and Gina okay?"

She glanced at Maggie.

"I gotta pack. We're leaving."

"Can I see the baby, please? I want to see she's okay."

Amelia glanced toward the stairs as if someone might be hiding, then threw open the door and hurried to her child. Gina was in a playpen, her face pinched and smeared with snot. She had dark hair, but looked nothing like Daryl. Amelia lifted her, jiggled her, and put her back in the playpen.

"Hcrc, you see? She's fine. Now I gotta pack, I got a friend coming. Rachel."

A faded blue wheelie carry-on was waiting by the door. A Samsonite suitcase older than Scott was open like a giant clam on the floor, half-filled with toys and baby supplies. She ran into the bedroom, and returned dragging a brown garbage bag fat with clothes.

Scott said, "Did Daryl say they would kill you?"

Amelia dropped the bag by the door, and ran back to the bedroom.

"Yes! That dumbass piece of shit. He said they'd kill us, and I ain't waiting."

"Who killed him?"

"The fuckin' killers. You're the policeman.

369

Don't you know?"

She ran back with a wastebasket filled with combs, brushes, hair spray, and toiletries. She upended it into the Samsonite, tossed the basket aside, and pushed a small velvet pouch into Scott's hands.

"Here. Take'm. I told the dumb fuck he was an idiot."

Scott caught her arm as she turned for the bedroom.

"Slow down. Listen to me, Amelia. Nine months ago. What did Daryl tell you?"

She sobbed, and rubbed her eye.

"He saw these masked dudes shoot up a car."

"Tell me exactly what he said."

"He said if they knew he saw, they'd fuckin' kill us and the baby, too. I want to pack."

She tried to twist away, but Scott held her. Maggie edged closer and growled.

"I'm here to stop them, okay? That's why I'm here. So help me. Tell me what Daryl said."

She stopped fighting him, and gazed down at Maggie.

"Is that a guard dog?"

"Yes. A guard dog. What did Daryl tell you?"

Scott felt her relax as she considered the

guard dog, and turned loose her arms.

"He was on some building somewhere, and heard a crash. Stupid Daryl went to see, and here's this truck and the cops and these men were around this Rolls-Royce, shooting the shit out of it."

Scott didn't bother to correct her.

"He said it was crazy. He was, like, fuck, it was Tarantino, these masked guys shootin' the cops and the Rolls. Daryl freaked, and slammed down off the roof, but it was all quiet when he hit the ground, and they were yellin' at each other, so idiot fuckass Daryl goes to see."

"Did he tell you what they were saying?"

"Just bullshit, hurry up, find the damned thing, whatever. They were scared of the sirens. The sirens were coming."

Scott realized he had stopped breathing. His pulse had grown loud in his ears.

"Did Daryl say what they found?"

"This one dude gets in the Rolls, and jumps out with a briefcase. They piled into this car and tore out of there, and stupid Daryl, he's thinking, rich people in this Rolls, he might get a ring or a watch, so he runs to the car."

Scott thought Daryl had embellished his story.

"With the sirens getting closer?"

"Is that fuckin' damaged? These two people are shot to shit, blood everywhere, and my moron boyfriend risks his life for eight hundred dollars and this —"

She slapped the velvet pouch.

"I said, you stupid shit, are you crazy? The money had blood on it. Idiot Daryl had blood all over, and he's freaking. He made me promise, we can't tell, we can't even hint, 'cause these maniacs would kill us."

"Did he see their faces?"

"You didn't hear what I just said? They had masks."

"Maybe one of them took off his mask."

"He didn't say."

"How about a tattoo, hair color, a ring or a watch? Did he describe them in any way?"

"All I remember is masks, like ski masks."

Scott thought harder.

"You kept asking my name. Why were you asking my name?"

"I thought you were them."

"Meaning what? He heard their names?"

"Snell. He heard this one guy say, 'Snell, c'mon.' If your name was Snell, I wasn't going to let you in. Listen, man, I gotta pack. Please. Rachel is coming."

Scott looked at the pouch. It was lavender velvet, closed by a drawstring, with a dark discoloration. Scott opened it, and poured seven gray rocks into his palm. Maggie raised her nose, curious about the pouch because Scott was curious. This was something he had learned about her. If he focused on something, she was interested. Scott poured the stones back into the pouch, and slipped the pouch into his pocket.

"When will Rachel be here?"

"Now. Any second."

"Pack. I'll help carry your stuff."

She was ready to go when Rachel arrived. Scott carried the Samsonite and the garbage bag stuffed with clothes. Amelia carried the little girl and a pillow, and Rachel carried everything else. Scott unclipped Maggie, and let her follow off-leash. At Scott's request, Amelia left her apartment unlocked.

When everything was in the car, Scott asked for her and Rachel's cell numbers, and took Amelia aside.

"Don't tell anyone you're with Rachel. Don't tell anyone what you think happened to Daryl, or what Daryl saw that night."

"Can't a policeman stay with me? Like in witness protection?"

Scott ignored the question.

"You hear about Marshall? He's in Men's Central Jail?"

"Uh-uh. I didn't know."

Scott repeated it.

"Men's Central Jail. I'm going to call you in two days, okay? But if you don't hear from me, on the third day, I want you to go see Marshall. Tell him what you told me."

"Marshall don't like me."

"Bring Gina. Tell him what Daryl saw. Tell him everything just like you told me."

She was scared and confused, and Scott thought she might get in the car and tell Rachel to never stop driving, but she looked at Maggie.

"I get a big enough place, I want a dog."

Then she got into Rachel's car and they left.

Scott let Maggie pee, then picked up his dive bag, and lugged it up to Amelia's apartment. He found a large pot in the kitchen, filled it with water, and set the pot on the floor.

"This is yours. We may be here a few days."

Maggie sniffed at the water, and walked away to explore the apartment.

Scott sat with the dive bag on Amelia's couch in Amelia's living room in Amelia's apartment, and stared at the wall. He felt tired, and wished he were living on the far side of the world under an assumed name, with a head that wasn't filled with anger and fear.

Scott opened the velvet pouch and poured out the pebbles. He was pretty sure the seven little rocks were uncut diamonds. Each was about the size of his fingernail, translucent, and gray. They looked like crystal meth, and the irony made him smile.

He poured them back into the pouch, and the smile went with them.

Interpol had supposedly connected Beloit to a French diamond fence, which led Melon and Stengler to speculate that Beloit had smuggled diamonds into the country for delivery, or had come to the U.S. to pick up diamonds the fence purchased. Either way, the bandits learned of the plan, followed Beloit's movements, and murdered Beloit and Pahlasian during the robbery. Melon and Stengler used these assumptions to drive the case until the same person who tipped them to Beloit's diamond connection later told them Beloit had no such involvement.

The I-Man. Ian Mills.

Scott thought it through. Melon and Stengler knew nothing of Beloit's diamond connection until Mills brought it to their attention. Why bring it up, and later discredit it? Either Mills had bad information when he cleared Beloit and made an honest mistake, or he lied to turn the investigation. Scott wondered how Mills knew about the connection, and why he later changed his mind.

Scott searched his dive bag for the clippings he collected during the early weeks of the investigation. Melon still ran the case at that time, and had given Scott a card with his home phone and cell number written on the back, saying Scott could call him anytime. That was before they reached the point Melon stopped returning his calls.

Scott stared at Melon's number, trying to figure out what to say. Some calls were more difficult than others.

Maggie came out of the bedroom. She studied Scott for a moment, then went to the open window. He figured she was charting the scents of their new world.

Scott dialed the number. If his call went to Melon's voice mail, he planned to hang up, but Melon answered on the fourth ring.

"Detective Melon, this is Scott James. I hope you don't mind I called."

There was a long silence before Melon answered.

"Guess it depends. How're you doing?"

"I'd like to come see you, if it's okay?"

"Uh-huh. And why is that?"

"I want to apologize. Face-to-face."

Melon chuckled, and Scott felt a wave of relief.

"I'm retired, partner. If you want to drive all the way out here, come ahead."

Scott copied Melon's address, clipped Maggie's lead, and drove up to the Simi Valley.

33.

Melon tipped his lawn chair back, and gazed up into the leaves.

"You see this tree? This tree wasn't eight feet tall when my wife and I bought this place."

Scott and Melon sat beneath the broad spread of an avocado tree in Melon's backyard, sipping Diet Cokes with lemon wedges. Rotting avocados dotted the ground like poop, drawing clouds of swirling gnats. A few gnats circled Maggie, but she didn't seem to mind.

Scott admired the tree.

"All the guac you can eat, forever. I love it."

"I'll tell you, some years, the best avocados you could want. Other years, they have these little threads all through them. I have to figure that out."

Melon was a big fleshy man with thinning gray hair and wrinkled, sun-dark skin. He and his wife owned a small ranch house on an acre of land in the Santa Susana foothills, so far from Los Angeles they were west of the San Fernando Valley. It was a long commute to downtown L.A., but the affordable home prices and small-town lifestyle more than made up for the drive. A lot of police officers lived there.

Melon had answered the door wearing shorts, flip-flops, and a faded Harley-Davidson T-shirt. He was friendly, and told Scott to take Maggie around the side of the house, and he would meet them in back. When Melon joined them a few minutes later, he brought Diet Cokes and a tennis ball. He showed Scott to the chairs, waved the ball in Maggie's face, and sidearmed it across his yard.

Maggie ignored it.

Scott said, "She doesn't chase balls."

Melon looked disappointed.

"That's a shame. I had a Lab, man, she'd chase balls all day. You like K-9?"

"I like it a lot."

"Good. I know you had your heart set on SWAT. It's good you found something else."

As they settled under the tree, Scott remembered a joke Leland loved to tell.

"There's only one difference between SWAT and K-9. Dogs don't negotiate."

Melon burst out laughing. When his laughter faded, Scott faced him.

"Listen, Detective Melon —"

Melon stopped him.

"I'm retired. Call me Chris or Bwana."

"I was an asshole. I was rude and abusive, and wrong. I'm ashamed of the way I acted. I apologize."

Melon stared for a moment, and tipped his glass.

"Unnecessary, but thank you."

Scott clinked his glass to Melon's, and Melon settled back.

"Just so you know, you were all that and then some, but, hell, man, I get it. Damn, but I wanted to close that case. Despite what you may think, I broke my ass, me and Stengler, shit, everyone involved."

"I know you did. I'm reading the file."

"Bud let you in?"

Scott nodded, and Melon tipped his glass again.

"Bud's a good man."

"I was blown away when I saw all the paperwork you guys generated."

"Too many late nights. I'm surprised I'm still married."

"Can I ask you something?"

"Whatever you like."

"I met Ian Mills —"

Melon's laughter interrupted him.

"The I-Man! Bud tell you why they call him the I-Man?"

Scott found himself enjoying Melon's company. On the job, he had been humorless and distant.

"Because his name is Ian?"

"Not even close, though that's what everyone says to his face. Now don't get me wrong, the man is a fine detective. He truly is, and he's had a scrapbook career, but every time Ian is interviewed, it's always, *I* discovered, *I* located, *I* apprehended, *I* take all the credit. Jesus, the I-Man? The ego."

Melon laughed again, and Scott felt encouraged. Melon enjoyed talking about the I-Man and seemed willing to discuss the case, but Scott cautioned himself to tread carefully.

"Were you pissed at him?"

Melon appeared surprised.

"For what?"

"The business with Beloit. Chasing the diamond connection."

"Him being hooked up with Arnaud Clouzot, the fence? Nah, Ian's the guy who straightened it out. Interpol had a list of Clouzot associates, and Beloit was on the list. It was bogus. Clouzot's business manager invested in a couple of Beloit's projects

381

along with a hundred fifty other people. That's not a connection."

"That's what I mean. Seems he should've checked it out first. Save everyone the trouble."

"Nah, he had to bring it. He had Danzer."

Scott thought for a moment, but didn't recognize the name.

"I don't know it. What's Danzer?"

"You know it. Danzer Armored Cars. Three or four weeks before Pahlasian, a Danzer car on its way from LAX to Beverly Hills was hit. The driver and two guards were killed. Bad guys got twenty-eight million in uncut diamonds, though you didn't hear it on the news. Remember now?"

Scott was quiet for a long time. Pressure built in his temples as he thought about the velvet pouch in his pocket.

"Yeah, vaguely."

"These big heists always end up with Special. Ian heard the rocks were going to France, so he asked Interpol for likely buyers. This was all weeks before Beloit was murdered, so his name meant nothing. But once he gets blown up, if you put Danzer in a world where Beloit is connected to Clouzot, you have to go with it. When you find out they're not connected, Beloit's just another Frenchman who got off the plane that night."

Scott watched gnats circling the avocados. The I-Man was like a gnat circling Beloit. Scott felt the pouch through his pants, and ran his finger over the stones.

Melon swatted the air at a gnat. He checked his hand to see if he had the gnat.

"I hate these damned things."

Scott wanted to ask Melon about the missing disc, but knew he had to be careful. Melon seemed fine with shooting the shit, but if he sensed Scott was investigating the investigation, he might pick up the phone.

"I get it, but I'm curious about something."

"Don't blame you. So am I."

Scott smiled.

"You guys tracked Pahlasian and Beloit from LAX pretty much all the way to the kill zone. Where'd he pick up the diamonds?"

"He didn't."

"I meant before you cleared him. Where did you think he picked them up?"

"I knew what you meant. He didn't. You know what happens when people steal diamonds?"

Melon didn't wait for Scott to answer.

"They find a buyer. Sometimes it's an

insurance company, sometimes a fence like Clouzot. If a fence buys them, you know what the fence has to do? He has to find a buyer, too. We believed Clouzot bought the diamonds earlier, had them in France, and resold them to a buyer here in L.A."

"Meaning Beloit was his delivery boy."

"We had LAX video, baggage claim, parking structure, the restaurant, the bar. Unless somebody tossed him the rocks at a red light — which I considered — it was more likely he carried them in. Not that it mattered. He wasn't in business with Clouzot, so the whole diamond thing was a mirage. You watch. Bud's going to find out one or both of these people borrowed from the wrong guy and couldn't hide behind Chapter Eleven."

Scott felt he had pushed enough. He wanted to learn about Danzer, and decided to wind up his visit with Melon.

"Listen, Chris, thanks for letting me visit. Reading the file is an eye-opener. You did a great job."

Melon nodded, and gave Scott a tiny smile.

"Appreciate it, but all I can say is, if you're reading that file, you must be getting a lot of sleep."

Melon laughed, and Scott laughed with

him, but then Melon sobered and leaned toward him.

"Why are you here?"

Maggie looked up.

Melon's eyes were webbed with lines, but clear and thoughtful. Melon had retired with thirty-four years on the job, and almost twenty in Robbery-Homicide. He had probably interviewed two thousand suspects, and put most of them in prison.

Scott knew he had crossed the line, but he wondered what Melon was thinking.

"What if Beloit had diamonds?"

"I'd find that interesting."

"Danzer unsolved?"

Melon's clear eyes never moved.

"Solved. Case closed."

Scott was surprised, but read nothing in Melon's eyes other than a thoughtful detachment.

"Did you talk to them?"

"Too late."

Scott read something in the unmoving eyes.

"Why?"

"They were found shot to death in Fawnskin thirty-two days after you were shot. They'd been dead at least ten days."

Fawnskin was a small resort town in the

San Bernardino Mountains, two hours east of L.A.

"The crew who took Danzer? Positive IDs?"

"Positive. Professional takeover bandits. Long records."

"That isn't positive."

"A gun matching the weapon used to kill the Danzer driver was found. Two uncut rocks were also found. Insurance company confirmed the rocks were part of the Danzer shipment. Positive enough?"

Scott slowly nodded.

"I guess it's supposed to be."

"Regardless, if I had to bet, I would bet they did it."

"Were the diamonds recovered?"

"Not so far as I know."

Scott found this an odd comment.

"Who killed them?"

"They were in a crappy cabin on the side of a mountain with no other cabins near by. The theory is, they hid out up there after the robbery, shopped for a buyer, and got ripped off."

"Two months after the robbery?"

"Two months after the robbery."

"You buy it?"

"Not sure. I'm trying to decide."

Scott searched Melon's eyes, and wondered if the man was giving him permission to ask more.

"Thirty-two days. You blew off Beloit before they were found."

"This is true, but closing Danzer was a nice capper. It put the knife in any lingering doubts."

"Who closed it?"

"San Bernardino Sheriffs."

"Danzer was our case. Who closed it for us?"

"Ian."

Melon pushed slowly to his feet, groaning like an old man.

"Sitting makes me stiff. C'mon, let's get you on your way. It's a longer drive than you think."

Scott once more debated showing the diamonds to Melon as they walked to his car. Melon had obviously been thinking about these things, but only offered cryptic answers requiring Scott to read between the lines. This meant Melon was still on the fence, afraid, or playing Scott to learn what he knew. Scott decided the diamonds would stay in his pocket. He could not reveal the diamonds or Amelia to anyone he didn't trust.

Scott let Maggie hop into the car, and turned back to Melon when a last question occurred to him.

"Did you watch the videos yourself?"

"Ha. Maybe Ian does everything himself, but I'm not the I-Man. A case this size, you delegate."

"Meaning someone else checked them."

"You trust what your people tell you."

"Who checked them?"

"Different people. You might find something in the file or the evidence log."

Scott expected this answer, but Melon also appeared to be giving him a direction. Then Melon added more.

"The I-Man makes out he's a one-man show, but don't you believe it. He has help. And you can bet they are people he trusts."

Scott searched the clear, thoughtful eyes, and realized he would find only what Melon allowed him to find.

"Thanks for letting me come out. The apology was overdue."

Scott slid in behind the wheel, started the engine, and rolled down the window. Melon looked past him to Maggie, who was already perched on the console.

"She doesn't get in your way, riding like that?"

"I'm used to it."

Melon shifted his gaze to Scott.

"I may be retired, but I'd still like to see

this case closed. Take your time driving home. Stay safe."

Scott backed out the long drive, and turned toward the freeway, wondering if Melon meant this as a warning or a threat.

Scott adjusted the mirror until he saw Melon, still on his driveway, watching.

34.

Scott climbed onto the Ronald Reagan Freeway, his stomach knotted and sour. He didn't believe Melon would give him up, but Melon had walked him in circles, giving only enough to get. Melon was good, better than Scott had ever imagined, but Melon had given him Danzer.

The Danzer Armored Car robbery had been just another news story to Scott when it happened, of no more importance than any other, and quickly forgotten. During his weeks in the hospital, Scott had no knowledge of the Danzer case, and had not known an overlapping investigation into an armored-car robbery was having a major impact on his own. He had now read a five-inch stack of reports and interviews about Eric Pahlasian, but Pahlasian had no connection with diamonds, so Danzer had not been mentioned. Danzer Armored Car felt like a secret that had been hiding in the file.

When Scott realized the total case file was four or five feet thick, he wondered how many more secrets were hiding.

The Santa Susana Pass was directly ahead, with the San Fernando Valley beyond it. After a while, Maggie left the console, stretched out across the back seat, and closed her eyes. After all the effort to make her sit in back, he missed having her next to him.

Scott rolled up his window, and checked his cell. His K-9 Platoon Lieutenant, the Metro Commander, and a woman who identified herself as an Internal Affairs Group detective named Nigella Rivers had left messages. Scott deleted them without listening. Budress had not called, and neither had Richard Levin. Joyce Cowly hadn't called, either.

Scott wanted to call her. He wanted to hear her voice, and he wanted her to be on his side, but he didn't know if he could trust her. He wanted to tell her everything, and show her the diamonds, but he could not put Amelia and her baby at risk. He had done this to Daryl. He had painted a target on Daryl's back, and someone had pulled the trigger.

Scott drove on in silence, holding the phone in his lap. He glanced in the mirror.

Maggie still slept. He touched the pouch through his pants to make sure it was real. He didn't know what to do next or where to go, so he drove the lonely miles across the top of the Valley, thinking. He could start with the Internet. Search old news stories about Danzer and the dead men found on the mountain. See if the I-Man was mentioned. Search the stories for someone named Snell.

Sooner or later, he would go back to Cowly, and he needed something to back up Amelia's story. He needed something that would convince her to help him without risking Amelia's life.

Scott's phone rang as he approached the I-5 interchange. He didn't recognize the number, so he let the call go to voice mail. When the phone told him a message was waiting, he played back the message, and heard a bright male voice he didn't recognize.

"Oh, hey, Detective James, this is Rich Levin, returning your call. Sure, whatever you want. I'm happy to answer your questions or help however I can. You have the number, but here it is again."

Scott didn't wait for the number. He hit the call back button. Rich Levin answered on the first ring.

"Hi, this is Rich."

"Scott James. Sorry, I was on another call."

"Oh, hey, no problem. We didn't meet before, did we? I don't remember your name."

"No, sir, we didn't. I've only been with the investigation for a couple of weeks."

"Uh-huh, okay, I see."

"You recall being interviewed by Detectives Melon and Stengler?"

"Oh, for sure. You bet."

"Regarding customers named Pahlasian and Beloit?"

"The men who were murdered. Absolutely. I felt so bad. I mean, here they were enjoying themselves — well, not here, but at the club — and five minutes later this terrible thing happens."

Levin liked to talk, which was good. More importantly, he was one of those people who liked to talk to police officers, which was better. Scott had met many such people. Levin enjoyed the interaction, and he would bend over backwards to help.

"The casebook here indicates you provided two video disc recordings from the night Pahlasian and Beloit were at the club."

"Uh-huh. That's right."

"Did you deliver them personally to

Detective Melon?"

"No, I don't think he was there. I left them with an officer there in the lobby. At that desk. He said that was fine."

"Ah, okay. And this was two discs, not one."

"That's right. Two."

"Two different discs, or two copies of the same disc?"

"No, no, they were different. I explained this to Detective Melon."

"He retired, so he isn't here. I'm trying to make sense of these files and log entries, and between me and you, I'm lost."

Richard Levin laughed.

"Oh, hey, I totally get it. Here's what happened. I burned one disc off the inside camera and one off the outside camera. They feed to separate hard drives, so it was easier that way."

Scott flashed on the parking lot outside Club Red, and felt an adrenaline rush.

"A camera covers the parking lot?"

"Mm-hm. That's right. I clipped the time from their arrival to their departure. That's what Detective Melon said he wanted."

Secret pieces appeared. One by one, they snapped together. A pressure in Scott released like a cracking knuckle.

Maggie sensed something, and stirred

behind him. He glanced in the mirror, and saw her stand.

Scott said, "I'm embarrassed to say this, really, but it looks like we lost the outside disc."

"No worries. That isn't a problem."

The man sounded so confident Scott wondered if Levin had walked them to their car, and could describe the entire evening.

"Do you recall what Pahlasian or Beloit did in the parking lot?"

"I can do better than that. I have copies. I'll burn a replacement for you. That way nobody gets in trouble."

Levin laughed when he said it, and the adrenaline burn grew fierce.

"That's great, Mr. Levin. We don't want anyone to get in trouble."

"I can send them or drop them? That same address?"

"I'll pick them up. Now, tonight, tomorrow morning. It's kind of important."

Scott drove on as they worked it out. Maggie climbed onto the console, and rode at his side until they left the freeway.

35.

JOYCE COWLY

At ten-oh-four the next morning, Cowly was in her cubicle. She stood, straightened her pants, and used the opportunity to check the squad room. Orso was in the LT's office, discussing Daryl Ishi's murder with Topping, Ian Mills, two Rampart Homicide detectives, and an IAG rat. The rat was grilling Orso about Scott's access to the case file. They were digging for some sort of administrative violation, and Orso was pissed. Cowly had already been questioned, and expected to be questioned again.

Two-thirds of the squad cubicles were empty, which was typical with detectives out working cases. The remaining cubicles were occupied, including the cubicle next door. Her neighbor was a D-III named Harlan Meeks, but Meeks was on the phone with one of his four girlfriends, flashing his perfect false teeth and shoveling bullshit.

Cowly sat, picked up her phone, and resumed her conversation.

"Okay, keep going. Does it match or not?"

The SID criminalist, John Chen, sounded smug.

"Tell me I'm a genius. I want to hear those words drip over your luscious, beautiful lips."

"You'll hear the sound of a harassment charge. Knock off the crap."

Chen turned sulky.

"I guess we were too busy flirting to pay attention in science class. Only iron and iron alloys rust, and rust, by definition, is iron oxide. Hence, all rust is the same."

"So you can't tell?"

"Of course I can tell. That's why I'm a genius. I didn't look at the rust. I looked at what's *in* the rust. In this case, paint. Both samples contain paint residue showing titanium dioxide, carbon, and lead in identical proportions."

"Meaning, the rust on the watchband came from the fence?"

"That's what I said."

Cowly put down her phone and stared at the picture of her niece and nephews. Her brother was making noise about a family cruise to Alaska. It was one of those ten- or eleven-day voyages where you sail from Vancouver, follow the Canadian coast from port to port, and end up in Alaska. See glaciers, he said. Killer whales. Cowly had her fill of killers on the job.

Orso and the others were still locked in conversation. Cowly got up, and wound her way past Topping's office to the coffeepot. She took her time, trying to eavesdrop. The faces in these meetings changed, but the talk remained the same, and Cowly found it troubling. People who should have no knowledge of such things discussed Scott James' psychiatric and medical history with authoritative detail as they debated a warrant for his arrest. It seemed like a done deal.

The I-Man noticed her lingering at the coffee machine, and closed the door. Cowly dumped the coffee and returned to her cubicle.

The phone rang as she settled into her chair.

"Detective Cowly."

Scott James asked her the damnedest question.

"Can I trust you?"

She straightened enough to glance next door. Meeks was still on with his girlfriend, laughing too hard at something she said. Cowly lowered her voice.

"Excuse me?"

"Are you a bad cop, Joyce? Are you part of this?"

His voice was so strained she grew scared the people in Topping's office were right. She lowered her voice even more.

"Where are you?"

"Someone broke into my home. The next night, someone broke into my shrink's office and stole my file. Dr. Charles Goodman. North Hollywood detectives Broder and Kurland have it. Call. So you know this is real."

"What are you talking about?"

"Call. Whoever stole Goodman's file is feeding the information to someone inside the department, and that someone is trying to frame me."

Cowly checked the squad room. No one was listening or paying attention.

"I don't like where you're going with this."

"I don't like living it."

"Why did you run? You know how bad that looks?"

"I didn't run. I'm getting it done."

"What are you getting done?"

"I have things to show you. I'm not far away."

"What things?"

"Not over the phone."

"Don't be dramatic. I'm on your side. I had SID check the rust on Daryl's watchband. It matches the rust on the roof, okay? He was there."

"I can beat that. I have the missing disc."

She checked Topping's office. The door was still closed. Meeks was still on with his girlfriend.

"The Club Red disc? Where would you get the missing disc?"

"The manager kept copies. You want to see this, Joyce. Know why you want to see it?"

She knew what he thought, and gave him his own answer.

"Someone doesn't want me to."

"Yep. Someone up there with you."

"Who would this be?"

"Ian Mills."

"Are you crazy?"

"That's what they say. Call North Hollywood."

"I don't need to call them. Where are you?"

"Left turn out of the building, walk across Spring Street. If it's safe, I'll pick you up."

"Jesus, Scott, what do you think will happen?"

"I don't know. I don't know who to trust."

"Give me five minutes."

"Come alone."

"I get it."

When Cowly put down the phone, she realized her hands were shaking. She rubbed them together as Topping's door opened, and the sudden surprise made them shake worse. Ian Mills came out, followed by the IAG rat and one of the Rampart dicks. Mills glanced at her, so she snatched up her phone and pretended to talk. He glanced at her again as he passed, but kept going and left the squad room.

Cowly continued her fake conversation, waiting to see if Orso emerged. She waited for thirty seconds, then put down the phone, slung her purse on her shoulder, and quickly left the building.

36.

Scott let the Trans Am idle forward. He watched the Boat's entrance from across City Hall Park. Maggie was on the console, with the AC blowing in her face. The cold air rippled her fur. She seemed to like it.

Scott hoped Cowly would show, but wasn't sure she would. Ten minutes had passed. He grew afraid she was telling Orso or the other dicks about his call, and the passing time meant they were figuring out what to do.

Cowly appeared beneath the Boat's glass prow and walked quickly toward Spring Street. She stopped at the corner for the light to change, and started across. Scott watched the prow, but no one appeared to be following her. He pulled up beside her at the next corner, and rolled down the window.

"Did you tell anyone?"

"No, I didn't tell anyone. Can you get this

dog out of the way?"

Maggie moved to the back seat when Cowly opened the door, almost as if she understood the front seat wasn't large enough.

Cowly dropped into the car, and pulled the door. He could tell she was angry, but it couldn't be helped. He needed her help.

"Jesus, look at this hair. It's going to be all over my suit."

Scott accelerated away, checking his mirror for a tail car.

"I wasn't sure you'd come. Thanks."

"I didn't tell anyone. Nobody's behind us."

Scott took the first turn, and kept an eye on the mirror.

"Suit yourself. Where are we going?"

"Close."

"This better be worth all the drama. I hate drama."

Scott didn't respond. He rounded the block, and a few seconds later badged their way into the Stanley Mosk Courthouse parking lot. Juror parking. They were three blocks from the Boat.

He found a spot in the shade and shut down the engine.

"There's a laptop on the floor by your feet. We'll watch, and you can tell me if I'm being dramatic."

She handed the laptop to him. He opened it to bring it to life, and handed it back. The disc was already loaded. The recording's opening image was frozen in the player's window. It showed a bright, clear, high-angle image of the Club Red parking lot illuminated by infrared light. There were hints of color, though the colors were mostly bleached to grays. The angle included the club's red entrance, the parking attendant's shack on the far side of the entrance, and most of the parking lot. Scott had watched the disc seven times.

Cowly said, "The Club Red parking lot?"

"Outside camera. Before you see this, you need to know a couple of things. I have more than a disc. Daryl saw the shooting. He told a friend about it, and I have the friend."

Cowly looked dubious.

"Is this person credible?"

"Let's watch. Daryl told his friend one of the shooters took a briefcase from the Bentley. I've cued it to the end, when they leave."

Scott leaned close, and touched the Play button. The frozen image immediately snapped to life. Pahlasian and Beloit emerged from the club, and stopped a few paces outside the door. A parking attendant scurried to meet them. Pahlasian gave him a claim check. The attendant ducked into his shack for the keys, then trotted across the parking lot until the camera no longer saw him. Pahlasian and Beloit remained outside the door, talking.

Scott said, "We can fast-forward."

"I'm good."

A minute later, the Bentley heaved into view from the lower right corner of the frame, moving away from the camera. The brake lights flared red, and Pahlasian stepped forward to meet it. The attendant got out, and traded the keys for a tip. Pahlasian got in, but Beloit walked past him to the street in the background. His murky image could be seen on the sidewalk, but he was too far out of the light to be seen clearly. Pahlasian closed his door, and waited.

Scott said, "It goes on like this for twenty-five minutes."

"What?"

"Beloit is waiting for someone. This is the missing time."

"I'm fine."

Two young women as thin as reeds arrived in a Ferrari. A single man left in a Porsche, followed by a middle-aged couple who left in a Jaguar. When the cars entered or left, their headlights flashed over Beloit, who paced back and forth on the sidewalk. Pahlasian remained in the car.

Scott said, "It's coming. Watch."

A car on the street slowly passed Beloit, and stopped. Beloit was lit by its brake lights, and could be seen moving toward the car. Once he passed the brake lights, he could no longer be seen.

Cowly said, "Can you tell what kind of car that is?"

"No. Too dark."

A minute later, Beloit walked from the darkness into the parking lot with a briefcase in his left hand. He got into the Bentley, and Pahlasian pulled away.

Scott stopped the playback, and looked at her.

"Someone in the investigation watched this, right? They told Melon and Stengler there was nothing worth seeing, and then they got rid of the disc."

Cowly slowly nodded. Her eyes seemed lost.

"A briefcase wasn't found in the Bentley."

"No."

"Shit."

"Not yet, but you will. Do you remember the Danzer Armored Car robbery?"

A deep line appeared between her eyebrows.

"Of course. Melon thought Beloit was here for the diamonds."

"Twenty-eight million dollars in uncut, commercial-grade diamonds, right?"

Cowly gave the slow nod again, almost as if she sensed what was coming.

Scott took the velvet pouch with the ugly stain from his pocket, and dangled it between them. Her eyes went to the pouch, and returned to his.

"Daryl didn't only describe what he saw. He gave his friend something he took off one of the bodies after the shooters left. What do you think they are?"

He poured the stones into his hand.

"Holy shit."

"Really? My guess is uncut, commercial-grade diamonds."

She stared at him, not amused.

"You believe the diamonds were in the briefcase?"

"That would be my guess. What's yours?"

"That this stain on the pouch scores a DNA match with Beloit."

"We're on the same page."

Scott poured the stones back into the pouch, and found Cowly still staring at him.

"Who gave these to you?"

407

"I can't tell you, Joyce. I'm sorry."

"Who did Daryl confess to?"

"I can't tell you. Not yet."

"These things are evidence, Scott. This person has direct knowledge. This is how you build a case."

"This is how you get someone killed. Someone up there murdered Daryl. Someone is trying to frame me for killing three people."

"If this is true, we have to prove it. That's how it's done."

"How, open a case? Go to Orso, and say, hey, what should we do about this? If one person up there knows, everybody knows, and I would be putting a target on this person's back just like I put one on Daryl."

"That's crazy. You didn't kill Daryl."

"I'm glad somebody thinks so."

"You have to trust someone."

Scott glanced at Maggie.

"I do. The dog."

Cowly's face turned hard as glass.

"Fuck. You."

"I trust you, Joyce. You. That's why I called *you.* But I don't know who else is involved."

"Involved in what?"

"Danzer. Everything started with Danzer."

"Danzer closed. Those guys were murdered up in San Bernardino somewhere."

"Fawnskin. One month after the briefcase you saw in this video was stolen from Georges Beloit. The diamonds were never recovered. These diamonds."

Scott dangled the pouch, then pushed it into his pocket.

"The Danzer crew — dead. Beloit and Pahlasian — dead. Daryl Ishi — dead. And the I-Man keeps showing up. West L.A. opened the Danzer case, the I-Man pulled it downtown, and used the West L.A. guys for his task force."

Her mouth was a tight, grim line as Cowly shook her head.

"That's totally normal."

"Fuck normal. Nothing about this is normal. The I-Man shoved Beloit at Melon to convince Melon that Beloit had no connection to the diamonds — the same diamonds Daryl Ishi took off Beloit's body."

"Why would he do that?"

"The same reason someone lied about what they saw on this disc. Because Melon or Stengler or you would eventually find out about Beloit and Clouzot. The I-Man put himself in a position to control what Melon knew. Melon wouldn't question him. Melon had to believe him. He did. Melon told me how it worked."

409

"You went to Melon?"

"I got a vibe, like he has doubts about Danzer, and how Danzer closed."

Scott could tell she was fitting the pieces together.

"We have to look at the people who opened the case, and see how they're tied with the I-Man. Melon gave me a hint. He told me the I-Man never does anything alone, and only with people he trusts. He wasn't implying they're honest."

"What do you want?"

"A head-shot case. Something so tight they're off the street before they know it, and can't kill anyone else."

"Sooner or later, we'll need Daryl's friend. We need a sworn statement. Whatever this person says has to be checked. We might need a poly."

"When you're ready to lock the cuffs, I'll take you to Daryl's friend."

"We'll need DNA from the pouch, and an order for SID to run it. We'll need the insurance company or some other authority to affirm these diamonds were stolen from Danzer."

"You can have everything."

"Great. Everything. Can I at least have the disc?"

"Why stir the water?"

Cowly sighed, and opened the door.

"I'll walk back. I'll see what I can find out, and let you know."

Scott gave her the last thing.

"Daryl heard a name."

She stopped with one leg out the door, and stared at him.

"One of the shooters called another by name. Snell."

"Are you holding back anything else?"

"No. That's it. Snell."

"Snell."

She got out, closed the door, and started away.

"Stay clear of the I-Man, Joyce. Please. Don't trust anyone."

Cowly stopped, and looked back through the window.

"Too late. I'm trusting you."

Scott watched her walk across the parking lot, and felt his heart breaking.

"You shouldn't."

He had pinned a target on Cowly's back now, and knew he could not protect her.

37.

JOYCE COWLY

Cowly brushed at the last of the dog hair stuck to her pants, and stepped off the elevator. She stared down a hall she had walked for over three years, only now the hall loomed taller and wider and went on forever, and everyone in it watched her. A sharp pain stabbed behind her right eye. She heard her mother's voice, I warned you not to watch so much TV, it must be a brain tumor. If only. Maybe her mother was right, and the tumor had made her as crazy as Scott. Only Scott wasn't crazy. Scott had the disc and the diamonds.

She pushed one foot forward and the next and after a while she entered the squad room. Orso was in his cubicle. Topping's door was open, but now her office was empty. Meeks checked the time like he was anxious to leave. Men and women she had known for three years worked and talked and got coffee.

Are you part of it?

Can I trust you?

Cowly went to the conference room, and sat down with the murder book. She sat facing the door so she could see if someone was coming.

Cowly had spent most of her walk back from the Stanley Mosk Courthouse figuring out how to find out who opened the original Danzer case file at West Los Angeles Robbery. She couldn't ask Ian or anyone who worked with Ian, and she couldn't call West L.A. Robbery. If Scott was right, and these guys were bad, any question about Danzer would be a warning.

Cowly had read the murder book twice and the complete case file once. She had only skimmed the sections referencing Beloit, Arnaud Clouzot, and Danzer. Knowing the Clouzot connection had been discounted by Robbery Special months earlier, she had seen no point in wasting time on a blind alley. She flipped through now, searching for the Danzer case number.

Cowly quickly found the number, and took it back to her cubicle.

She brought up the LAPD File Storage page, and was typing in the number when Orso surprised her.

"Have you heard from Scott?"

She swiveled to face him, trying to draw his eye from her computer. He glanced at her screen before he looked at her.

"No. Is he still in the wind?"

Orso's face was pinched.

"Would you mind calling him?"

"Why would I call him?"

"Because I'm asking. I left a message, but nothing. Maybe he'll call you back."

"I don't have his number."

"I'll give it to you. If you reach him, try to talk sense to him. This thing is getting out of hand."

"Okay. Sure."

He glanced at her computer again, and turned away.

"Bud. You think he killed those people?"

Orso made a face.

"Of course not. I'll get his number."

Cowly cleared her screen, and fidgeted until Orso returned. She typed in her file request as soon as he was gone. Officers were only allowed to request materials relevant to a case they were working on, so Cowly provided the number for an unsolved homicide that had been on her table for two years.

Case #WL-166491 appeared as a PDF. The first document was a closure form filled

414

out and signed by Ian Mills, along with a three-page statement describing how Dean Trent, Maxwell Gibbons, and Kim Leon Jones, all deceased, were found and identified as the perpetrators of the Danzer Armored Car robbery. Mills cited and referenced SID and San Bernardino Sheriff's Department reports tying a weapon found as having been a weapon used in the Danzer robbery, as well as Transnational Insurance Corporation documents affirming that the two diamonds found were among those stolen in the robbery. He concluded that the three perpetrators of the robbery were now dead, and as such, the case was rightfully being closed.

Boilerplate bullshit.

Cowly skimmed the documents Ian attached, until she found the beginning of the original West L.A. file. It opened with a couple of form documents filled in and signed by the detectives who caught the case, followed by a scene report describing how the detectives received their orders to report to the scene, and what they found when they arrived. Cowly didn't bother reading it. She skipped to the end. The report was signed by Detective George Evers and Detective David Snell.

Cowly blanked her screen.

Orso was in his cubicle, talking on the phone. Topping's door was closed. She stood, took in the room, then sat and stared at the screen.

She said, "You sonofabitch."

Cowly abruptly stood, and walked down the hall to the Robbery squad room. Same cubicles, same carpet, same everything. A Robbery detective named Amy Linh was in the first cubicle.

"Is Ian here?"

"I think so. I just saw him."

Cowly walked back to Ian's office. The I-Man was scribbling something on a report when Cowly walked in. He looked surprised when he saw her, and maybe a little watchful.

"Ian, you have more names to go with those white sideburns? We gotta bust these low-life, scumbag pieces of shit. We gotta fuck'm up."

She wanted to see him. She wanted to say it.

"I hear ya. I'll get you those names as soon as I can."

Cowly stalked back to her desk.

George Evers.

David Snell.

She wanted to find out everything about them, and she knew how to do it.

38.

IAN MILLS

Robbery Special Section kept extensive files on people who stole for a living, whether they were actively being sought on warrant or not. Not chickenshit perps like teenage car thieves or the clowns who knocked over an occasional gas station, but hard-core professional thieves. Fifty minutes after Cowly left his office, Ian was searching this database for likely white-haired drivers when his email chimed, and he saw the note.

His shoulders tightened when he saw it was an auto-notification from the Storage Bureau. Such notifications were available at the option of the commanding bureau, unit, or closing officer, and Ian had opted to be notified when any of his closed cases were requested. He did this for every case he closed, but he only cared about four. The others were only a cover story.

Ian got up, closed his door, and returned

to his desk. He had only received three notifications since the LAPD adopted the new system. Each time, he was afraid to open them, but all three had turned out to reference meaningless cases. It took him a full thirty seconds to work up his nut before opening it now. Then his belly flushed with acid.

Danzer.

The information provided by the notification was slight. It did not include the name of the requesting officer or agency, only the date and time of request, and the requesting officer's active case number.

The case number told him plenty, and he didn't like what it told him.

The number bore an HSS designator, which meant it was a Homicide Special Section case. Any dick on the Homicide side could walk forty feet, and ask whatever they wanted about Danzer, but someone had chosen to keep him out of the loop. This wasn't good. An active case number was required to process the retrieval, which meant their case file was locked, but Ian had a work-around.

He phoned down the hall, calling Nan Riley. Nan was a civilian employee, and Carol Topping's office assistant.

"Hey, Nanny, it's Ian. Are you as beauti-

418

ful now as you were ten minutes ago?"

Nan laughed, as she always did. They had flirted for years.

"Only for you, baby. You want the boss?"

"Just a quick answer. You guys have an active down there —"

Ian read off the number.

"Who's on it?"

"Hang on. Let's see here —"

He waited while Nan typed in the number.

"That's Detective Cowly. Joyce Cowly."

"Thanks, babe. You're the best."

Ian put down his phone, and liked this even less. If Cowly was interested in Danzer, he wondered why she didn't mention it when she came to his office. Instead, she had shoveled up some bullshit about nailing the shooters in the Pahlasian case. He mulled over what this might mean, then gathered his things and walked down the hall to Homicide Special.

Cowly was in her cubicle. She was hunched over her computer, and appeared to be on the phone.

He walked up behind her. He tried to see what she was reading, but her head blocked the screen. She spoke so quietly he couldn't hear what she was saying.

"Detective."

She jerked at his voice, and visibly paled

when she turned. She pressed the phone to her chest, and leaned sideways to cover the screen. This wasn't a good sign.

Ian held out the list of names.

"The names you wanted."

She took the page.

"Thanks. I didn't expect it so soon."

He watched shadows move in her eyes. She was afraid. This left him wondering how much the Ishi kid had told Scott James, and how much James told Cowly.

"Happy to help. You going to be here a while?"

"Ah, yeah. Why?"

"I'll try to come up with some others."

Ian returned to his office, closed the door, and used his cell phone to call George Evers.

"We have a problem."

Ian told Evers what he wanted him to do.

39.

Three hours after their earlier meeting, Cowly texted Scott that she had the information about Danzer. They agreed to meet in the Stanley Mosk parking lot, same as before. Scott thought she looked tight and compressed when she got into his car.

"I talked to a friend at Bureau Personnel about Evers and Snell, strictly on the down low. I told her I was thinking about using them on a task force, and needed top people. She understands. This woman was my first supervisor."

"What did you find out?"

"They suck."

Scott wasn't sure what he was supposed to do with that.

"Snell has a rep for smart, efficient case work, but he's sketchy. He likes to take chances and cut corners. He has no history with Ian, but Evers and Ian are hooked through the ass. Jesus, I'm already covered with fur. Look at this."

Maggie was laid out across the back seat.

"I haven't had time to brush. What about Evers?"

Cowly brushed uselessly at her pants, and went on with her report.

"Evers and Ian were partners for four years in Hollenbeck. Evers was the lead, but it was common knowledge Ian carried him. Evers got himself in the tall grass and made a mess of his life. He was drinking, the wife left him, all the usual blue nonsense. Ian covered for him and kept him going, but too many complaints were filed. When Ian jumped to Special, Evers was sent to West L.A."

"What kind of charges are we talking about?"

"Deep-shit charges. You know finders keepers?"

It was cop slang officers joked about, only for bad cops it wasn't a joke. If they found a bag of cash when they made a bust, they left enough to meet the felony statute, and took the rest for themselves. Finders keepers.

"I know. Did any of the dirt stick to the I-Man?"

"Ian came out like a rose. He propped Evers up until Evers got his shit together."

Scott looked at Maggie, and touched her. She opened her eyes.

"It flows both ways."

"What flows?"

"If Ian cleaned up after Evers, there were times Evers cleaned up after Ian."

"Whatever. So now Evers is in West L.A., and his partner is Snell. They had Danzer for all of four days, then Ian sucked it up, and made them his front men. The very next day, that's six days after the robbery, Evers obtained wiretap warrants on Dean Trent and William F. Wu."

Scott had no idea who these people were, but Cowly rolled on like an express train.

"Two months later, Dean Trent, Maxwell Gibbons, and Kim Leon Jones were found murdered in the San Bernardino Mountains."

Scott remembered this from Melon.

"The crew who took Danzer."

"So it's believed, and it's probably true."

Also what Melon said.

"Who's Wu?"

"A fence in San Marino. He deals jewelry and art to rich people in China, but he's hooked up in Europe, too. What makes this telling is Dean Trent and Wu are known to have a long relationship. If Dean Trent steals jewelry or art, you can bet he's going to Wu."

Scott realized where she was going.

"Evers and Snell knew Trent had the diamonds."

"Had to. Maybe one of Ian's informants tipped him. It was only six days after the robbery, and they knew or suspected Dean Trent's crew took the score. So they wired up Trent and Wu, and listened to these guys for the next three weeks. The case file contains no transcripts. None. Zero."

Scott felt numb.

"They heard Wu make the deal with Clouzot. They knew Beloit was arriving, and when and where he would pick up the diamonds. They wanted to steal the diamonds."

Scott looked at Maggie. He touched the tip of her nose, and she play-bit his finger.

"Is this enough to make our case?"

Cowly shook her head.

"No. I wish it was, but it isn't."

"It sounds like enough to me. You can connect the dots from start to finish."

"Here's what Ian would say, we received information from three independent reliable sources Trent was attempting to move the diamonds through Mr. Wu, who we know to have an established history with Mr. Trent. Acting on this reliable information, we obtained the required judicial warrant for wiretap service, but failed in our efforts to obtain incriminating information. We are left to believe Mr. Trent or Mr. Wu communicated only in person or using disposable phones. You see? Nothing here hurts him."

Scott felt himself growing angry.

"Evers, Snell, and Mills make three. Five men hit Beloit."

"No one in what I've seen jumped out at me. Let's focus on who we have. If we can bust these guys, they'll give us the other two."

Scott knew she was right.

"Okay. Are Evers and Snell still on the job?"

"Snell is on the job, but Evers retired six days after the murders."

"That isn't smart."

"I don't know. He had the years. He's older than Ian, so it's not out of line."

"Old enough to have white hair?"

"Jesus. I don't know. I've never seen either one of these people."

Scott thought if Evers was old enough to retire, maybe he was the white-haired, blue-eyed driver, and his DNA would match with the hair follicles recovered from the getaway car.

"Evers is the point man here. You have his

address?"

Cowly leaned back.

"What do you think you'll find, the diamonds? The diamonds are gone. The guns are gone. Every piece of that night is gone."

"We need a direct connection between these people and the robbery, something that puts Evers or Snell or the I-Man there on the scene, right?"

"Yes. If you want this so-called slam-dunk case, that's what we need."

"Okay, I'll nose around. Maybe I'll get lucky."

"Weren't you paying attention when we lectured you about the watchband? Nothing you find will be admissible. Your testimony about whatever you find will not be admissible. It will do us no good."

"I heard you. I won't take anything. If I find something useful, you'll come up with a work-around."

Cowly looked disgusted, but dug through her papers, and found George Evers' address.

"I should have my head examined."

"Have faith."

Cowly rolled her eyes, pushed open the door, and hesitated. She looked concerned.

"You have a safe place to stay?"

"Yeah. Thanks."

"Okay."

Scott watched her get out of the car, and wanted to say more.

"Can I drive you back?"

"I'll walk. It gives me time to pick off the fur."

Scott smiled as she walked away, and pulled out of the parking lot. He went to find George Evers.

40.

JOYCE COWLY

Cowly cut through the Stanley Mosk parking lot, making her way toward the Boat. She picked away dog hair and brushed at her pants as she walked. That German shepherd was a beauty, but she was also a fur machine.

Cowly reached the end of the parking lot, and stepped over a low chain barrier onto the sidewalk. She didn't think they were doing this the right way, and now she worried Scott would contaminate the case. Cowly absolutely believed a conspiracy linked Danzer and the murders of Beloit and Pahlasian, and, by extension, Stephanie Anders, but she and Scott weren't playing it the right way. She knew better, even if he didn't, and she was irritated with herself for going along.

Criminal police conspiracies had always existed, and always would, even within the

428

finest police department in the world. There were protocols for dealing with such investigations, which often had to be conducted in total secrecy until charges were levied. Cowly had a friend who once worked with the Special Operations Division, and planned to ask her advice.

"Detective Cowly! Joyce Cowly!"

She turned to the voice, and saw a nicely dressed man trotting toward her, waving a hand. Tan sport coat over a medium blue shirt and darker blue tie, jeans; he could have trotted off the pages of a Ralph Lauren catalog. His sport coat flapped as he ran, revealing a gold detective shield clipped to his belt.

He slowed to a stop, smiling.

"I hope you don't mind. I saw you at the Mosk."

"Have we met?"

He touched her arm, stepping aside for two women hurrying toward the courthouse.

"I'd like to talk to you about Robbery-Homicide. You going back? I'll walk with you."

He touched her arm again, encouraging her to walk, and fell in beside her. He was relaxed, boyish, and totally charming, but he stood too close. Cowly wondered why he assumed she had come *from* the Boat, and was now going *back.*

A dark blue sedan slid past them and slowed.

Cowly said, "You work Homicide or Robbery?"

"Robbery. I'm good at it, too."

He touched her arm again, as if she should know him, and Cowly felt irritated.

"Now isn't a good time. Give me your card. We can talk another time."

He flashed the boyish smile, and moved so close she teetered on the curb.

"You don't remember me?"

"Not a clue. What's your name?"

The sedan's rear door swung open in front of them.

"David Snell."

He gripped her arm hard, and pushed her into the car.

41.

Sunland was a working-class community in the foothills north of Glendale. Down in the flats, it was arid and dry, and deserving of its name. The neighborhood streets between the freeway and the mountains were lined with small stucco ranch homes, but as the land climbed into Tujunga Canyon, eucalyptus and black walnut trees gave the neighborhoods a rural, country feel. George Evers lived in a clapboard house that might have been a converted barn. He had a large rocky yard, a satellite dish, and a metallic blue powerboat parked on the side of his house. The powerboat was covered, and looked as if it hadn't seen the water in years. Evers had a carport instead of a garage, and the carport was empty.

Scott drove past, turned around, and parked two houses away. Police officers rarely have listed phone numbers, but Scott tried Information, asking for a George Evers in Sunland. Nothing. He studied Evers' house for a while, wondering if anyone was home. The empty carport meant little, but the alternative was to stare at the house forever.

Scott was glad he was wearing civilian clothes. He tucked his pistol under his shirt, let Maggie out, and didn't bother with the leash.

He went to the front door, had Maggie sit to the side out of sight, and rang the bell twice. When no one answered, he walked around the side of the house into the backyard. Scott found no alarms, so he broke the pane from a kitchen window and let himself in. Maggie stretched to reach the window, and whined to follow.

"Sit. Stay."

He opened the kitchen door, called, and Maggie trotted inside. Scott knew she was alerting by her expression. Her head was high, her ears were forward, and her face was furrowed in concentration. She went into a high-speed search, trotting wavy patterns throughout the house as if a scent here concerned her and she was seeking its source.

Scott realized it could only be one thing.

"You got him, don't you? This prick came into our house."

432

The kitchen, dining room, and family room contained nothing out of the ordinary. Worn, mismatched furniture and paper plates speckled with crumbs. Two framed photos of LAPD officers from the thirties and forties, and a poster from the old TV series *Dragnet,* with Jack Webb and Harry Morgan holding revolvers. It didn't look like the home of a man who banked a five-million-dollar split from the diamonds, but that was the point.

Maggie was calmer when she rejoined him in the family room.

A short hall off the living room led to the bedrooms, but the first room they reached was part storage and part Evers' I-love-me room. Framed photographs of Evers and his LAPD friends dotted the wall. A young, uniformed Evers at his Academy graduation. Evers and another officer posed beside their patrol car. Evers and a blond, sad-eyed woman showing off the gold detective shield he had just received. Evers and a younger Ian Mills at a Hollenbeck crime scene. Scott recognized Evers because Evers appeared in all of the pictures, and as he changed through the years, Scott felt the floor drop from beneath him.

George Evers was bigger than anyone else in the photos. He was a large, thick man with a big belly over his belt, not a soft, flabby belly, but hard.

Scott had no doubt. He knew it in his soul.

George Evers was the big man with the AK-47, and in the moment he realized this he saw the rifle flashing, flashing, flashing.

"Stop."

Scott made himself breathe. Maggie was beside him, whining. He touched her head, and the flashing disappeared.

Nothing on the wall would connect Evers with the crime scene or the diamonds, but Scott couldn't turn away. He glanced from photo to photo until one photo held him. A color shot of Evers and another man on a deep-sea fishing boat. They were smiling, and had their arms across each other's shoulders. The other man was a few years older, and smaller. He was crowned by white hair, and had vivid blue eyes.

Seeing him triggered Scott's memory, which unfolded like a film: The getaway driver lifted his mask as he shouted at the shooters, exposing his white sideburns. The driver faced forward again as the shooters piled into his car, pulled off his mask, and Scott saw his face — this man's face — as the Gran Torino roared away.

Scott was still in the memory when the vibration in his pocket broke the spell. He checked his phone, and found a text message from Cowly.

I FOUND IT

A second message quickly followed the first.

MEET ME

Scott texted back.

FOUND WHAT?

It took several seconds for her answer to arrive.

DIAMONDS. COME

Scott typed back his answer.

WHERE?

He ran to his car, and Maggie ran with him.

42.

MAGGIE

Maggie rode on the console, watching Scott. She noted the nuance of his movements and posture and facial expressions as completely as she noted his scent. She watched his eyes, noting where he looked and for how long and how quickly. She listened to his sounds even when he was not speaking to her. Every gesture and glance and tone was a message, and her way was to read him.

She sipped his changing scent, and tasted a familiar stew — the sour of fear, the bright sweetness of joy, the bitter rose of anger, the burning leaves of tension.

Maggie felt her own anticipation growing. She recalled similar signs in the moments before she and Pete walked the long roads, Pete strapping up, gathering himself, the other Marines doing the same. She remembered their words. Strap up. Strap up. Strap up.

Maggie whined with excitement.

Scott touched her, filling her heart with joy.

They would walk the long road.

Scott was strapped up.

Maggie danced from paw to paw, anxious and ready. The fur on her spine rippled from tail to shoulders as the taste of blood filled her mouth.

Pack would seek.

Pack would hunt.

Maggie and Scott.

War dogs.

43.

Scott left the Hollywood Freeway only a few blocks from the Boat, and crossed the First Street Bridge to the east side of the Los Angeles River. The east side was lined with warehouses, small factories, and processing plants. He drove south between lines of big rig trucks, searching for Cowly's location.

"Take it easy, baby. Settle. Settle."

Maggie was on her feet, nervously moving back and forth between the console and back seat. When she was on the console, she peered through the windshield as if she were searching for something. Scott wondered what.

He turned between two bustling warehouses, and spotted the empty building behind them, the remains of a bankrupt shipping company set well back from the street. It was lined with loading docks built for eighteen-wheel trucks, and marked by a big FOR SALE OR LEASE sign by the entrance.

"There she is."

A light tan D-ride was parked by the loading dock. The big loading door was closed, but a people-sized door beside it was open.

Maggie dipped her head to see, and her nostrils flickered.

Scott pulled up beside the D-ride, and sent a quick text.

HERE

He was getting out when he received Cowly's reply.

INSIDE

Scott let Maggie hop out, and headed for the door. He wondered how Cowly learned about this place, and why the diamonds were here, but didn't much care one way or the other. He wanted this to be the needle that slid into Evers' vein; Evers, the I-Man, and the rest of them.

The warehouse was dim, but lit well enough. The great, empty room was wide enough for four trucks, thirty feet high, and broken only by support pillars as big around as trees. Doors on the far side of the warehouse led to offices. One of the doors was open, and showed light.

Maggie lowered her head, and sniffed.

"Hey, Cowly! You in there?"

Scott stepped inside, and Maggie moved with him. He wondered why Cowly hadn't waited in her car, and why she hadn't come out when he arrived.

Scott called to the open door on the far side of the warehouse.

"Cowly! Where are you?"

Cowly didn't answer. Not even a text.

Scott was moving deeper into the building when Maggie alerted. She froze in place, head down, ears forward, and stared.

Scott followed her gaze, but saw only the empty warehouse and the open door on the far wall.

"Maggie?"

Maggie suddenly looked behind them, and faced the door to the parking lot. She cocked her head and growled, and her growl was a warning.

Scott ran back to the door, and saw two men with pistols coming from the end of the building. One was a man in his thirties wearing a tan sport coat, and the other was George Evers' white-haired fishing buddy. Scott felt sick. His heart pounded. The instant he recognized the white-haired

440

driver, he realized Mills and Evers knew. They had taken Cowly or murdered her, and baited him into a trap.

Then the white-haired man saw Scott, and fired.

Scott shot back, and scrambled away. He thought he hit the older man but he was moving too fast to know.

"Maggie!"

Scott ran through the warehouse toward the far door. The younger man appeared behind him, and fired twice. Scott cut sideways, fired again, and took cover behind the nearest support pillar. He pulled Maggie close.

The man in the tan jacket fired twice more, and a bullet slammed into the pillar.

Scott made himself as small as he could, and held Maggie tight. He glanced at the offices, and prayed Cowly was alive. He shouted as loud as he could.

"COWLY! ARE YOU HERE?"

Stephanie Anders, Daryl Ishi, and now Joyce Cowly.

His personal body count was climbing, and he might be next.

Scott checked the front door, then the door to the offices behind him. He was so scared and angry he trembled. If Evers and the I-Man and the other shooter were there,

they had him boxed. Sooner or later someone with a gun would show in the office
door, and finish what they started nine
months ago. They would kill him, and probably kill Maggie, too.

He pulled her closer.

"No one gets left behind, okay? We're
partners. Cowly, too, if she's here."

Maggie licked his face.

"Yeah, baby. I love you, too."

Scott ran for the office door. Maggie ran
with him, then stretched out and ran ahead.

"Maggie, no! Come back here."

She ran for the door.

"Heel!"

She ran through the door.

"Maggie, out! OUT!"

Maggie was gone.

Maggie

Maggie felt Scott's fear and excitement
when they entered the building, and knew
it as her own. This place was rich with the
scent of threats and danger. Loud noises
like she heard on the long road, the intruder's fresh scent, and the scents of others.
Scott's own rising fear.

Her place was with him.

Please him and protect him.

If Scott wanted to play in this dangerous

place, it was her joy to play with him, though each loud noise made her cringe.

Scott ran deeper into the big room and Maggie ran at his side. More loud noises came, and Scott held her close. Approval! Praise!

Alpha happy.

Pack happy.

Her heart was joy and devotion.

Maggie knew the intruder was ahead, as clearly as if she could see through the walls. His fresh, living scent grew brighter as the scent cone narrowed.

Scott ran, Maggie ran, knowing she must protect him. She must drive the intruder away or destroy him.

Maggie lengthened her stride, seeking the threat.

Scott commanded her to stop, but Maggie did not stop. She was strapped up.

Alpha safe.

Pack safe.

Maggie knew nothing else. The air was alive with the scents of intruders and other men, some familiar, some not; she smelled their fear and anxiety. She smelled gun oil and leather and sweat.

They were strapped up, too.

Maggie reached the door well before Scott, and saw another door ahead. The intruder and another man were waiting beyond it.

Ten thousand generations filled her with a guardian's rage.

Scott was hers to care for, and hers to keep.

She would not let him be harmed.

She would rather die.

Maggie ran hard up the cone to save him.

Joyce Cowly

Snell and Evers left Cowly tied and gagged in the I-Man's trunk like a stupid girl victim in an old TV show. Cowly had stayed her own execution with a call-your-bluff play. She told them Orso knew. She identified the captain friend at Bureau Personnel who had given her the background on Evers and Snell, and her story rang true enough to make Ian hesitate. Better for him to check out her story than kill her too quickly. Staying his hand might mean the difference between beating the rap and taking the needle.

But Ian would not stay his hand forever. Cowly could identify four of the five men who murdered Pahlasian, Beloit, and Stephanie Anders. The white-haired driver was George Evers' older brother, Stan. The fifth man was not present, though she had learned his name was Barson.

Cowly knew too much to live. Ian would kill her as soon as he checked her story and came up with a work-around to explain her death.

So now Cowly was in the trunk, furious, and fighting down the pain. She wasn't stupid and didn't intend to be a victim, on this day or any other.

The plasticuffs cut down to the bone. She lost a deep flap of meat on her hand, but she twisted free. She found the trunk release, and let herself out. Blood ran from her hand like water from a faucet.

Ian and Stan had parked behind the warehouse. Her gun and phone were gone, so Cowly tried to get into their cars, but both were locked. She found a lug wrench in Ian's trunk.

Cowly was still blinking at the harsh California light when she heard gunfire within the warehouse. She could have run down the street for help, but she knew Ian had used her phone to text Scott. Ian planned to kill them that day, and he might be killing Scott now.

Cowly ran toward the building, leaving a blood trail in the dust.

Maggie

Maggie sprinted into the dim room and reached the end of the cone. The intruder loomed tall and large, with his scent burning as brightly as if he was on fire. Maggie knew the second man's scent, but ignored him even though he spoke.

"Watch out! The dog!"

The intruder turned, but was slow and heavy.

Maggie snarled as she charged, and the man threw up his arms.

Maggie caught him below the elbow. She bit deep, snarling and growling as she savagely shook her head. The taste of his blood was her reward.

The man stumbled back, screaming.

"Get it off! Get it!"

The other man moved, but was only a shadow.

Maggie twisted, trying to pull down the intruder. He stumbled backwards into a wall, flailing, screaming, but stayed on his feet.

The other man shouted.

"I can't get a shot! Shoot it yourself, damnit! Kill it!"

Their words were meaningless noise, as Maggie fought hard to pull him down.

"Kill it!"

Scott James

Scott ran harder, afraid for his dog. She was trained to enter houses without him, and face danger alone, but she did not understand what she faced. Scott knew, and was scared for both of them.

"Maggie, OUT! Wait for me, damnit!"

Scott heard Maggie snarling as he reached the door, and found himself in a short hall. A man screamed.

A gunshot boomed behind him, and a bullet snapped into the wall. Scott glanced back. The man in the sport coat was chasing him.

Scott steadied his pistol against the door, and squeezed off one shot even as the snarls and screaming grew louder.

The man in the sport coat went down, and Scott turned toward the snarls.

Ian Mills shouted.

"I can't get a shot! Shoot it yourself, damnit! Kill it!"

Scott thought, *I'm coming.* He ran toward the voice.

The hall opened into a large, barren utility room with dirty windows. Ian Mills was on the far side of the room, waving a gun. George Evers was stumbling sideways along the wall with Maggie hanging from his arm. Evers was big, a big strong man with a big

447

belly, maybe even bigger than Scott remembered, but he couldn't escape her. Then Scott saw his pistol, and the pistol swung toward Maggie.

The muzzle kissed her shoulder.

A voice in Scott's head screamed, or maybe the voice was his own, or maybe Stephanie's.

I won't leave you.

I'll protect you.

A man does not let his partner die.

Scott slammed into the gun, and felt it go off. He did not feel the bullet, or his ribs break when the bullet punched through him. He felt only the pressure of hot gas blow into his skin.

Scott shot George Evers as he fell. He saw Evers wince, and clutch at his side. Scott bounced on the concrete floor as Evers stumbled sideways. The I-Man was in the shadows, but was swept by light when an outside door opened. Joyce Cowly may have come in, but Scott was not sure. Maggie stood over him, and begged him not to die.

He said, "You're a good girl, baby. The best dog ever."

She was the last thing he saw as the world faded to black.

Joyce Cowly

The gunshots were loud, so loud Cowly knew they were on the other side of the door. She pushed into the warehouse, and found Ian Mills in front of her. Scott was on the floor, Evers was down on a knee, and the dog was going crazy.

Mills turned at the sound of the door, and looked surprised to see her. He was holding a gun, but it was pointed the wrong way.

Cowly swung hard, and split his forehead with the lug wrench. He staggered sideways and dropped the gun. Cowly hit him again, above the right ear, and this time he fell. She scooped up his gun, checked him for other weapons, and scored his cell phone.

The dog stood over Scott, barking and snapping in a frenzy as Evers crabbed past, trying to reach the far door.

Cowly pointed her gun at him, but the damned dog was in the way.

"Evers! Put it down. Lower it, man. You're done."

"Fuck you."

The dog was acting like she wanted to gut Evers, but she wouldn't leave Scott to do it.

"You're shot. I'll get an ambulance."

"Fuck you."

Evers fired a single wide shot and scrambled into the warehouse.

Cowly called the Central Station's emergency number, recited her name and badge number, told them she had an officer down, and requested assistance.

She checked Mills again, then ran to help Scott, but the dog lunged at her and stopped Cowly cold.

Maggie's eyes were crazy and wild. She barked and snarled, showing her fangs, but Scott lay in a pool of blood, and the red pool was growing.

"Maggie? You know me. That's a good girl, Maggie. He's bleeding to death. Let me help him."

Cowly edged closer, but Maggie lunged again. She ripped Cowly's sleeve, and once more stood over Scott. Her paws were wet with his blood.

Cowly gripped the gun, and felt her eyes fill.

"You gotta move, dog. He's going to die if you don't move."

The dog kept barking, snarling, snapping. She was wild with an insane fury.

Cowly checked the pistol. She made sure the safety was off as tears spilled from her eyes.

"Don't make me do this, dog, okay? Please don't."

The dog didn't move. She wouldn't get

off him. She wouldn't leave.

"Dog, please. He's dying."

Maggie lunged at her again.

Cowly aimed, crying harder, but that's when Scott raised a hand.

Scott James

Scott was floating in darkness when he heard her call.

Scotty, come back.

Don't leave me, Scotty.

Scott drifted toward her voice.

I won't leave you.

I never left.

I won't leave you now.

He drifted closer, and the darkness grew light.

The voice became barking.

Scott opened his eyes, and reached up.

Maggie

Maggie attacked the intruder with primal ferocity, and fought to bring him down. Her fangs had been designed for this. They were long, sharp, and curved inward. They sank deep, and when he tried to pull away, his own struggles forced them deeper, making his escape even less likely. Her fangs, as was her bone-crushing jaw, were gifts from her wild ancestors before her kind were tamed.

451

The tools for killing were in her DNA.

Scott safe.

Pack safe.

She had ranged ahead to protect him, but now her heart soared when Scott entered the room.

They were pack.

A pack of two, they were one.

Scott attacked, fighting beside her and for her, fighting as pack, and Maggie's soaring heart filled with bliss.

A loud, sharp crack ended it.

Scott fell, and his changing scents confused her. His pain and fear washed through her as if they were her own. The smell of his blood filled her with fire.

Alpha hurt.

Alpha dying.

Maggie's world shrank to Scott.

Protect. Protect and defend.

Maggie released the intruder, and turned to Scott. She frantically licked his face, whined, cried, and snarled her rage at the intruder as he crawled past them. She stood over Scott, and snapped her jaws as a warning.

Protect.

Guard.

The intruder ran away, but the woman approached. Maggie knew her, but the woman was not pack.

Maggie snarled, warning the woman. She barked and snapped. Maggie slashed the woman's arm and held her at bay. Then she felt Scott's calming touch.

Maggie's heart leaped with happiness. She licked his face, healing him with her heart, as his heart now healed her.

Scott opened his eyes.

"Maggie."

She was instantly alert.

Maggie looked into his eyes, watching, waiting, wanting his command.

Scott glanced toward the big room beyond the door.

"Get'm."

Maggie leaped over Scott without hesitation and sprinted after the intruder. His fresh blood scent was easy to follow.

She powered up the scent cone, stretching and pulling, and closed on him in seconds. She flashed through the warehouse, outside into the sun, and saw the man who hurt Scott stumbling toward a car.

Maggie ran harder, joy in her heart, for this was what Scott wanted.

She will get'm.

The man saw her coming, and raised a gun. Maggie knew this was an act of aggression, but this was all she understood.

His aggression fueled her rage, and darkened her purpose.

She stared at his throat.

She will get'm.

Scott safe.

Pack safe.

Maggie launched herself into the air, baring her fangs, jaws open wide, her heart filled with a terrible, perfect bliss.

She saw the flash.

44.

Eleven Hours Later
Keck/USC Hospital
Emma Wilson, ICU/Recovery Nurse

Three female nurses and two female surgeons told her the waiting room was filled with hunky young cops. Emma was dying to see, even though they also warned her about the nasty old Sergeant who scowled and shouted. He'll be on you like an attack dog, they told her.

Emma was curious about him most of all, and she wasn't afraid. She had been a head floor nurse for almost twenty years, and damn few doctors had the balls to stand up to her.

She put away Officer James' chart, told her staff she would be back in a minute, and pushed through the double doors into the hall.

Emma Wilson had seen this kind of thing before when officers were brought in, but the sight always moved her.

Dark blue uniforms spilled from the waiting room, and crowded the hall. Male officers, female officers, officers in civilian clothes with their badges clipped to their belts.

"What in hell is going on in there?"

His voice cut through the hall, and every officer turned.

Emma wheeled around, and thought, yep, you're him.

A tall thin uniformed Sergeant pushed through the crowd. Bald on top, hair short and gray on the sides, and the nastiest scowl she had ever seen.

Emma held up a hand, motioning for him to stop, but he stalked right up to her until his chest touched her hand. He scowled down his nose.

"I am Sergeant Dominick Leland, and Officer James is *mine.* How is my officer doing?"

Emma stared up at him, and lowered her voice.

"Take one step back."

"Goddamnit, if I have to go back there to —"

"One. Step. Back."

His eyes bulged so wide she thought they would pop from his head.

"Please."

Leland stepped back.

"The surgeon will be out to give you more details, but I can tell you he came through the surgery well. He woke a few minutes ago, but now he's sleeping again. This is normal."

A murmur swept through the officers filling the hall.

Leland said, "He's okay?"

"The surgeon will answer your questions, but, yes, he appears to be doing fine."

The fierce scowl softened and the Sergeant sagged with relief. Emma thought he seemed older, and tired, and not nearly so fearsome.

"All right then. Thank you —"

He glanced at her name tag.

"Nurse Wilson. Thank you for helping him."

"Is Maggie here?"

Leland stood taller, and the edge returned to his eyes.

"Officer James is in my K-9 Platoon. Maggie is his police service dog."

Emma didn't expect Maggie to be a dog, but she was touched by the idea, and nodded.

"When he woke, he asked if Maggie was safe."

The Sergeant stared, and seemed unable to speak. His eyes filled, and he blinked hard to fight the tears.

"He asked after his dog?"

"Yes, Sergeant. I was with him. He said, 'Is Maggie safe?' He didn't say anything else. What should I tell him when he wakes?"

Leland wiped his eyes before he answered, and Emma saw two of his fingers were missing.

"You tell him Maggie is safe. Tell him Sergeant Leland will look after her, and keep her safe until he returns."

"I'll tell him, Sergeant. Now, as I said earlier, the surgeon will be out shortly. All of you rest easy."

Emma turned for the double doors, but Leland stopped her.

"Nurse Wilson, one more thing."

When she turned back, Leland's eyes were filled again.

"Yes, Sergeant?"

"Tell him I will continue to pretend I have not seen that dog limp. Please tell him. He will understand."

Emma assumed this was a private joke, so she didn't ask for an explanation.

"I'll tell him, Sergeant. I'm sure he will be happy to hear it."

458

Emma Wilson stepped through the double doors, thinking how wrong the others were about the scowling Sergeant. He was a sweetheart, once you got past the fierce scowl, and stood up to him.

All bark and no bite.

45.

Sixteen Weeks Later

Scott James jogged slowly across the field at the K-9 training facility. His side hurt more now, after the second shooting, than it had after the first. A full bottle of painkillers was back at his guest house. He told himself he should stop being stubborn and take them, but he didn't. Being stubborn was good. He was stubborn about being stubborn.

Dominick Leland scowled as Scott lurched to a stop.

"I see my dog here is responding to her injections. I have not seen her limp in almost two months."

"She's my dog, not yours."

Leland puffed himself up, and swapped a glare for the scowl.

"The hell you say! Every one of these outstanding animals is my dog, and best you not forget it."

Maggie gave him a low, menacing growl.

460

Scott touched her ear, and smiled when her tail wagged.

"Whatever you say, Sergeant."

"You may be the toughest, most stubborn sonofabitch I've ever met."

"Thank you, Sergeant."

Leland glanced at Maggie.

"The vet tells me her hearing is better."

After the warehouse, Leland and Budress noticed that Maggie didn't hear so well with her left ear. The vets tested her, looked in her ears, and determined she had suffered a partial hearing loss. Something about nerve trauma, but the loss was temporary. They prescribed drops. One drop in the morning, one every night.

Leland and Budress decided it happened when she ran down George Evers in the parking lot. He tried to shoot her at point-blank range. He missed, but she was only inches from the gun when he fired. Evers survived, and was currently serving three consecutive life sentences, as were Ian Mills, David Snell, and the fifth member of their crew, Michael Barson. These were the terms of a sentencing agreement they accepted to avoid the needle. Scott was disappointed. He wanted to testify at their trials. Stan Evers died at the warehouse.

Scott touched Maggie's head. It was a

close call.

"She hears fine, Sergeant. Comes when I call her."

"She gettin' those drops?"

"One in the morning, one at night. We never miss."

Leland grunted approvingly.

"As it should be. Now, they tell me you are still refusing to accept a medical retirement."

"Yes, sir. That would be true."

"Good. You stay stubborn and tough, Officer James, and I will be with you every step of the way. I will back you one hundred percent."

"Gettin' my back?"

"If you choose to see it that way. And when all the back-gettin' is done, and you can move faster than an old man like me, you and this beautiful dog will still be here. You are a dog man. This is where you belong."

"Thank you, Sergeant. Maggie thanks you, too."

"No thanks are necessary, son."

Scott offered his hand, and Leland shook.

Maggie made the growl again, and Leland broke into a wide, beaming smile.

"Would you look at yourself, growling like that? You lived in my house for damn near two months, and you were my lapdog! Now you are back with our friend here, and you got nothin' but growls!"

Maggie growled again.

Leland burst into a great booming laugh, and headed back to his office.

"My God, I love these dogs. I do so love these fine animals."

"Sergeant —"

Leland kept walking.

"Thanks for pretending. And everything else."

Leland raised a hand, and called over his shoulder.

"No thanks are necessary."

Scott watched him walk away, and bent to stroke Maggie's head. Bending hurt, but Scott didn't mind. The hurt was part of the healing.

"Want to jog a little more?"

Maggie wagged her tail.

Scott set off at a slow lurch. He jogged so slowly, Maggie kept up fine by walking.

"You like Joyce?"

Maggie wagged her tail.

"Me, too, but I want you to remember, you're my best girl. You always will be."

Scott smiled when she nuzzled his hand.

They were pack, and both of them knew it.

OF NOTE

Readers knowledgeable about the LAPD K-9 Platoon or PTSD will note several differences between the facts of these subjects and their portrayal in this novel. These differences are not mistakes of research. They are choices made to increase drama or facilitate the telling of this story.

Post-traumatic stress disorder in humans and canines is real. Symptoms such as exaggerated startle response are difficult to treat, and the timeline for improvement is longer than is presented here.

LAPD K-9 Platoon is an elite organization of superbly trained individuals and police service dogs. My thanks to Lt. Gerardo Lopez, Officer in Charge, for his help and cooperation. The training time needed for Scott to become a certified K-9 dog handler was compressed for this story. The actual LAPD training facility, also known as "the K-9 field" or "the mesa," is located in

465

Elysian Park near the Police Academy. The facility depicted in this novel does not exist. Rules governing canine care, feeding, and housing are stated in the LAPD's *K-9 Platoon Procedures and Guidelines Handbook.* The approved K-9 diet does not include baloney. Additional thanks to Deputy Chief Michael Downing and Capt. John Incontro, Commanding Officer of Metro Division.

Acknowledgments and thanks once again go to Meredith Dros and her production team, Linda Rosenberg (Director of Copyediting) and Rob Sternitzky (proofreader), whose efforts at the wire are heroic. Copy editor Patricia Crais has the most difficult c/e job in publishing, with the lost sleep to prove it. Neil Nyren and Ivan Held could not have been more supportive; they almost certainly believe I am disordered. Not without reason. Aaron Priest remains my hero. Thanks go to Diane Barshop for sharing her knowledge about German shepherds. Also to Joanie Fryman. Kate Stark, Michael Barson, and Kim Dower — thanks for believing.

Any and all mistakes in this book are my responsibility.

ABOUT THE AUTHOR

Robert Crais is the author of many *New York Times* bestsellers, most recently *The First Rule, The Sentry,* and the #1 bestseller *Taken.* He lives in Los Angeles.